VAINGLORIOUS
SUN

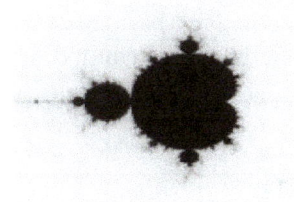

Mark D. Longo

SOPHIC PRESS
Palo Alto, CA

First edition released as The Shaman: Science, Nature, Prophecy 2008

ISBN: 978-0615621487

Dedicated to Sir David Attenborough and Drs. Stephen Jay Gould and E.O. Wilson. These men have been my Jared Foster, opening my eyes to the wonder of it all.

Author's Note

This is an indie publication and thus will not benefit from any sizable marketing campaign. If you enjoy this book, please consider recommending it to your friends and posting a review on Amazon.com or Goodreads.

Regarding the likelihood of said enjoyment, I should probably also mention that I am not a professional novelist and this is not a standard novel. My goal was a hybrid between a scientifically informed thriller *à la* Michael Crichton, a non-fiction meditation on the wonders of nature *à la* Stephen Jay Gould, and a spiritual adventure *à la* Carlos Castaneda. Frankly, as much as I love each of these authors, I don't know how well these genres mix and how successful this little experiment has been. I do know that I put everything I had into this book and believe that if you invest the time to read it you will be rewarded with a rich storyline, a dollop of cutting-edge scientific and philosophical thought, and an epic adventure at the bounds of rationality. As a bonus, you may even uncover a few laughs. Thank you very much for taking a look, and please feel free to contact me with questions and thoughts at VaingloriousSun@gmail.com.

Acknowledgements

Though I had always considered myself more *Sinbad the Sailor* than *Dilbert*, it seemed my fate was to navigate a sea of cubicles rather than the open ocean. Some time ago I decided I'd had enough. I quit my corporate job, fixed up an old Land Cruiser, and just started driving. I didn't know where my journey would lead but I did know I was in for an adventure. I am grateful to my close friends and family who not only encouraged (or at least tolerated) this decision, but also provided me with incredibly positive feedback when I started writing essays about my travels. It was during this period that I was inspired to write *Vainglorious Sun*, and it was all that praise which gave me confidence to do so.

So thank you to Dan Galperin, Mark Tracy, Jasmine Becker, Nikki Delaney, Dan Hereid, Nadav Enbar, Linda Eberling, Chase Adams, Ben Birndorf, Ray Wrigley, Matt Holmberg, my brother Eric Longo, my mother Liliana Longo and my father, D. Thomas Longo Jr. Many from this same group provided invaluable advice regarding early drafts of the book (previously released as *The Shaman: Science, Nature, Prophecy*), but I have to give particular thanks to my father who gave my manuscript several thorough readings and likely saved it from the trash bin.

Revisions which led to the final version of this book benefited from critical reviews by Bill Anderegg, Chelsea Wood, Noa Lincoln, Rachael Garrett, Henri Folse, Holly Moeller, Deborah Rogers, Jennifer Berkowitz, Megan Minsky, Julie Granka, Danny Karp, and Victoria Curtis. Again my father provided much appreciated editorial advice. This time around I had the benefit of a wonderfully supportive girlfriend to share in the joys and tribulations of writing. Olivia Borsje's unflagging encouragement and penetrating critiques helped to mold Vainglorious Sun into the book it is.

My high school English teachers, Ms. Stubbs and Mr. Roylance, deserve special mention because they were the first to plant a seed in my mind that I should pursue creative writing. It took a while for the seed to germinate, but you are holding the end result of their praise in your hands. Thanks also to my mentors in Biology at the University of Colorado, Drs. William Adams and Barbara Demmig-Adams, and to the many others who have supported and encouraged me through the years.

Prologue
Guardians of the Forest

The men gaped at their view from atop the crumbling temple ruins. Before them, a sea of mist-shrouded rainforest met a sky ablaze in the setting sun. Symphonies of animal cries swelled from the treetops as brightly plumed birds burst through the air. George Verderber and Reginald Sloan considered their surroundings and shared one overriding thought. They were going to make such an *ungodly* amount of money mowing it all down.

"Think of it," Verderber whispered, sweeping his arms across the horizon, "a vast eco-community anchored by picturesque parks and ancient ruins."

Sloan sopped up the sweat pouring from his brow. He was a head shorter than Verderber, bald but for a few dark wisps of hair, and built like an egg. His words wriggled past pendulous jowls like flatulence bubbling through water. "You were right, George. A few solar panels and a monkey on the cover of our brochures and it'll be bumper-to-bumper hybrids all the way to the airport!"

The men smiled at one another and basked in the sweetness of the moment. They were elated to see their plans coming to fruition. From an empty wilderness they would conjure a dream, and earn a great deal of money in the process. They were heroes of progress! Kings of industry! And marketing geniuses to boot!

Their cheer abated when they noticed a dark wall of storm clouds charging in from the horizon. Realizing it was getting late and not wanting to get drenched, they clambered down the temple steps.

When they reached the forest floor they were happy to see their Guatemalan government liaison and his driver waiting patiently inside their all-terrain van. Nearby, a group of military men surrounded a hulking transport.

"Okay *amigos*," Verderber said, studying the darkening sky, "let's get back to Flores before it gets too late."

He and Sloan climbed into the back of the van and relaxed in anticipation of the journey back to town. Their faces radiated tranquility as they gazed out of their windows, for in their minds the green leaves around them were like just so many gently swaying dollar bills.

Verderber stared passively at the back of the liaison's head as it bobbed up and down and side to side. The agent was light-skinned and wore an immaculately tailored suit. Verderber knew that status in Latin America was often directly proportional to the degree of one's European ancestry. This man looked like a pure-blooded Spaniard.

The liaison turned to face his guests. "*Señores*," he crooned, "on behalf of the Guatemalan people I would like to thank you for your consideration of the development of this untapped region of our country. It is through the promise of such economic prosperity that we may ensure political tranquility. The Petén is our most remote and economically backward region. Your development of its rich natural gifts can only help to stabilize the area. I can assure you of our utmost cooperation in its exploitation."

Verderber thought the word "exploitation" was an interesting choice. Sometimes translations could be awkward. "Absolutely," he said with amusement, "we will happily exploit the hell out of this area and bring in plenty of hard cash to help you fight the Indians."

The liaison's eyes darted to the driver, a compact

man with a dark complexion. He clearly had little European blood, if any at all.

"Furthermore," Verderber continued, retrieving an envelope from his attaché case, "my partner and I have put together a care package for you and your associates. We want to show how much we appreciate your assistance in this grand endeavor."

"*Gracias, señores, muchas graci-,*" the liaison started, when he was jarred by an abrupt turn.

"Now why did we go this way?" Sloan asked, tightening his seatbelt. His jowls burbled with each bump. "I thought we took that main road all the way back to town."

Verderber leaned forward. "*Amigo, que pasa?* Is this the way we came?"

The liaison repeated the question in Spanish. Eventually, the driver muttered a response. "I am sorry, *Señor* Verderber," the agent offered. He nodded toward the chauffeur. "This man, he says he is taking a faster way back but I am not so sure that is the case." Lowering his voice, the agent continued, "This morning I was notified that my regular driver was ill. I do not know this person. He does not speak Spanish well, he is *indigena*. I do not recognize this way back to Flores. It seems we are going deeper into the Petén."

As the van continued along the wretched road, patters of rain transformed into great tumbling sheets of water. What little light that remained in the day quickly vanished under the deluge.

Verderber cracked his knuckles and pulled out his smartphone. Moments later the device had a geographical fix on the van. It was suddenly quite obvious that they were traveling in exactly the wrong direction. "We're going the wrong way!" Verderber grumbled. "Could you please tell this little miscreant to turn the car around?"

Yet despite repeated exhortations, the driver did not deviate from his path.

"I apologize, *señor*," the liaison said. "I will contact our security escort to let them know our situation. They must also be wondering where we are going." The man proceeded to release an anxious flood of Spanish into a two-way radio he retrieved from the glove box. A crackling voice responded with military brusqueness. Momentarily, the passengers heard the engine rev in the vehicle behind them as their escort started to overtake them.

Unfortunately, the road was barely wide enough for one car, let alone two. On either side of the track grew towering trees and impenetrable undergrowth. There was simply no room for the military transport to do anything but follow. The convoy continued deeper into the jungle.

Sloan sat motionless in the back. Only his eyes moved, flitting back and forth between the driver and Verderber.

"George, what's going on? Did you bring the...."

"Yes, don't worry," Verderber mumbled as he surreptitiously pulled a pistol from his pocket. "Look, buddy," he said to the liaison, keeping his pistol low, "you assured us many times that you had this area under control. It's becoming clear this little communist is trying to kidnap us for ransom or worse but-" Verderber's face flushed in anger mid-sentence as he noticed the driver's lips purse into a smirk. At that moment, they all heard a catastrophic groan behind them. They turned just in time to see a titanic tree tumble to the ground. Although their military transport avoided a collision, it could no longer follow them. Only the scattered rays of its headlights could penetrate the swaying wall of branches and leaves before it.

The two-way radio burst into chatter. The liaison yelled in response while looking wild-eyed at the man next to him. "*Ven, Ven, Ven!*" he hissed into the radio.

That was it! Verderber had had enough! He pressed the muzzle of his pistol against the driver's temple and demanded that he stop, immediately, or Verderber would splatter his filthy Indian blood all over the van. The driver did not flinch. He kept driving, faster now, around a corner and onto another road. Onwards he raced, ignoring the increasingly desperate threats of the men around him.

Abruptly, he stopped the car. He turned, said something unintelligible, and eased his gaze to the front of the vehicle. Everyone's eyes followed his. There, in the glow of the van's headlights, barely visible past the driving rain, shone a pair of luminous, golden discs. Everyone sat transfixed. The eyes obviously belonged to a massive creature, perhaps a jaguar, but in the dim light nobody could quite make out its shape. The animal itself was dark and slinking closer.

"*Que Diablo!*" the liaison whispered.

The driver smiled. He calmly turned off the van's engine, opened his door, and walked into the jungle.

"Stop him, he's got the keys!" squealed Sloan as Verderber launched himself outside and ordered the driver to return. Shots rang out – *bang! bang! bang!* – but the driver had already disappeared behind the foliage on the side of the road.

"Dammit!!" Verderber cursed. A chill raced along his spine as he remembered the presence lurking behind him. Instinctively, he whirled around. He saw nothing but darkness, the van's filthy headlights illuminating just a sliver of road ahead. He scrambled back inside the vehicle and slammed his door shut.

The liaison jabbered furiously into the radio. Sloan sat curled into himself in his seat. His lips worked but no words came out. Finally, he managed to speak. "Wha...wha...what do we do now?"

"Dammit, Dammit, Dammit!!" Verderber fumed. "Well, let's see what Numnuts here has to say about our escort."

"They are coming on foot," the liaison exhaled dramatically.

"Whew!" said Sloan. Color rushed back into his face. "Wait a minute," he added, the color draining just as quickly as it had returned, "wha…wha…who's there?"

Before them, where the eyes had been moments before, loomed a hulking silhouette. With grotesque musculature rippling over powerful limbs and fearsome animal forms jutting from an enormous headdress, it seemed the murderous appendage of a bristling forest. The monstrous man-thing clenched and unclenched its fists as it stared into the van.

Suddenly, the military man on the other end of the walkie-talkie shrieked so loudly that the speaker distorted with the intensity of his calls. Everyone glanced at the radio. The transmission stopped. They looked back up. The figure was gone, vanished in the instant they had averted their eyes.

Verderber, Sloan, and the liaison looked nervously at one another and began frantically wiping condensation from their windows. They peered outside cautiously. Through the rain and mist it appeared as though the entire forest was writhing, as though the trees themselves were breathing.

A horrendous thud beat against the side of the van. In panic, Verderber let go of round after round from his pistol, shattering the window beside him.

Then, for a brief moment, all was still. They heard only their own jagged breaths. Tendrils of fog crept into the vehicle from the empty window frame. Sloan's jowls undulated in waves of fear. Droplets of sweat swam down his forehead to sting his twitching eyeballs. Ever so slowly he moved to clear a bit more condensation from his window. The instant his hand touched the glass, something enormous exploded through his window and heaved him, whimpering, into the darkness outside.

Verderber spun around and let loose of everything he had left in his gun. To his horror, his quick reflexes produced nothing more than a pathetic series of clicks.

The liaison's expression bespoke sheer terror, all bulging eyes and mouth agape. Staccato pleas shot from his mouth when he too was ripped violently from the van.

Verderber froze, shoulders hunched around his neck, trying to hide within his own body. He felt like a mouse trapped in its burrow as something unspeakably sinister probed for a claw hold. He even squeaked like a mouse when, finally, he peeked outside the van. He looked back and forth and side to side in rapid succession, trying to see all directions at once, straining his senses for any clue as to who or what might be out there hunting him. He saw nothing but nebulous black and heard only muffled rustling on the side of the road.

He had to do something. The thought of leaving the van filled him with dread but staying where he was would be sure suicide. Taking a deep breath, he worked his face into a visage of courage. He had made his decision. George Verderber would not just wait around and die, dammit! With that, he opened his door and stumbled into the darkness.

His courage abandoned him the instant he left the confines of the van. He ran with the panic gait, arms waving in front of him to move aside any branches that might hit his vulnerable eyes. He cleared barely twenty paces before getting mired in mud. Then he heard an eerie fluttering behind him. Reflexively, he struggled off the road and into the jungle.

The undergrowth he found there lay thick with

thorny, stabbing vines and trees. The harder Verderber fought the more tangled he became in the vegetation and the deeper he sank into the morass of liquid earth. Within moments he found himself torn, bloody, and immobile, utterly snarled by the angry jungle.

And then came the fluttering sound again.

He whipped around to see a shadow creeping toward him. Desperately, he flailed to get free. His breaths were pathetic stabs at air. He was near losing consciousness from fright. He patted the ground to his sides searching for a stick or a rock, anything he could use to defend himself. A snake hissed as he wrapped his hand around its body. A bird bit him as he tried to pull himself up on a vine. A monkey just out of arm's reach screeched and threw feces in his face.

He spun to avoid the assault and was startled to see the enormous man that had been standing in front of the van now towering directly above him. The mist surrounding the giant rippled and swelled amidst the animal forms carved into his headdress. Howler monkeys roared in the distance as the man ripped Verderber free from the bramble. He lifted him like a doll so their faces stood only inches apart. His expression was twisted with rage. He snapped his jaws and snarled as his eyes tore into Verderber's terror stricken soul.

Chapter 1
The Hero Twins

The character lines in his face didn't seem used to smiles, but Jared Foster was happy at the moment and forcing the lines to adapt. In the soft light of a bay window, he stood peacefully misting a tray of plants as his dog looked on curiously. Jared froze mid pump. He'd noticed a casualty.

"Oh, sorry buddy!" he said, watering one particularly frazzled looking *crassula*, "I must have forgotten you last time. You've *gotta* be thirsty!" He gently touched the plant to let it know he still cared and then caught himself.

"What?" he asked the rumpled mutt sitting next to him, "Something wrong with a grown man talking to his succulents? I talk to you, don't I?"

The dog looked away, as though it had actually posed such a ridiculous question.

Jared heard a chime indicating a new email had arrived. His face reverted to its usual concerned countenance as he glanced at the video monitor on his desk. He could just make out the subject line of the message: Dinner tonight?

No time for that, he thought. *I've got plenty of food in the fridge.*

He turned back to his plants and felt tranquil once again as he marveled at their diversity. They each seemed to have their own personalities, or "plant-alities" really. "Slow down, spanky," Jared admonished one particularly boisterous *kalanchoe* spilling out of its pot. "We've got limited space here." He started changing the plant's container when his attention was diverted to the radio.

"War in the Middle East continues to rage as oil

prices reach an all-time high," the newscaster announced with a little too much enthusiasm, as though he were selling something.

Jared grimaced. *I should really turn that off.* He finished changing the pot and gazed at the mountains outside. Flurries of snow were falling over a backdrop of evergreen and granite. The scene calmed Jared and he went back to work, moving the plants carefully so they could share the light.

"The stock market took a tumble today," droned another announcer. "Consumer confidence is low, but analysts say the best thing we can do for our economy is to go out and spend spend spend..."

Nonsense! thought Jared as he accidently impaled his thumb on a cactus spine. *Too much spending is the cause of all this--* The email chime went off again. Jared looked over at his desk. Someone was kindly offering to sell him pills to increase the girth of his penis.

Jared huffed in disgust and squeezed a drop of blood from his wound. He considered ripping all the electric plugs from their sockets.

"...a tragic tale of heroism from the floods in the south..." The first newscaster was back on, though his tone seemed more earnest this time.

Floods, good. Flush...it...all...AWAY! Jared cleaned his finger and went back to work.

"Young Davie Prevoir" continued the newscaster, "age nine, from Esperance, Louisiana, was trapped in a car with his mother and younger brother when rescuers arrived."

Jared unfolded a wet towel to reveal a series of plant cuttings.

"Rescuers could retrieve only one person at a time and when they went to grab Davie he insisted that they take his younger brother instead, who he claimed could not swim."

Jared carefully arranged the cuttings so they would be covered by just the right amount of water. Too much and they would drown.

"Younger brother, Timmy Prevoir, insisted that it was his older brother who was the one that could not swim and asked the rescuers to take him first. In the end, rescue workers decided that the youngest boy would be the most vulnerable and succeeded in pulling him to safety, but just then the car was rocked free by the current and submerged in the raging waters. Older brother Davie Prevoir and his mother are presumed dead."

Jared's head dropped. He kneeled next to his dog and gently patted its head. "That's a sad story," he said. "Nature is so beautiful, but she sure can be a bitch."

The email application chimed once more. Jared looked at the monitor. This time he welcomed what he saw. He climbed on a chair and read on. One of his former professors had written him with good news:

Jared,

I understand you're in a bind to hire a production assistant immediately. I put out some feelers and believe I've found a promising candidate. His name is Christopher Burgeis and he is currently studying toward a Master's degree in anthropology with a focus on the Maya. While he doesn't have much experience making films, he is apparently quite knowledgeable about the Petén region and is eager to join your expedition. If you're interested in following up you'll find his contact info below.
Warm regards,
Barbara

Jared ran his fingers through his turbulent river of hair and tapped a thank you note to his former professor. She had been his PhD advisor in ecology and, despite his unceremonious dismissal from the program years ago, she continued to be one of his biggest supporters. He rummaged through his desk for his OnePod smartphone, eventually finding it tucked underneath a recent issue of *National Geographic*. Glancing absently at the magazine's cover, he dialed Chris's number. The picture of Jared was a good likeness of him, he thought, though he looked a little haggard for his thirty-two years. He certainly looked fit – all that rock climbing had chiseled his physique. They'd managed to capture so much in just that one photo. In it, Jared held his favorite video camera in one hand and a tiny monkey in the other.

The line went to voicemail. "Chris isn't here," said the greeting. "This is his conscience. Please leave a message and I'll guilt him into calling you back. *Beeeep.*"

Jared determined he would need to meet Chris in person before committing to anything.

He left a quick message and began typing an email to confirm his potential assistant's interest in the job. He looked at the date on the screen. They would need to leave in just a few days, he wrote, and would be gone for several weeks. He knew it was short notice, but it would be great to have the company and making nature documentaries was infinitely easier with two people. He could offer Chris a small salary as well as food, board, and transportation. Most importantly, it would be the adventure of a lifetime and would grant Chris the opportunity to see the archeological sites in person that he may have only read about up until now.

Jared paused to scratch his dog's chin. "I wish you could come," he said, "but we'll be crossing the border. And don't look at me like that; it's just a filming trip. What could happen?"

Jared reviewed his note, added a few more logistical details, and crossed his fingers as he pressed the "Send" button.

Just across town in Boulder, Colorado, Christopher Burgeis was making the most of the information age, simultaneously chatting on the phone, surfing the Internet and instant messaging. He was chuckling at his friend's joke when he heard the chime indicating a new email had arrived. He had to drill down past one web browser displaying a series of Mayan hieroglyphic translations and another serving as an online sports score ticker before he got to his email application. There was one message in particular that he was hoping to receive and there it was, a note from *the* Jared Foster asking Chris if he wanted to join him on a filming expedition to the Petén region of Guatemala.

"Gotta go!" Chris said excitedly as he hung up the phone and turned his full attention to the email. Jared explained that the purpose of the trip would be to capture the remarkable beauty of the Petén in order to raise awareness of its special status as one of the last great vestiges of wild rainforest left on Earth. There was some degree of urgency to the project in that portions of the Petén were being actively considered for development by some unscrupulous American investors. The trip itself would last for several weeks. Apparently much of that time would be spent driving to Guatemala in Jared's custom expedition vehicle. He had opted to drive rather than fly because doing so would allow him to film along the way and would provide a secure means to transport his expensive camera gear. Driving would also enable the two travelers to explore remote locations they would otherwise not be able to reach.

Chris leaned back to consider the invitation. He had already been excited about the possibility of this trip. The Petén, after all, was the cradle of the Maya, whose ancient civilization served as the subject of Chris's research and the main focus of his recent thoughts. At its height, during the Classical Period from 200-900AD, Maya culture reached a level of sophistication that rivaled anything that existed in the world at that time. Across the Petén, cities of tens of thousands of individuals boasted spectacular temples and palaces, and Maya art reached its full flowery expression. Of course much of that expression dealt with the horrors of human sacrifice and other pagan misdeeds, but that was one of the many things that Chris found fascinating about the culture.

Since that time, all of the Classical cities had been abandoned and the rainforests had enjoyed a thousand year period of regeneration. Going with Jared would mean that Chris would get to see, touch, smell, and feel those mysterious sites now buried deep within the jungle. He would have the opportunity to read from the original carved glyphs himself and solemnly climb the steep temple steps just as the divine god kings of old had. He would get to experience the ancient Maya firsthand who he had previously known only through books.

But Chris had had no idea they would be *driving* down. The prospect of an epic road trip only augmented his enthusiasm. The timing was good as he had already finished all of his coursework and was thus free to leave anytime. Chris leaned in to double check the dates in the email and started giggling to himself. In fact, the timing couldn't have possibly been more perfect! He couldn't believe his luck. Chris and Jared would be in the Petén, the very heartland of the ancient Maya civilization, at the single most important date in the history of history, December 21st of that year!

Predictions regarding what exactly would happen on that date varied widely and Chris had his own theories. Some predicted an apocalyptic end of all civilization as we know it. Others focused on curious astronomical events due to occur at that time. And still others thought the whole thing was bunk. Two things were very clear to Chris.

First, December 21 marked the end of the five-thousand year Maya "Long Count" calendar. The ancient Maya believed the universe went through cycles of birth and death. They considered the beginning of this current cycle of their "Long Count" calendar to be the beginning of this current manifestation of existence, and the end of that cycle would represent the birth of a new world.

The second thing Chris knew for certain is that all the movies made so far about this impending rebirth were complete crap and he wished someone would do the topic justice. I mean, come on, what could be cooler than an ancient prophecy of apocalypse?

Thinking of theories related to the Maya calendar, Chris suddenly remembered something. He shuffled papers on his desk and pumped his fist in excitement as he picked one up. Not only would this be the most epic adventure imaginable in exotic lands coinciding with one of the most significant dates ever, but one of his favorite Maya scholars was due to give a lecture in Guatemala at just about the time they should be arriving there. In Chris's mind, Dr. Jason Conroy, had *the* answer regarding what was really going to happen on December 21. To actually be there in Guatemala to hear one of his favorite scholars talk about one of his favorite subjects, Ahhhh! It was overwhelming!

Chris started writing Jared back with an enthusiastic "yes!" when he heard a voice in his head that sounded suspiciously like his mother. The voice was blathering on about something or another to do with safety. Oh, it was his conscience. Now previous concerns tumbled onto the center stage of his mind, tossing aside his enthusiasm which had just moments earlier been singing like a diva. In discussing the possibility of this trip with friends, Chris had been subjected to a parade of stern warnings about the risks associated with travel through Central America. And they were all right, friends and voices of conscience alike – this wouldn't be a very fun trip if Chris died.

He decided to play it safe and research the issue further before committing. He typed "Guatemala" and "danger" into his web browser's search bar. Six hundred and forty two links returned. Chris's trepidation only increased as he read a recent U.S. State Department Consular Country Report on Guatemala:

> Violent criminal activity continues to be a major problem in Guatemala with more assaults against foreigners annually than any other Latin American country. Armed attacks have been particularly common on the northern roads leading from Guatemala City to Flores.

Flores was the gateway to the Petén. Apparently, Jared and Chris would be heading into the most dangerous part of the most dangerous country in the Americas. The rest of the report was similarly ominous.

Chris shook his head and got up to walk around and think. He hadn't ever even seen a real gun, he realized, and he was as physically intimidating as a puppy dog. He cursed his meager musculature and wished he'd hit the gym, at least once in his life.

Sighing heavily, he looked at his collection of baseball memorabilia hanging on the wall. At the center of this display was a poster showing a reenactment of a Classical Maya ballgame. The precise rules of the game were lost to history, but the outcome was well known. Losing the game meant losing one's head.

Chris had been a lifelong sports nut. Long before he had discovered the wonders of past civilizations, he had basked in the arcana of baseball statistics and the excitement of championship showdowns. His path to the Maya had been through the serendipitous discovery of their ballgame. Once he learned about it, he had to know more about a culture that took the ritual aspects of a game so seriously that the very lives of its players were at stake.

Also hanging on the wall was a mask that a friend had given him as a gift from his travels in Guatemala. The mask was carved into the shape of a fierce jaguar and was meant to portray the "Mundo," a guardian forest spirit worshipped by the Maya from ancient times to this day. The mask and poster were portals to another world, rich with meaning and history. Chris looked at the State Department warning and back and forth between these two links to the exotic.

To hell with it, he decided. Jared had traveled extensively and must have seen the warnings as well. The danger must be overblown. And even if it wasn't, Chris would be so upset with his own timidity if he didn't go that he would pose more of a threat to himself than anything he was likely to encounter down south.

He wrote Jared back excitedly. Of course he was interested in helping! This was the opportunity of a lifetime! He could be ready in no time, he just needed to know what to bring!

Chris then switched browser windows, excited to do more research related to his upcoming trip. He began to navigate to the Mayan hieroglyphics page but got sidetracked by the sports ticker. His New England Patriots had won again, cementing their undefeated winning streak. What a glorious, blessed day!

***

"You're weak, Jared," the sweet angel hissed. "You're fucking pathetic. You don't know how to treat a woman."

Jared couldn't reconcile his feelings for the girl with the verbal assault he was enduring. He tried to defend himself but it was no use, she was inconsolable.

"Please," he pleaded, "you know I'm doing all I can." He was sitting on her stomach, surrounded by black void. She was all that existed. She was all that mattered. He had to get through to her.

Her expression belched disgust. "It's too late for Mr. Nice Guy," she foamed, spittle raining on his face. Her head started twisting from side to side. "I need a real man! I need a man who knows what he's doing!" As she spoke, an enormous hand reached out of her mouth and grabbed the side of her face. Jared scrambled to his feet and stumbled back. The hand was followed by an arm, and then another hand and arm emerged. A giant man-thing heaved itself out of the woman's mouth and stood tall, towering over Jared. It was dark, grotesquely muscular, and glowered with pitiless eyes. Its body trembled with power as it took a step toward Jared.

Jared fled in terror as the lumbering thing took chase and the woman continued to spew venom. He didn't understand. She'd been so kind to him in the past. This wasn't her.

The pounding footsteps drew closer.

She'd been mean before, sure, god could she be a bitch, but never like this.

"You're nothing Jared! Come back here!"

When she was sweet, she was such an angel, such a sweet, fragile angel. Jared had devoted himself to her. He was so confused, so hopeless.

And then suddenly he reached the end of a pier.

He could go no further. It would be only moments before the thing caught up with him.

Jared didn't know what to do. He kneeled, closed his eyes, and prayed for an answer, though he'd stopped believing in gods and spirits long ago. He didn't so much hear an answer, as feel it. *She was just one. Love her, but recognize the rest.* When he opened his eyes again, Jared was surrounded by women. The tempestuous girl hurling insults at him was only one of a multitude. They were radiant, endless, an infinity of color and form extending in all directions forever. How could he have been so blind not to see this before?

The giant was upon him, but Jared remained calm. It reared back for the killing blow and Jared focused on the radiance. He knew what to do. The giant swung and Jared stepped behind him swiftly. He gently nudged the thing forward, off the pier, and into oblivion.

Jared woke. What a crazy dream. His jujitsu lessons sure were working – they'd even made his subconscious safer. He'd used the giant's own strength against him just as his instructors suggested.

Why had he dreamt of the girl? He hadn't seen her in so long. And why had he envisioned her as so cruel? She'd summoned that monster. Her words had turned into that thing. Jared loved her so much, too much for his own good. He knew that. But what did it all mean?

Maybe nothing. Not all dreams were meaningful. Some were just random neurons firing.

Suddenly Jared realized why the woman was on his mind. But, man, was he being paranoid. The chances were so slim, sooo slim. Mexico was a big country after all.

***

The next few days were a blur of frenetic activity. There were so many errands to run, so much equipment to buy and so many loose ends to tie up, but somehow he had managed and now Chris was just about ready to leave. He whistled the "Rocky" theme as he dressed. He was even more upbeat than usual, and who could blame him? In just a few minutes he was about to hit the road with Jared Foster for what was sure to be the biggest adventure of his life.

Chris put some hair product into the tawny mop on top of his head and tried in vain to tame some of its curls. Giving up quickly, he turned his attention to his teeth. He smiled cheesily into the mirror. Sparkly white. He looked at his face. His freckles weren't too prominent today. They weren't usually too bad this time of year. It was the sun that really brought them out. Chris had just switched to whistling Black Sabbath's "Iron Man" when he heard his OnePod chiming.

"Hello," he said.

"Hey Chris, how are you? It's Jared."

"Jared! I'm great! I'm so excited about this trip I can't stand it!"

"Same here. Did you manage to get all the gear I recommended?"

"Sure did." Chris kneeled on top of his suitcase in an effort to close it. "Do you really think I need to bring that much bug spray? I didn't think the bugs were that bad in the rainforest."

"Yes, I do. Maybe you don't realize this, but 'rainforest' is just a PC word for 'bug-infested jungle.' We'll need a lot of spray."

"And you really think that I'll need that many batteries for my flashlight?"

"Trust me. You said you haven't camped much. You'll need lots of bug spray and plenty of batteries. We're heading into a wilderness."

"Well, I got everything you asked me to and I'm just about packed up."

"Excellent. Sherpa and I will be there in about

two minutes."

"Okay, I'll be outside waiting for you....Who's Sherpa?"

But Jared had already hung up. Chris finished packing, put on a warm coat and his favorite, well-worn Red Sox cap and then stumbled out the door with his luggage just in time to see Jared pull up in a beast of a 4x4 vehicle. It was a much older model, probably mid-eighties, sort of a bluish-grey color, and looked tough as nails.

Jared stepped out of the truck and the two men greeted each other. Although they had met in person earlier to discuss their trip, Chris was still struck by Jared's presence. With his cascades of dark brown hair, flannel shirt, and rugged good looks he had the appeal of a grunge rock star, albeit it with broader shoulders than usual. The dark five o'clock shadow that covered his lean jaw bordered on becoming an actual beard and his intense emerald eyes recalled a forest ablaze.

Jared glanced at Chris's overstuffed suitcase. "Is this everything you're bringing?" he asked.

"Well, that and this too," Chris replied, motioning to a grocery bag filled with potato chips and an assortment of cheese puffs.

Jared chuckled. He opened the rear of the truck, pressed a lever and a large cabinet rolled out. After moving aside a few boxes, he placed Chris's suitcase and grocery bag next to his own gear.

Chris started to step into the vehicle but got distracted. The truck was just too cool. From the burly brush bar up front to the stomping 4x4 tires below there was absolutely nothing about it that didn't scream independence and adventure. The machete and shovel mounted on the sides of the roof rack cinched it.

"This truck is amazing" he said.

"Thanks. This is Sherpa. She may not look like

much, but she's a James Bond car on the inside."

"No, she definitely looks like she means business. It's a Land Rover, right?"

"Nope, Land Cruiser, '87."

"Right. It's just so…real…like it's built for a purpose other than just showing off. How many miles does it have?"

Jared was halfway in the truck. He stepped back out and put the keys in his pocket. He could always spare a few minutes to talk about Sherpa.

"Well, over two hundred thousand on the chassis, but I just replaced the engine. She's biodiesel now. Here, let me show you a couple of things."

Chris nodded eagerly.

Jared spent the next few minutes demonstrating some of the highlights of his truck. Suddenly his somewhat imposing demeanor was replaced by that of a happy child showing off his treasured pet earthworm.

"This is called a brush bar" he said, pointing to what looked like a small battering ram mounted in place of the front bumper of the vehicle, "though with the three-inch steel tubing you could take down a lot more than twigs. Then of course we have the auxiliary driving lights here, super bright, and the winch here, very handy if we get stuck."

Jared opened the hood.

"Just about everything in the engine compartment has been upgraded. There are two batteries, one to start the truck and the other for all the secondary electronics. There are also two alternators. This second one serves as a welder. Oh, and this is the hot shower."

"Whoa. Sweet! Where does the water come from?"

Jared explained that the shower needed an external water source. It had a built-in pump which circulated the water around the engine, thus heating it and allowing for the luxury of a steaming hot shower anywhere.

"I love this truck!" Chris said, his mind already racing through adventures that would require full use of all of Sherpa's James Bond car features.

"That's just the start!" Jared pointed out a number of other modifications. There was a steel safe console mounted between the front bucket seats containing a top-end stereo. There were also power inverters, a huge fuel tank ("almost 1200 miles between fill-ups"), an air compressor, a custom cabinet system, custom roof racks, an alarm, and Jared was sure there was something else...

"Oh wait, I have to show you this! I can't believe I forgot one of the most important things." Jared walked to the rear of the vehicle and opened the tailgate. He carefully removed a panel of trim and pulled out a peripheral device cable from the opening.

"So this cable goes to an on-board computer system." he said. He plugged the cable into his OnePod and the words "Connecting to Satellite" scrolled across the device's screen. "The computer communicates with low orbiting satellites to send and receive GPS coordinates for tracking and navigation purposes, and it can also be used to send emails from anywhere in the world."

"Can't you just use a OnePod to send emails?"

"Those only work if there is a mobile phone network around. There are still plenty of places in the world without cell phone service. With this thing you could be literally anywhere, even out to sea, and you'd be able to communicate."

"Too cool," Chris said. He was sure they'd have to use this feature to save the world at some point during their trip.

Jared beamed.

Chapter 2
Intelligent Spirits

Two bulging eyes funnel information to the terrified mind. The mind tries to process these mixed gifts of vision, but the mind does not understand. It does not understand why it is here and what the brooding figure at the other end of the darkened room is doing.

The brooding figure is an extraordinarily large man with a dark complexion. He sits at an old wooden lectern illuminated by candlelight. The muscles of his bare back ripple with each minute movement of his arms as he slowly leafs through what appears to be an ancient manuscript. The book is built like an accordion, its deeply yellowed pages folded over and stacked on top of one another. The man's hands are so enormous that they seem to have lives of their own, like they might turn around, roar, and scurry off the desk at any moment, but they move with delicate grace as he applies diaphanous coats of liquid to the pages of the tome. Perhaps the liquid is a sealant to protect the pages from the suffocating humidity of this place. The walls glisten with moisture, reflecting the candlelight like mirrors. Incessant drips from the ceiling provide the only sound.

The mind wonders desperately what the large man intends to do. If only it could understand what was written on the pages of the book it might have some clue, but the book is far away and all the mind can see are abstract symbols and drawings of strange half-human creatures.

The large man, of course, understands everything written in the book because its symbols are pictographic representations of his native tongue. He knows that the book is the oldest surviving text of his ancestors, the Classic Maya of the Petén. All the rest of the sacred codices were burned by the Europeans or lost to the ravages of the humidity. Bark paper and deer hide did not last long under these conditions.

But for generations the man's ancestors have protected

this text against invaders and rot, and now the man himself is caring for the book. He reads from its pages as he does so. To him, the mysterious glyphs and drawings tell the timeless tale of the two deities known as the Hero Twins, who descended to the Underworld and, through their knowledge and sacrifice, managed to defeat the Dark Gods that dwelled there. The Twins then brought their beloved father, the Maize God, back to life, thus restoring the world's cyclic harmonies of life and death.

To succeed, it was critical that the Twins gained a deep understanding of nature because the final battle was to take place in the realm of the spirits. The man knows that spirits are nothing more than the incorporeal aspects of the material world, intertwined and interpenetrated parts of the same whole. He understands that to know one realm is to gain insight into the other, and he smiles as he realizes that his ancestors probably knew more of the fundamental nature of reality through their myths than modern science has learned through all its frantic efforts at measurement and calculation. He reaches the final glorious scenes of the epic and is once again inspired.

"Knowledge and sacrifice," sighs the man, as he gently folds the book and tucks it into a crumbling wooden case. He rises from his chair and walks across the room to a corner where clothes hang from hooks on the wall. He puts on a t-shirt and slips into a long, white lab coat stained with streaks of crimson. He pulls on a pair of latex surgical gloves, slapping each one back at the palm to ensure proper fit, picks up an old doctor's satchel, and turns to the terrified eyes.

"Sacrifice, Sloan," he says in a deep, resonant tone, "The key to balance is knowledge and sacrifice."

***

Jared and Chris spoke about their upcoming trip and spent some time getting to know each other as they chugged south in Sherpa toward New Mexico. Chris learned that Jared was an only child. His father had worked in the oil industry and as a result Jared had spent his early years moving from one remote drilling location to another. He had studied biology and ecology at school and was on his way to getting a doctorate when he had a falling-out with some professors regarding his "unorthodox" ideas. He didn't elaborate. His favorite activities were hiking and mountain biking and he had a passion for all kinds of music, "even country." He also had a weakness for animals (not surprising) and such a green thumb that he was regularly able to nurse fallen leaves back into whole plants. Noticing that Jared never mentioned his mother, Chris cautiously asked about her and immediately regretted his nosiness. Apparently she had died when he was young and they had been very close.

Chris said that he, on the other hand, had not had nearly so unusual a childhood. He was a city kid. He hailed from Boston and was one of five siblings. His father was a self-proclaimed inventor who had yet to actually invent anything useful and his mother was a devoted housewife. Chris admitted to being an accomplished student and a champion chess player, though he seemed embarrassed by both facts, and he boasted that he could recall every joke he'd ever heard. His great love was baseball. He said that the closest he'd gotten to raw environments like the ones Jared had apparently grown up in were the times that he had watched Jared's nature documentaries; however, when Jared asked him which documentaries he liked best Chris demurred. The fact was he'd seen only part of one, once, while flipping channels during a commercial, but he had liked it, sort of.

As they drove Chris began to feel more comfortable asking Jared about rumors he had heard regarding his past. Although Jared was a well-known documentary filmmaker, he remained somewhat of an enigma. He never gave interviews ("I'm not what's important" he'd say) and so it was hard to tell fact from fiction. There was one thing Chris had read that he was more curious about than anything.

"Is it true that you lived in a tree for three months?" he asked.

Jared's face took on a serene aspect. "Yes."

"I can't even imagine. You were trying to prevent people from cutting down the forest?"

"That's right. I was trying to protect an old growth grove. In the end they tore me out. But I tried."

Chris thought about Jared living on top of a tree in a remote wilderness for months on end. The logistics of it were perplexing.

"How did you eat?" he asked finally.

"The other protesters sent up a bucket of food every morning."

"Where did you go to the bathroom?"

"Another bucket." Jared laughed. "Different bucket."

"Didn't you get bored?"

Jared squinted, refocusing to his mind's eye. He was quiet as they passed an office complex jutting like an alien growth from the prairie. The structure looked as though its architectural plans had spawned from a computer's "autodesign" feature. Then Jared started talking about the forest he had grown to know so well. He talked about its damp, earthy smells and constant hum of birds and insects. He mentioned laying on soft moss, breathing cool mist, and watching owls silently glide by at dusk. He spoke about feeling connected.

"You get used to being there," he said, "and then you start noticing details. Once that happens, the details keep you entertained."

"What kinds of details?"

"I wouldn't know where to start. You sit there

and after a while you just kind of blend into the environment. You begin to wonder where you end and where your surroundings begin. Then when a storm blows through you can really appreciate it. You feel as though you can hear each of the individual rain drops landing, and when they fall on the earth it's as though they're falling on your own skin. Something as simple as a rain shower becomes a full-on 3-D sensory experience. It's definitely not boring."

Chris reached into his jacket and pulled out a packet of cookies. He offered one to Jared who politely declined.

"I'd lose it," Chris said, pensively chomping. "I'd need to know how my BoSox are doing. But that sounds trippy. Did you eat a bunch of mushrooms or does your body just naturally produce hallucinogens?"

Jared laughed. "I guess I produce them naturally. Spend some time out in nature and you might too. It's a good thing."

As they reached Pueblo, Jared's mood darkened visibly. The traffic increased and it seemed as though every square inch from the road to the horizon was occupied by one housing subdivision after another. Where houses didn't snuff out the land there were other bland lessons in real estate profit maximization – shopping malls, office buildings, movie complexes.

Chris looked back and forth between Jared's pained expression and the development around them. As he made the connection between the two, he decided to hazard his next question.

"So," he began carefully, "I also heard you used to be an eco-terrorist."

Jared scowled and then quickly softened.

"I prefer the term eco-activist," he said.

"Did you set any buildings on fire?"

"No comment."

"I heard you blew up a Bear Mountain ski lift because they were trying to expand the resort into wilderness area."

"That wasn't me."

"I also heard you painted all the Hummers in Aspen pink one summer."

"Nope. That's pretty funny though."

"And that you torched the Rock Creek construction site outside of Boulder."

"It's amazing how rumors build on themselves. That wasn't me either, though I'm certainly not opposed to limiting urban sprawl. But I realized a long time ago that destroying stuff was not an effective way to protect the environment. Moneyed interests buy insurance and they end up getting even richer when their property is damaged. It's counterproductive."

"So you gave up?"

"No, I changed tactics. I decided the best way to protect our wildernesses would be to capture as much of the magic and mystery of the natural world as I could on film and to share that beauty with the public. That's why I started making documentaries. My hope is that by increasing our appreciation of natural places we will be more apt to protect them. That's the whole point of this trip south. In fact, that's the whole point of my life."

As Jared and Chris continued through Colorado and into New Mexico, scenic valleys and snowy passes gave way to earth-toned mesas and wide expanses of desert. They were approaching their first stop of the trip.

"So you said we'll be doing some filming in Portal?" Chris asked.

"Well, for the most part we'll just be retrieving

data from time-lapse equipment I have set up near there, but we will do some live shots tomorrow morning."

Chris imagined capturing dramatic footage of mountain lions battling bears. Or maybe eagles fighting snakes, or bears fighting eagles.

"What kinds of shots are we after?" he asked excitedly.

Jared's words fell heavily on the whoopee cushion of Chris's enthusiasm. "The time lapse shots are of plants and live shots will be of ants."

Plants? Ants? What could possibly be more boring?

"Oh. Is that it then?"

Jared chuckled. "Try to keep an open mind. There's a lot more going on there than you might think."

It was already dark by the time they reached the Southwestern Research Station at the border of New Mexico and Arizona. This was one of Jared's favorite places in the world. The station, given its location at the intersection of an archipelago of mountains and a sea of desert, was a hotbed of biological diversity and ecological research. Its grounds comprised a number of Spartan but comfortable cottages and meeting houses tucked in a woody grove between towering peaks. A stream ran through its center, and in the summer, a pool and dining hall bustled with activity. Now, in the middle of winter at night, all was quiet.

Jared and Chris parked Sherpa and made their way to one of the rustic cottages. Jared reached for the door handle. "Ronny should have left it unlo--hello buddy." A confused chickadee hopped through the doorway and flew away peeping. Jared laughed. God he loved this place. You couldn't even keep nature out of the rooms.

The two travelers were exhausted after a full day on the road and were asleep almost before they hit their beds. Chris couldn't believe it when the OnePod's alarm chimed. He turned over and put his pillow over his head. It couldn't be time to get up yet, could it? It was still dark out. But Jared was already out of bed getting dressed.

"What time is it?" mumbled the voice under the pillow.

"Four-thirty. Rise and shine. We're meeting the others in thirty minutes. The ants are only active in the morning so we need to get to the desert soon."

Ants, thought Chris. *Ants!* He whimpered out of bed and into his clothes.

A few minutes later they were in Sherpa rumbling toward their filming destination in the desert just outside the mouth of the Chiricahua mountain range. There they would meet a team of university researchers who were studying the ecology of the red harvester ant, *Pogonomyrmex barbatus.* The same area containing about three-hundred colonies of ants had been the subject of studies for the past thirty years, providing a rare continuity of research that was helpful in determining long range ecological patterns.

They reached a nondescript area of desert fenced with wooden rails and parked next to a battered mini-van. Three people, all wearing headlamps, shuffled through the brush nearby. There seemed to be a large machine next to them but in the darkness it was hard to make out.

"Come on, we're late," Jared said. He walked briskly to the rear of his truck and pulled out a cabinet drawer to reveal a treasure of film equipment. He packed a bag full of microphones, tripods, lenses, batteries, cleaning supplies, and two heavy-duty video recorders and started toward the researchers.

As they walked through the desert Chris was surprised to see just how rich it was with life. From the road the previous day it had looked featureless. Now, in the glow of his flashlight, he was greeted with a cabaret of strange plants – spiny aloe vera looking things, scraggly vines and a hundred variations on the cactus theme.

They reached the researchers and Chris had to muffle a chuckle. They were funny in their safari hats with their socks pulled over their pants. There was one tall young African American guy, an older, enthusiastic-looking lady and a mousy kid that looked as though he was about twelve but was probably older since he must have been in college. They each carried a shovel. Next to them was a large backhoe.

"Jared!" the woman said. "You made it!"

"Hi, Dr. Ross," Jared replied, smiling. He gave her a hug.

"Jared, meet my graduate student, Marty Styles."

Jared shook hands with the tall researcher. He was lanky and had a face that seemed perpetually ready to tell a joke.

"Nice to meet you, Mr. Foster, I've watched all your shows."

"Thanks Marty, I really appreciate that."

"And this is Arnold Tzang," continued the professor, "an undergrad honors student."

Arnold Tzang was small and with his giant glasses and the dangling straps of his headlamp he looked a little like an ant himself.

"Pleased to meet you," said Jared. "This is my production assistant, Christopher Burgeis. It's his very first day filming."

"Oh, you're in for a treat!" promised Marty.

"Yeah?" Chris was dubious, but he was admittedly enjoying this experience more than he thought he would. Unfortunately that was for reasons that had nothing to do with what they were about to film. The whole situation was comical to him, researchers spending their time dressing ridiculously and looking at bugs.

"We're going to rip this bad boy up," Marty said, motioning to his side. For the first time Chris noticed the large mound of pebbles next to them. It was at least a meter across. Chris had never seen an ant mound that big. Were these giant mutant ants? Suddenly he realized what the shovels and backhoe were for.

"We didn't want to start before you got here," Dr. Ross said. "There's something interesting happening on the mound. Come look."

Jared and Chris walked over and shined their flashlights on the next entrance. Slender black ants, each about the size of a pencil eraser, were busily piling stones on top of the mound.

"It's really unusual to see this happening this time of year," continued the professor. "It's usually too cold for the ants to do much of anything. But it's been a mild winter."

"Coooool," oozed Jared. "So those must be *Aphaenogaster*?"

Chris was confused. He didn't know why this was interesting or what the significance of it was. Marty must have heard his thoughts.

"They're plugging the nest entrance of the pogos," he explained. "Both species of ants compete for the same food. The *Aphaenogaster* are nocturnal. If they plug the nest entrance of a pogo colony, they can sometimes prevent that colony from foraging the next day, which leaves more food for the *Aphaenogaster* the following night."

Chris still didn't see the big deal. Ants. *Ants*!

"I don't know if you know much about ants," the professor said to Chris, perhaps noticing his lack of a response, "but the thing to keep in mind as we dig into this colony is that there is nobody in charge here. There are no directors or managers running the show. The 'queen' just sits in the ground and lays eggs."

"But we'll find her," Marty promised, "and when we do, Arnold will mate with her."

"Hah, hah, hah, very funny Martian, very funny!" Arnold had some spunk to him. "Actually, we're here to capture the queen and some of the colony to bring back to the lab for Marty's research. So he's the one that will probably end up mating with her back on campus."

"Mind if I film this for a few minutes?" Jared asked.

"No problem," the professor replied. "Take your time. We're just digging up colonies today so it doesn't matter whether we catch them being active or not."

Jared started setting up his equipment. Lighting would be interesting here – little shadows would be hugely magnified in the super zoom shot.

"Oh, they'll be active once we start excavating," Marty said in an ominous tone. "Chris, you may want to pull your socks over your pants. Pogos have really nasty stings. There'll be around ten or twenty thousand very angry ants swarming around here pretty soon."

Oh, thought Chris, that wasn't just a bad fashion choice. He didn't even know ants had stingers; he thought they just bit. Taking a risk at seeming stupid, he asked if Marty really meant "stings." He did. Ants were descended from wasps. The resemblance was clearer with the queens who still had wings during parts of their lives but in reality ants were basically ground wasps. Twenty-thousand angry ground wasps didn't sound fun. Chris pulled his socks up as high as they could go.

"So are these shots going in the *Intelligence in Nature* documentary you were telling me about?" the professor asked Jared. "You know I think that's such a neat idea. And you know what I think about what happened to you in your PhD program. It was a great thesis proposal. They were small-minded."

"Thanks, Dr. Ross. Yes, all the footage we're capturing here will go into that project. We're also collecting time-lapse shots of plants."

"Oh, I'd love to see that!" the professor said. Her face seemed custom built to express the sense of wonder.

Chris was busy watching the *Aphaenogaster* working to sabotage their competitors but overheard Jared and the professor. In the back of his mind he wondered what ants and plants might have to do with intelligence, but mostly he was trying to figure out how the ants he was watching knew to do what they were doing. If there was nobody in charge, how did they know where to put the rocks? How did they even know to start the process, there, at that nest, at that time, all together? It was weird. Ants, he thought, *Ants!* But he didn't mean it quite as much this time.

"Okay, let's get going!" whooped Marty as Jared wrapped up his shot. Arnold climbed on the backhoe and started the ignition. The ground began to dance with vibrations from the engine.

"You're certain you've had enough practice with that thing?' the professor asked.

"Yes, Dr. Ross! Clear the way please!"

Jared handed Chris one of the large video recorders on a tripod. "You're certain you've had enough practice with this thing?" he asked jokingly. In truth, Jared had given Chris only a quick tutorial in the days before they'd left on their trip, but Chris was pretty confident he could press 'record'. Looking at Arnold wildly yank on the backhoe control levers, he wasn't as sure about that plan.

The *Aphaenogaster* scattered.

"Ants don't like vibrations." Marty yelled above the noise, "They think it's an earthquake. Our Pogos are going to wake up fast."

Arnold pressed a lever and the backhoe's claw crashed into the ground, jolting the front of the vehicle up three feet. Dr. Ross and Marty exchanged concerned expressions.

"Sorry, sorry!" Arnold said as he lifted the claw back up. He eased the backhoe into position and extended its stabilizers. The idea wasn't to dig up the nest directly with the machine, but to carve a trench alongside it. They would then use more delicate means to try to find the queen among her twenty-thousand companions.

Arnold scooped the first claw full of dirt. Ants flooded out of the nest. They were huge, by ant standards, each as big as a fly. And they were not happy, viciously biting and stinging anything in the vicinity of their nest.

"Sorry," Dr. Ross said, looking down. She seemed sincere.

Arnold continued to scoop large swaths of earth away from the side of the nest. The pile of debris grew and grew until it was as high as a man and wide as a car. Chris was dumbfounded to think the ant nest could extend as far into the ground as the backhoe had reached.

Eventually Dr. Ross asked Arnold to stop. He looked like a child whose ice cream cone had just been taken away mid lick. It must have been fun getting behind the wheel of the real version of a toy he had played with many times as a boy.

Marty handed gloves, shovels, and hats to Chris and Jared and everyone jumped into the trench and starting digging toward the nest beside it. The top of the trench extended a foot above their heads. Small avalanches of dirt and angry ants fell from above and bounced off the hats that Chris now recognized as critical survival gear. The hazy light of impending dawn cast an eerie pale to the earthen walls around them. They dug until their arms ached and their sweat met the cool morning air. Finally, they broke through to the first nest chamber.

"Whoa, OK, time to move to dental," Dr. Ross exclaimed.

Dental? Chris stopped digging as instructed. Jared climbed out of the hole and retrieved a camera. Arnold brought out a box full of small metal implements and passed them around.

"We have to be very careful now," Marty explained. "All of this is for naught if we can't find the queen or if we accidently kill her. And in this species, she doesn't look much different than the workers – she's just a little bigger. So we use dental tools for this part."

The next few hours were spent tediously teasing the nest chambers into view and sifting through the ants and debris within them in search of the queen. The researchers also collected a fair number of workers and larvae which would form the base of the new colony in the lab.

The more they dug, the more puzzled Chris became. How was this possible? Through their efforts, they had revealed an enormous subterranean Antopolis. Hundreds of baseball-sized chambers of varying shapes lay connected by narrow tunnels spread out across meters of earth. What was most bewildering, beyond the fact that this giant structure could be built without any sort of leadership, was the extreme organization found within each chamber. Some were filled with piles of seed, each type neatly separated in rows. Others were filled with eggs and larvae in various stages of development. Still other chambers contained refuse and some nothing but full-grown workers. How did the ants know where to put what? Who made the decisions regarding how many chambers to build in what configuration? How did they know how much food to collect? It was clear somebody or something or somehow these decisions were getting made.

Chris made a comment expressing his confusion. "Now you're getting it," Marty said excitedly. "That's just the start though – think about all the other things they need to decide how to do - how many foragers to send out each day and when and where, how many queens to make versus workers, how many ants to send out to defend the nest when there's an invasion, who does what tasks in the nest and outside. It's endless. They have this amazing colony-level coordination and yet nobody is in charge."

"And this species faces relatively simple challenges," Dr. Ross commented. "Other types of ants carry on more complex operations, tending aphids like cows, nurturing vast underground fungal gardens—"

"Oh yeah, the leaf cutter ants," Marty added. "They use the leaves they collect to grow the fungus that they eat. Those nests are HUGE, as big as a house underground."

"And then there are the slave driver ants," Dr. Ross said, "capturing larvae from the nests they invade to serve as their unwitting servants when they grow into adults. How do they decide which nests to invade, where, and when? How many larvae to take? What strategies to use in their assault?"

The word *instinct* came to Chris's mind, but it was just a word. It didn't explain anything.

"Science is magic," Arnold mused, carefully placing larvae into a plastic box. Dr. Ross looked over at this comment and just shook her head. Science wasn't magic of course, it was an effort to understand the magic, but it was the mystery that made it worthwhile.

"Whoa! Whoa! Whoa!" Marty stuttered as he froze.

"The queen?" Arnold asked excitedly.

"I think so."

Chris was surprised that even he could make her out. She really wasn't much bigger than the workers bustling around her, an ant pin in a swarmstack, but she moved so slowly, so regally through the tumult around her. She was built to be served, and her demeanor showed it.

"That's her," said Dr. Ross smiling. Marty scooped up the queen gently and smiled as he put her in her new plastic throne room.

The sun had swept a wide arc across the sky by the time Jared and Chris left the researchers to continue with their day's chores. Chris was so deep in thought about what he had just seen that he barely even noticed the change in scenery from parched desert to verdant valleys as they proceeded toward the sites where Jared had his time-lapse photography equipment set up. Collecting the data was relatively easy. Each site involved a short hike, a few minutes of downloading images to laptop, and some camera maintenance. By the time the sun had eased behind the mountains, Jared and Chris were back at the research station.

The on-site chef was off for the winter so they were on their own for dinner. Chris inspected their groceries with concern. Jared's mostly vegetarian diet did not promise a satisfying meal. As it turned out, there was no need to worry. From pedestrian produce, they conjured a meatless miracle.

Chris munched happily at the long dining room table and admired the various mobiles dangling from the ceiling. Iron ants spun round each other like planets of a solar system, birds fluttered in an arc, and a school of fish gently swam through the air. Inspired by the art, Chris wondered how flocks of birds and schools of fish decided what to do. How did they determine what direction to go and when? As with ants, it was clear nobody was in charge. Every time a flock or a school changed directions, it changed leaders.

Seated next to him, Jared let loose a chuckle of wonder at the time-lapse images he was reviewing. Chris dug into a chunk of asparagus and wondered what Jared might be watching. Probably just some pretty images. Jared's fascination with shrubbery was amusing. Granted, plants could be beautiful and, Chris chewed a bit, they were certainly good to eat.

"Oh yeah," Jared whispered appreciatively.

Chris paid no notice. He moved on to a spinach-mushroom concoction. He didn't actually like spinach, or mushrooms, but together they took on a whole new aspect. It was funny how ingredients could interact to create something altogether new. Chris reached for the salt. Perfect example – sodium was a shiny metal and chlorine a poisonous gas but, together, they made a vital nutrient, table salt. Come to think of it, this was even true of musicians and bands. Guns and Roses rocked, but its singer, Axl Rose, was as noxious as chlorine as a solo artist. Maybe something like this explained what was going on with ant colonies – together ants created something that transcended what each individual could do alone. Chris noticed a fourth hanging mobile. This one was really clever. As it spun, its metal panels aligned to simulate a flower unfurling from a bud.

"Oh ho ho! Springtime in the valley!" Jared said.

Chris was tempted to look over. The fact was that he had seen something unexpectedly interesting things in ants. But plants? *Plants?* He was quite confident that nothing short of doing taxes could compare to the boredom inherent in all things plant. Nevertheless, he was getting curious about what Jared could possibly be finding so entertaining. Maybe just one more bite and he would take a closer loo-

A dramatic movement on the screen beside him caught Chris's eye. Now here's the thing about plants, which Chris only realized later. They do things, many absolutely amazing things, but they work at a different time scale than people. Time lapse photography brings their slow motion operas to life. On the screen, Chris was astounded to see delicate tendrils of vines probing, like a blind man, for a holdfast. They twirled around, gently at first, and then in an increasingly frantic manner as they lashed about in a desperate search. When they finally sensed something to grab, they calmly ceased their probing, curled around the objects they had found, and lifted the plants steady.

How could plants "sense" anything? And how did they "know" to expand the vigor of their efforts if they didn't find anything close by?

Jared noticed Chris's shift of attention and smiled. He loved playing this role. He flipped to another camera. Flowers were pulsing open and closed as days went by in seconds in the time-lapse shots.

"Better to close them at night for protection," Jared commented.

Chris's mouth was half-open. He hadn't even finished chewing his last bite. In the screen next to him, plants followed the sun, dancing with the rhythms of day and night. Jared switched cameras. Weeds tumbled and wrestled with one another to reach the light.

Jared accessed a previous collection of footage. He glanced at Chris. He had him on the ropes.

A spindly vine dangling from an epiphyte encircled an enormous tree. The vine eased down the side of its host until it reached the forest floor. Tapping the water and nutrients it found there, it expanded dramatically. Its thin stem engorged to the width of rope, then to the girth of an arm. It dug into the trunk it encircled. It was choking the tree. *It was murdering the tree!*

"Strangler figs," Jared explained, as he retrieved photos of full grown specimens to show the end result of their efforts. The hollow cores of the towering adult stranglers provided the only testimony of their dark essence.

Chris finally gulped down the food in his mouth.

"Coooool," he oozed.

Chris stared into space as Jared edited the plant footage beside him. Ants. Plants. *Ants! Plants!* How was this possible? As hard as it was to understand how ant colonies could display such coordinated behaviors and make decisions with nobody in charge, it was even harder to understand how plants could "behave" at all. They didn't even have brains! Chris's curiosity had almost burned a hole through his skull by the time the ant research crew came laughing into the room.

"Arnold mated with all the queens!" Marty exclaimed.

Arnold strutted to the water cooler to pour himself a drink. "I guess that makes me a king," he said proudly.

Dr. Ross shook her head.

They were freshly clean and wore that weary but contented air that came with a good day's work. Marty and Arnold grabbed some sandwiches from the fridge and took off. "Gotta get back to the ladies in the lab," Marty apologized. "See you guys!"

Dr. Ross pulled out her own sandwich and sat by Jared, observing the images. "Oh yes, that's wonderful," she said.

Chris couldn't stand it any longer.

"How's it work?" he asked. "How do they do it?"

"The ants?" Dr. Ross asked.

"Yes, and the plants, everything. I feel like I just woke up in the middle of a giant conspiracy of mind and I have no idea how it works."

"Well, Jared can tell you a bit about that, can't you, Jared?" Dr. Ross said warmly. "Isn't that exactly what you're after in your *Intelligence in Nature* documentary?"

"And exactly the topic that got me booted from the program," Jared replied, with a hint of bitterness in his voice.

"Your PhD program?" Chris asked.

"Yeah." Jared laughed, shaking it off. "In retrospect I just should have been more careful with my language."

"Well, what did you say that was so controversial?"

Jared looked at Dr. Ross. She nodded encouragingly.

"Basically," Jared started, "I tried to make that point that what we typically call intelligence or mind goes way past what happens in our brains, or in brains in general – that life is mind, in a way. See, living things, all living things, don't passively accept their environments, like rocks would, they interact with them. You kick a rock and it goes flying. Kick a dog and you may get any number of responses. Shine sunlight on a rock and it heats up, shine sunlight on a free living cell and it might heat up, or it might crawl away, or it might swim closer to the light to photosynthesize. The reason the reaction isn't always obvious is because living things have a degree of autonomy, thanks to their ability to harness energy, which allows them to actively interact with their environments. And at every stage of those interactions, living things need to make decisions. Those decisions require some element of mind, or proto-mind."

"What do you mean 'mind'?" Chris asked. "Are

you saying that even a single cell can think? That it's got some kind of consciousness?"

"I don't know about consciousness, but I do believe all living things have aspects or processes which are in many ways analogous to those involved in thought. These include perception, intention, and mood."

"Maybe 'state' is a better word than 'mood'" Dr. Ross offered.

Jared laughed. "You're right, 'state' is better. Where were you when I was writing my thesis proposal?"

"I still don't know what you mean," Chris said. "Cells perceive?"

"Yes. They sense and interpret their environments. That's actually not controversial. Pick up any biology journal and you'll see words like 'perception,' 'sensing,' 'learning,' all these really cognitive terms, all over the place, even when the researchers are talking about single cells. It's generally recognized that living things have these abilities – they must if they're going to sense and make sense of their environments in order to make good behavioral or metabolic or developmental 'decisions.' But nobody's really been explicit about it and made connections regarding what these processes have in common across living forms. That's what I've been trying to do."

"So how's it work? What connections?"

"I wish I had a detailed answer for you. Really I just have some ideas. Think about how brains work. Neurons exchange electro-chemical signals in dynamic waves of interaction. Learning occurs as these cells adjust their synaptic connections in response to sensory inputs. The specific changes that occur depend on how a stimulus is perceived, which depends on one's state of mind. That state of mind is what we'd call an emotion or a mood if we're talking about the short term, or a personality if we're talking about the long term. Resulting changes in the connections between brain cells then bias future electro-chemical flows, and so the process goes on iteratively through time."

Chris looked curiously at Jared. There was a clearly a lot more going on within the man's head than just a desire to capture pretty pictures of nature. "I think I follow," Chris said. "Thought arises through the dynamic interactions of neurons, and our experiences with our environments change the structures of our brains, which then effects how we interact with our environments in the future."

"Right"

"So what's the connection to life in general?"

"The connection is that analogous processes occur in all living things across all scales. Even an individual free living cell, like an amoeba, is just a bundle of interacting molecules and energetic flows, all coupled to environmental inputs, biased by past events, and changed by experience to influence its future behaviors. In this case, instead of neurons we have interacting molecules, but the general idea is the same. Activated receptors on the cell surface sense the cell's environment and induce molecular cascades within the cell body, which combine with what's already going on to create new dynamic structures, which then determine how the cell will "make sense" of its input and subsequently react.

"And the same principles hold true for any organism. Instead of talking about neurons within brains or molecules within cells we can talk about cells within bodies, animals within groups, or individuals within societies."

"Animals within groups…" Chris repeated. "You mean like ants within colonies?"

"Bingo."

Chris stared at the blossom mobile and saw its

form come together as its various components aligned. He was getting it. Colony behaviors emerged from interacting ants as thoughts emerged from interacting neurons as life emerged from interacting molecules in a cell. "And the same would hold true for plants," he offered, "with interactions between cells determining how the plant would develop and 'behave', like the whole plant is a brain."

Jared and Dr. Ross exchanged smiles.

"Yes," Jared said, "and they are just as moody-"

"They have just as many 'states,'" corrected Dr. Ross.

"They have just as many 'states' as other living things. Try not watering a plant for a while, till it's near death. Then pour a bunch of water in its pot. Will it instantly spring back and start to grow? Probably not. It doesn't 'know' if the drought is really over. It's not willing to let go of its defensive state that easily. So one watering might not make a difference, but water it regularly and over the course of time it might change its outlook and grow new shoots. These are all relatively short-term changes, analogous to moods. In the long term, the 'personality' of a plant would be captured in its actual physical form, just as the personality of a person is captured by the physical structure of his or her neural connections. This plant 'personality', or maybe 'plant-ality' is a better term, would be affected by the plant's experience in life, as well as the experiences of its ancestors as recorded in its genes. Think of the 'careful' attitude of a bonsai tree stunted by lack of resources at an early age, or the permanently 'careful' behavior of desert plants, tuned by natural selection to expect the worst."

Chris was starting to feel bad for all the plants that had withered in his care. "But..." he started. He was stretching his knowledge of biology to its breaking point. Though he understood Jared's points about collective interactions producing decisions and the importance of 'moods' and 'personalities' in determining behavior, one thing still confused him.

"Yes?" Jared asked.

Dr. Ross finished her sandwich and began collecting her things.

"But where's the intention come from?" Chris asked. "You mentioned perception, mood, and intention as universal traits in living things. I understand now what you mean by perception and mood, but I don't see where the intention comes from in something like a single cell or a plant. I mean, we do things because we want to. Why do single cells or plants do what they do? Those things don't even have brains to 'know' or 'want' anything. Something has to have made the connection between the behaviors and outcomes. It's hard to imagine how it works without consciousness."

"I think it comes back to evolution," Jared said. "I'd say that 'thought,' that intention, if it exists, exists within the genetic 'mind.' Genes work together just like neurons but instead of building thoughts they build bodies and brains. Evolution tunes the way those genes work together so that the ants, or neurons, or cells act in ways that lead to reproductive success. I don't think I'd call it a consciousness, but the end result is something like intention in all living things."

"Crazy," Chris said. "That's one of the coolest things I've ever heard."

Dr. Ross laughed. "And on that note I'll say goodnight." She gave Jared a warm hug and proud look and shook Chris's hand. "I can tell you two are going to have some fun conversations during this trip."

Chris's neurons interacted frantically. Connections formed between the most unlikely brain regions. His thoughts were fiery tendrils probing for a holdfast and though he lay comfortable in bed the likelihood of sleeping was negligible. Not only had the discussion earlier that night opened whole new ways for him to view life, but this new input had joined the existing structure of Chris's brain, which had previously focused on quite different subject matter, to form the most unexpected of connections between science and spirit.

It was what Jared had said on the way back to their room that had launched this train of thought. He had talked about how viruses fit into his theories. The example he had used was rabies. Now, viruses weren't even really alive; they were just bits of DNA or RNA surrounded by proteins, but nevertheless, they displayed remarkably adaptive "behaviors."

The first thing the rabies virus did when it infected its mammalian host was to make its way to its host's brain and multiply. But it didn't just infect any part of the brain; it specifically disrupted the circuits responsible for aggression. At the same time, other virus particles migrated to the host's salivary glands. As they multiplied there, they made it excruciatingly painful for their host to swallow. As a result, the new viruses accumulated in massive amounts in the host's mouth.

The result was an aggressive host frothing with virus-laden saliva and eager to chomp on anything that crossed its path. This proved a very effective recipe for the spreading of the rabies virus, but the really amazing thing was that this brilliant reproductive strategy evolved without brains or bodies or even cells. Or rather, it evolved without a central focus on any of these physical forms. Over the course of its life cycle, the virus moved through them all. It was nearly impossible to pin down as a concrete thing since it was different things at different stages – sometimes the virus manifested as a discrete particle, sometimes it was embedded within the metabolic machinations of its host.

This all fit within Jared's ideas – it was natural selection and the memory of the genetic mind that allowed the emergence of this "intelligence" in the form of the rabies life cycle. But it was the fact that viruses didn't have bodies or brains of their own that created a neon beacon in Chris thoughts. This was important. To an observer, this "intelligence" would seem to come out of nowhere.

"Jared, are you still up?" he asked.

"Mmm."

"The thing about viruses, it's, well, I've been thinking…"

"Mmm, hmm."

"I've been studying ancient cultures forever and one thing they all have in common is a belief in spirits. Every time I came to the word 'spirit' in a document I just had to kind of gloss over it and thought it was kind of sad that they could be so deluded."

Jared opened one eye sleepily. Chris was sitting upright in his bed, talking excitedly.

"But what you were talking about tonight, well, with the rabies virus for instance, you're talking about this sort of 'intelligence' that seems to come out of nowhere but has the ability to affect the material world."

Jared sat up attentively.

"I mean that's exactly what a spirit is, isn't it? I don't mean like ghosts or immortal souls going up to heaven or anything like that, but like the 'spirit' of a forest, or a 'death spirit,' or even 'team spirit.' To an observer, a forest would seem to have an intelligence, like it knows how to heal itself and carry on, but that intelligence would just emerge from the interactions of all the things that compose the forest. And like you said, 'mood' is important. So a forest in a particular mood may or may not be able to regenerate itself after damage since its ability to do so would depend on its past and what the state of the forest was when it got damaged. And then with death spirits, well, I've read so much about how they could be wrathful or merciful, which I always thought was just superstitious bunk, but now I'm thinking of a disembodied virus plague. Its 'mood' would seem to change depending on how many people were infected – as the density of people for it to infect increased, people would think a wrathful spirit were at work because more people would become infected and die. As population density decreased, infection rates would go down and people might think the spirit was showing mercy. And then there's team spirit. That sure seems to have real effects, and mood is the whole thing there. I'm starting to think these things are as real as any material object. Or rather, they are material, they're just diffuse. Even though they're so decentralized that they're hard to pin down as concrete things, they're as real as anything else that can affect the material world."

Jared was wide awake. He rubbed his chin thoughtfully. "I stopped believing in spirits, gods, and Santa Claus all at the same time," he mused. "But what you're saying, thinking of spirits the way you're saying, takes some of the voodoo out of the subject. Maybe we shouldn't be looking for wailing apparitions; we should be looking for intelligent behaviors that seem to come out of nowhere. I think you're on to something very…important."

"And that means spirit possession is possible too," Chris said, staring far past the confines of their room. Worlds of interpretation were throwing open their doors to his probing thoughts. "You hear people talking about ancestor spirits a lot. Now I realize those spirits can be considered as real as anything, so long as they affect our actions. It's the same thing – the spirits of our ancestors are composed of bits and pieces of the collective memory. When those memories come together, either within or between minds, and interact with what's currently going on, they can affect our behaviors."

"So what's the possession part?"

"Well, I'm thinking that if someone tunes into that kind of collective spirit, it could have really good or bad material effects. I mean, consider Hitler. Hitler tapped into something. A man doesn't have that kind of demonic power. A man can't kill fifty million other people through the sheer force of his will. Hitler was more than a man; he was an incarnation – of the seething rage of his countrymen after defeat in the first World War. When he spoke it was the 'spirit' of that entire nation speaking and it was the fury of the people that gave his acts impossible strength. It wasn't the man but the spirit channeled through the man that led to the horrors of the age."

"Whoa."

"Yeah, pretty dark. But holy shit, Jared, spirits exist."

Chapter 3
Music of Nature

  Sloan watches as the large man next to him places his satchel atop a stainless steel gurney. He squints as the man turns on a powerful examination lamp. Now the contraption surrounding Sloan is clearly visible. He sits strapped in a dentist chair with twisted metal appendages dangling from its sides and back.

  "Wha...what are you going to do to me?" Sloan snivels.

  The man reaches behind the chair for a head brace, which he fits over Sloan's cranium. He pauses. "The spirits anguish, Sloan. I will help you to hear them as I do." He tightens belts and screws expertly. With his head now immobile, Sloan must strain his eyes to follow the man as he walks to a corner of the room. There are electronics there and a video monitor. The man manipulates knobs and Sloan hears rhythmic ocean waves crashing against a shore. With the turn of a few more dials, the air flushes with calls of forest creatures, a choir of joyous birds, a million leaves rustling under pattering feet. More knobs bring forth a warmth of coos and purrs, the whoosh of curious wind, and the eerie beauty of whale song. The air becomes so thick with sound that Sloan can almost feel it pour into his lungs when he breathes.

  As Sloan listens, he realizes that the disparate sounds are interleaving to form a rich harmony. Despite his horrifying situation, he finds himself relaxing into the music. The large man seems to be doing the same. He faces the ceiling, eyes closed, an expression of rapture on his face.

  And then a distinctly unnatural tone pierces through the sonic edifice. Sloan can't quite place it, but it is definitely not an animal. It is there again, a furious gnawing. A chainsaw. Explosive snapping announces the violence of falling trees, followed by more chainsaws and more tumult of tearing timber. Other grating sounds emerge, metallic noises –

whirs, pops, twists and impact blows. Engines redline at high pitch, horns and alarms blare, and raging fires moan and crackle. The animal calls transform. Pleasant murmurs turn to cackles and harsh bellows. Monkeys scream wildly, wolves howl in despair, and pigs squeal in terror. It is as if the worst nightmares of all the creatures on Earth had burst open and flooded the room with anguish.

The large man's face has changed as well. It is no longer serene. He turns to Sloan, trembling with fury and sneering viciously. Sloan wets himself and begins to weep.

***

Crossing the border to Mexico was uneventful. Hints that Jared and Chris had entered a foreign country included a sharp change in the condition of the buildings and cars around them as well as a shocking increase in the number of men wearing cowboy hats. Houses sported more colorful hues, and pick-up trucks advertised lax driving laws through their impressive numbers of cargo bed passengers.

On their way to their next destination in the Copper Canyon, the two travelers continued south through a Dr. Seuss panorama of dusty plains and strange desert plants. Parched desert slowly transitioned to mountainous pine forests. Sherpa struggled up steep passes and across scenic valleys. Arteries of paved highway branched into capillaries of increasingly primitive dirt roads. At one point it became clear that the track they were following had transformed into a dry creek bed, or maybe it was a road sometimes and a creek at others. They continued for several more miles until a river confronted them. Sherpa muscled her way over several large boulders and eventually they reached a perfect camping spot along the river bank. Verdant cliffs with peaks covered in chiffon veils of snow surrounded them. The river ahead ran strongly and the forest around them protected them from the wind.

"This'll do," Jared said contentedly.

This was Chris's first camping experience and Jared was happy to show him the basics of setting up tents and starting a fire. Leaving Chris to prepare dinner, Jared retrieved sound recording equipment from Sherpa and headed to the river bank. Grumbles from Chris's stomach marked the time until eventually wafts of savory scent announced that dinner was ready. Chris tried a bite and ambled to the riverside to find Jared. He rounded a bend to see his friend engulfed by a lattice of microphones and stands arranged in a geometry Pythagoras would have admired. Jared wore headphones and worked the controls of a console to which all of the electronics were attached. Chris was about to say something when Jared motioned for him to be quiet. A moment passed and Jared waved Chris over as he removed one side of his headphones.

"Can I talk?" Chris mouthed silently.

Jared adjusted a knob on the mixer. "Yup, sorry, just had to get the levels right."

Chris stepped into the lattice of recording equipment and marveled at the construction around him. Microphones pointed in all directions. Some were trained at the forest, others at the sky above, and an entire army of sharp shooters took aim at the river beside them. "Dinner is…um…what is all this?"

"The Symphonator - my mobile recording studio. The music of nature is the soundtrack to my films."

Chris's recording experience had never extended beyond using the built-in microphone on a laptop. This all seemed over the top. "But why so many mics?" he asked.

Jared sat on a boulder and gestured to a spot next to him. "Take a seat," he suggested. "Listen for a minute."

Chris sat. He heard rushing water and the occasional bug chirping in the surrounding woods. It was certainly relaxing, but he didn't understand why someone would expend so much effort trying to capture these sounds. He shrugged.

Jared smiled as if he knew a secret. "Sometimes it's hard to notice the symphony, but it's always there. All this equipment...well, have you ever been to rock concert?"

"Of course."

"They're fun, but there's so much going on that you usually can't hear the music well at all. In the studio, engineers know how to bring out the sound, to accentuate it, bring out its essence. Once you've heard the studio version of a song, even if you can barely hear the instruments at the live show, you'll know what's there; you'll be better able to appreciate it."

Chris nodded.

"Try these," Jared said, handing Chris his headphones.

It was glorious. The dull roar of the river instantly transformed into an epic three-dimensional tapestry of interweaving sounds. What had at first seemed to be one loud drone revealed itself to be an almost infinite number of varied whispers. Chris glanced in rapid succession at the turrets of microphones pointed at the river and understood – each was highlighting some small portion of the sonic tapestry. Delicate swirls of eddies mixed with bubbling waterfalls as countless streams shooshed against all manner of rocks. Waters raced past submerged branches and trees to weave their own timbres into the mix and every minute bend and variation in the river added another layer of tonal complexity.

Chris fumbled off the headphones and listened

directly to the water. How had he never noticed this? Jared was right - within the drone, all the sounds were there.

He put the headphones back on. The river constituted just one aspect of the symphony that caressed his ears. Whorls of wind formed a cavalcade of whistles as it pranced through the leaves and branches of the forest. Cicadas, crickets and other forest creatures made their own contributions, each playing a slightly varied note, together creating complex rhythms and harmonies. Above the rest soared exultant birdsong, its singers reveling in their roles as lead instruments in the natural chorus.

Chris removed the headphones. He laughed in amazement. The sounds were all there.

"Coooool," he oozed.

Jared beamed.

They talked over dinner. The setting sun painted the mountains and clouds with its warm farewells. Jared was as at home as a baby in a womb. He marveled at their surroundings and shared his belief that the music of nature wasn't just limited to the auditory realm. It was everything around them – the sights, the smells, the sensations. It was the colors of the setting sun playing off the clouds, the branches and leaves swaying beside them, the sweet air they breathed. To Jared, nature *was* music, and what could be done to bring out the latent complexities of soundscapes could be done with anything to make the infinite richness of reality more salient. That was his biggest challenge as a filmmaker. The trick was making the most of one's limited senses to discern the wonder of what was really there, and then capturing the essence of that subtle richness in video and sound.

A rhythmic rumbling in the distance interrupted

their conversation. They scanned their surroundings in an effort to determine its source. The racket ricocheted off the mountains. As the strident tones grew more distinct, they both realized what it was.

"A helicopter?" Chris said, incredulous. He thought of the beautiful recordings Jared was capturing by the river. Ruined, for the moment anyway.

Jared winced.

The sound grew deafening. Eventually a monstrous helicopter burst through the air above and groaned out of sight. No sooner had it disappeared than they heard a bellowing horn, followed by the telltale chugging of a train locomotive. The train's screeching wheels drowned out the singing birds and gently flowing water.

Jared hunched over as if he were in pain.

"You alright?" Chris asked.

It was a long time before Jared sat back up. When he spoke, his voice was subdued. "You know, earlier, I was imaging that I was recording the spirits of this place. I'd never thought of such a thing before. I imagined the spirits would want nothing more than to exist within the natural symphony of the area, but they're constantly being assailed by the screeching tones of humanity. Our singing is thoroughly out of tune."

Chapter 4
Nature on the Run

Sloan burbles in terror. The sounds of destruction and suffering around him have fused into a furious thunder of misery. The thunder ebbs and flows, reaching crescendos that burn into his mind and press into his gut. Through this dense synchronous swirl he sees the large man begin to speak but cannot hear his words. The giant's voice blends unintelligibly into the tumult around him. It seems as though it is the animal screams themselves that are emanating from his mouth. The man walks slowly towards Sloan. Now the occasional word becomes distinguishable. "…all things…" he says, "…toxic in excess…"

Poison, is he going to poison me? wonders Sloan. He tries to shake his head "No" but cannot because of the dome restraint. "What do you want?" he pleads, his tiny voice barely audible through the din.

The man does not answer. He stands tall in front of Sloan. His mouth once again moves but Sloan hears only the roar of the loudspeakers. Then Sloan hears a piercing fizzle and his eyes dart to the electronics. They have gone dark.

Did the audio blow a fuse? But the sounds are still there, plaintive and tortured, pulsing, throbbing, coming from, coming from where?

The man reaches into the leather satchel laying on the gurney.

"Majestic mountains…" he says, "…denuded…"

What the hell does that mean?

"…trimmed…"

"…like manicured poodles…where once there were wolves!"

The man retrieves a clamp from the bag. He palms Sloan's chin and pulls the flesh of his face forward with his fingers until he has a firm grip on his lips. His voice is booming *now, stentorian in tone. Each word released through his clenched jaws is a fist pummeling Sloan's brain.*

"...no respect!"

The man fixes the clamp onto Sloan's mouth.

"...to build!"

"...to cut! "

"...to mock the power of the Earth!"

The man reaches once more into his satchel. More words, or screams, or both, come hurtling from his mouth.

"...disfigured..."   he   seethes   viciously, "...disgustingly disfigured!"

Sloan squirms against his restraints. He sees the glint of a scalpel and begins to squeal in abject horror. His desperate cries add just one more voice to the wailing chorus of suffering around him.

***

Despite two days of hard driving along twisting roads from the Copper Canyon to the Pacific Coast, Jared was upbeat. Fond memories of his next filming destination corralled his wandering mind toward happy thoughts. In his recollection, the lagoons around the town of Abundancia were a celebration of living diversity. There, at the interface of ocean and land, a vast expanse of mangrove forests marched deep into the watery domain, providing shelter along the way for a teeming variety of life. Roseate Spoonbills feasted on legions of crustaceans; Cormorants, Wood Storks, Herons and Egrets enjoyed a rich bounty of fish; crocodiles and turtles lounged in the sun; and dozens of other species of birds and bats flew through a languid air bursting with song.

The plan was to camp or find a hotel near Abundancia and hire a boat to take Jared and Chris deep into the mangrove forest. There, Jared would collect footage for his "Living Hope" project, a collage of particularly spectacular natural displays. The last time he had been in the area, almost ten years earlier, Jared had made a mental note to return one day to capture its splendor. That day, in fact, that hour, now approached.

Navigating, Chris indicated a well maintained road branching from the highway as the turnoff to Abundancia. This didn't seem right to Jared. He distinctly remembered a much more primitive route. In his experience, dirt roads often led to good things, but the approaching turnoff looked more like an entry to a shopping mall parking lot than a path to an enchanted wilderness.

They took the turn and Jared's confusion grew. The agricultural tracts and irrigation ditches that he saw extending to the horizon juxtaposed harshly with the forests and scrublands of his memory. True, it had been some time since Jared had been to the area but this degree of change was hard to believe. Maybe the road he was thinking of was farther along.

Disbelief locked horns with disappointment in his head. Where Jared remembered flourishing mangrove forests along the coast, he now saw only isolated archipelagos of trees separated by neat rectangular pools. "It's all gone!" Jared's disappointment moaned from beneath blankets of denial. "There must be another explanation," replied his disbelief. Jared noticed another change. The last time he had driven this route, he had passed only the occasional battered truck, but now waves of shiny new cars zoomed by. "Paid for by all this development no doubt," Jared's disappointment claimed accusingly. "Maybe," replied his disbelief, "or maybe these were just tourists who had come to visit parts of the forests that were preserved up ahead." Minutes passed. "Oh, is that a preserve?" Jared's disappointment asked with mock sincerity. They drew closer. "Oh, dear," it went on, "it's just some stumps, where there *used* to be trees."

An hour after taking the turnoff, Jared and Chris reached their destination. The welcome sign before them settled the argument. Jared's disappointment grabbed his disbelief by the scruff of its neck and drop-kicked it off a cliff. The sign read "Bienvenidos a Abundancia de Los Camarones." The good citizens of Abundancia, proud of their fruitful dominion of the land, had changed the name of their town to "Abundance of Shrimp." The mangrove wonderland of Jared's memory had been replaced by an endless grid of shrimp farms.

Sickened, Jared tried to concentrate as he drove through a modern downtown he now barely recognized. Chris tried to cheer him up by pointing out the benefits of the area's recent development. The citizens were clearly better off, materially at least. And people had to eat. Food had to be grown to feed the burgeoning human population. This was progress. This was investment in a brighter future.

Jared groaned like a man who'd just been reassured that at least the cancer devouring his body was thriving. "We're a plague," he mumbled dourly. He glanced forlornly around him, each eyeful a soul-sucking demon slurping hope from his heart. "You know there used to wild lions and elephants in the U.S.," he said, "and camels and cheetahs and horses, just ten thousand years ago?"

Chris shook his head. He was afraid to say the wrong thing and further upset his friend.

"Know what happened?" Jared continued. "We ate them. We *ate* them! We crossed the land bridge from Asia to North America and feasted all the way down to Tierra del Fuego. Same with the dodo in Mauritius, same with the large marsupials of Australia, same everywhere we go – we find Eden, swallow it, and shit it out to make a place like this."

Chris nodded. He certainly wasn't as bothered by development as Jared, but recognized his friend's anguish and let him go on.

"What's the exchange rate for a person and a tree anyway?" Jared asked bitterly. "Or a person and a tiger, or a panda? We've got a measly five-thousand tigers left in the entire world, a couple hundred wild pandas, and a growing population of seven billion human beings. Don't those ratios seem a little off? How many more people do we need?" He shook his head as though trying to clear away the scene, but reality didn't dissipate so easily. "Shrimp!" he cried, throwing his arms in the air. "Abundancia de fucking shrimp!"

Eventually Jared calmed. He decided the last thing he wanted was to stay the night in this town and so began looking for a camping spot. He learned from a townsperson that the entire area from Abundancia to the coast and all the way back to the highway was jealously guarded private land. They would thus need to find a space in an official campground or a room in a hotel, or they would earn an unwelcome lesson in Mexican law. They tried one pitiful campground on the outskirts of town. Its grounds consisted of a field of mud and one remaining tree. Despite its lack of appeal, it was filled to capacity. They drove to another site, and yet another. There were no vacancies anywhere. Eventually, they gave up and tried to book a room in a hotel back in town. Even that was a challenge. Apparently, the entire region had recently experienced an enormous population boom. This, along with the large number of travelers who came to do business related to the area's burgeoning economy, made it surprisingly hard to find lodging.

After much struggle, they secured a room in a rickety guesthouse. They learned from the guesthouse proprietor of a wildlife sanctuary one town over, which they planned to visit the following morning. Exhausted and dejected, they ate dinner in silence and retired for the night.

Jared's mind swam through layers of depression to poke its head into consciousness. He opened his eyes reluctantly. The morning sun can be so generous, he thought, with its gifts of light and hope. But not today. A swollen blanket of dark clouds drowned the morning cheer, and the only thing to be hoped for in this town was a good deal on a shrimp taco. Jared and Chris both dressed quickly and left, but soon found that their next destination offered no reprieve. The wildlife sanctuary was the exclamation mark at the end of a tragic sentence.

The sanctuary occupied a ramshackle series of wooden buildings surrounded by barbed wire fence. Each building had its own courtyard and specialized in its own genre of endangered species. The reptile and amphibian wing contained a crocodile breeding center and frog pond, as well as a sea turtle "museum" (i.e., a dilapidated shack featuring the painted carapace of a sea turtle and a basket of shellacked eggs). The mammal wing held an assortment of singularly miserable animals in cages, and the bird arena served as a hospice for the last remaining survivors of a variety of doomed species.

Chris was confused when Jared abruptly left the center and came back with an armful of video equipment. "This isn't exactly prime nature habitat for shooting," he said.

Jared sighed heavily as he set his equipment down and began to clean the lens of one of his cameras. "I had hoped to capture video for my Living Hope project," he said, "but obviously we're too late for that. We can use this footage for my 'Nature on the Run' documentary."

"Is that like the flipside of the Hope project?"

"Exactly. You know, I try not to be preachy in my work. I try to focus on the beauty of our natural treasures and let people make their own decisions. But for whatever reason, sometimes it's hard for us to recognize the value of things until they're gone. We only recognize the depth of a girlfriend's warmth and devotion after the breakup, the cool shade of the tree after it's cut. 'Nature on the Run' is designed to increase our appreciation by highlighting our loss."

After getting permission from the sanctuary staff, Jared and Chris began recording video of the crocodile breeding area. Jared worked the camera while Chris handled lighting. A khaki-clad staff member, with soulful eyes and the pendulous face of a sad clown, looked on and told them about the history of the center and the current state of its denizens. Apparently, the species of crocodile they were videotaping had been inadvertently exterminated from the surrounding area. While hunting had played some role in its demise– this species provided excellent meat, hide, and eggs –it was the loss of habitat associated with the recent development that had pushed its fortunes off the ledge. Though the staff member was optimistic about the center's crocodile breeding efforts, he lamented that there was no place to release the captive animals – they had no homes left to go to.

The crocodiles were sleek and beautiful, raw nature expressed in muscle and jaw. These animals had no clue how screwed they were, thought Jared, as a memory lurched from his subconscious and dragged him into the past. He was a child once more, arriving at his father's summer house in Florida to see a baby alligator floating in the swimming pool.

The alligator was at that stage in life when it needed to find its own territory. So it had wandered, probably for days, across disjointed swamp lands and then through the suburbs that had replaced those lands, and had eventually found what it must have thought was succor, a shimmering blue pool uninhabited by any competitors. But the pool was a mirage of goodness. Its chlorine killed any plants and prey before they had a chance to grow while its concrete borders prevented the comfort of shade trees. It was a man-made aquatic siren, luring unwitting creatures with its beauty to a sad and confusing end.

Of course the alligator didn't understand this. Its genetic program told it that water meant food, but no food was forthcoming in this artificial world. So it sat and waited and grew thinner. By the time Jared had found it, there was barely anything left of the alligator at all, just a pathetic rag of hide draped over a thin, doomed body, floating, endlessly hopeful, in the empty water.

Jared cleared his throat. Another memory rapped at the door of his attention. He tried to ignore it – he'd buried this one deep in his subconscious for many years – but what Jared was seeing resonated so strongly with that earlier experience that the crystal cup of his repression exploded into a billion razor-sharp shards of painful imagery. Those ducks, the highway and that poor brave man. It was Los Angeles, an eight-lane freeway. A duck waddled through the road, her downy ducklings following in single file. Streams of cars roared by. The mother duck had no ability to understand the gravity of her situation. Any second she or her babies would be killed. The whole scene was so wrong, so bizarre and unnatural, so cruel. That road wasn't supposed to be there. It was an abomination. Where did it come from? Who had the right to bisect the world so rudely? Jared stopped his truck. The shoulder was thin. This was a dangerous situation. A car ahead of him also pulled over. Its driver, a young man, carefully opened his door. He motioned for his passenger to stay inside, turned and was promptly hit full speed by a black limousine. Tires squealed and horned blared. The limousine kept driving. Jared raced toward the scene, passing a shower of feathers on the way. As he knelt over the broken man he noticed a movement beyond the crowd gathering around him. The mother duck lay squirming, half crushed under a tire, as her brood peeped frantically around her.

Jared cleared his throat again, more vigorously this time. His knuckles were white from the force of his grip on the camera. The fierce determination etched in his face contrasted sharply with the tears raining from his eyes. This was going to be a long day.

Chapter 5

Syncretism

The heavy steel door closes with a thud. The room is silent once more. The dentist chair is empty, the large man covered in blood. He turns to a corner where flickering candlelight illuminates an altar laden with carved figurines. Some of the sculptures are human-like, some animal, and some so worn with time that only stubs remain of their original forms. All face the dentist chair.

The man kneels before them. He lights fragrant copal incense and dabs their mouths with blood. He chants rhythmically as tendrils of smoke rise to explore the room. His voice seems to synchronize with the meanderings of the mist, or perhaps it is the smoke that swirls in time with his words. A light knocking on the door threatens to pull him out of his trance but he does not respond. The door creeps open and two small men enter, backs hunched in servitude. They tip-toe to the lectern and gently deposit a stack of documents there, as well as a small glass vial. Their eyes widen as they notice ephemeral forms moving through the mist. Bowing repeatedly, they carefully back out of the room.

The man continues his worship until the incense burns to ash and the smoke dissipates. With both hands, he reverently lifts a gnarled wooden cross and holds it high above his head. He pleads for forgiveness and pledges more nourishment for his pantheon. Lowering the cross to his lips, he kisses it gently, and places it back on the altar, careful to maintain its unobstructed view of the dentist chair. He then walks to his lectern and begins to examine the documents that his men have deposited there.

***

Jared's mood brightened as he and Chris drove

along the coast. Crashing waves framed picturesque beaches on one side of them while mountains and valleys swam in and out of existence on the other. The temperature served as their odometer, rising with each southward mile. Jared estimated they would reach Guatemala within a day, in time to hear Chris's favorite scholar give a lecture on the true meaning of the Maya apocalypse, but he could not be certain given Mexico's wide variation in road quality. A journey of an hour as the crow flew could take a week as the truck drove. As it turned out, the roads twisted along the coast but were in good repair and the two travelers made quick progress toward the border.

Interesting discoveries punctuated the beauty of the scenery chugging by. First, there was the town of Viento, aptly named for the wailing winds that roared through the surrounding valley. The vegetation in the area was forced to grow to one side, like hair trailing in the wind. Jared found the existence of such a place remarkable. It had never occurred to him that stable rivers of wind existed. In his experience, air was like a capricious infant, throwing windy tantrums in random directions, but here it always flowed along the same route. Even more fascinating was the interplay between the physical and organic– each new gust both molded and was molded by the shape of the trees. History engaged the present in dialogue to determine the future.

Another sight was stranger still. Endless caravans of men, women, and children ran along the roads. They went barefoot, wore bandanas and wooly vests, and carried torches. A van or pickup truck, decorated with garlands of flowers and featuring framed paintings on their roofs, led each group. The vehicles honked their horns, blared their alarms, and flashed their lights. Runners filled the highways and city streets, often backing up traffic for miles, though nobody seemed to care.

For a time both Jared and Chris could not understand the significance of what they were seeing, however, once Chris got a good look at one of the mounted paintings the whole phenomenon became clear. "They're worshippers," he explained, "running in devotion to Virgin of Guadalupe. Her festival must be coming up."

This explanation dispelled some confusion, but one question still remained. Why did the runners dress the way they did? With their bare feet, fur vests, and occasional feathered headdresses, they seemed from another time, closer in style to traditional indigenous garb than modern Catholicism. To understand that aspect of the ritual, Chris suggested, one needed to recognize that the Virgin of Guadalupe was not simply Mexico's version of the Virgin Mary. She was an entity unto herself.

To support his claim, he pointed out the fact that what is now the country of Mexico was once the heartland of the Aztec nation. In fact, the name 'Mexico' meant 'The Land of the Aztecs.' Despite the victories of the conquistadors, this nation's assimilation of European culture had not been wholesale. Some Aztec beliefs had been replaced outright, but others had melded with European traditions to create something altogether new. The case of religion illustrated this complex interplay. Though the Aztecs adopted Catholicism, the depth of their true 'conversion' was debatable. Given that the Aztecs had already been burning incense, worshipping images, undertaking elaborate pilgrimages (like the ones Jared and Chris were now witnessing), and worshipping a primary deity (the Maize God) who had died and later been resurrected, much of their transition to Christianity seemed an exercise in adaption and name changing versus outright substitution.

The story of the Virgin of Guadalupe fit within this pattern. As the story went, an Aztec peasant provided his local bishop with evidence of an encounter with the Virgin in the form of a ghostly image emblazoned on his tunic. Upon seeing this evidence, the local bishop ordered that a church be built on the spot where the peasant had received his vision. That spot had previously been the location of an important Aztec temple devoted to the Earth goddess, Tonatzin. Thus, once the new church was built, the Aztecs could go right on worshipping their old goddess in the same holy spot, and could continue their pilgrimages of devotion unchanged except in name.

Given these various lines of evidence, Chris held that the reverence the Mexicans demonstrated toward the Virgin of Guadalupe represented as much an Aztec loyalty to a pagan deity as a modern nation's acceptance of a foreign god. There was even a general term for this sort of religious melding – it was called 'syncretism.' Old beliefs died hard. Their twisted leaves and branches had their own say in the way the winds of change would blow.

Eventually, Jared and Chris reached the border. After dealing with a chaos of paperwork, sketchy characters, and fees paid to individuals who may or may not have had any anything to do with the official border staff, they continued into Guatemala. Worried that they would miss Dr. Conroy's lecture, Chris asked Jared if they could go any faster. Unfortunately, the terrain was incredibly steep, with Sherpa alternating between exhausting trudges almost straight up mountains and dizzying descents, the grades of which would have prohibited road construction back home. To make matters worse, their maps were insults to cartography.

The fact was that good charts of Guatemalan roads simply did not exist. Nor could they rely on their OnePods, which now showed only vague outlines in place of detailed geographic information. Despite these challenges, Chris coaxed the proper cardinal directions from the tools he had at his disposal and they slowly made their way.

The long shadows of late afternoon indicated time was running out. Chris found what looked like a shortcut on his map but there was no way to judge how much time it would save given the unknown of road quality. They decided to gamble and turn. What started as a road in good repair quickly degraded into a mule track. As Sherpa bucked and bounced along dutifully, the scenery more than made up for their slow progress. This region had no notion of "flat." Majestic mountains wearing royal robes of green bathed in a fine mist. The emerald earth heaved forth to meet a jagged, fractal sky. They had stumbled upon the scenic route of an already scenic road system.

They began to notice patches of cultivation, angular fields extending halfway up the towering peaks. Judging by the traditional dress of passersby, Chris surmised that this area was inhabited by ethnic Maya. The men wore small capes and the women richly embroidered huipils. Both Jared and Chris commented on the beauty of the youths they passed, with their delicate features and bronze skin. Chris had read something of the area and knew a thing or two about the Maya. Most saliently, and contrary to popular belief, the Maya had never 'disappeared.' Their classic civilization may have fallen, but just as the descendents of the Romans were still very much alive sipping cappuccinos by the ruined buildings of their ancestors, something like seven million Maya still inhabited these lands. They continued to speak variants of their ancient tongue and lived much the way they always had. Or at least they tried to live that way. As a general rule their Spanish conquerors had not left them with the easiest lands to cultivate. How exhausting it must have been to plow the rocky soils of these steep mountainsides!

The two travelers pressed on, occasionally pausing to let trains of livestock amble across the road. Eventually they reached a small village set in a valley surrounded by corn. A few villagers shuffled by with firewood on their backs. Others sat peacefully in the soft afternoon sun. A prominent chapel centered the town. Its stucco walls explored every nuance of white and its rustic roof acted as a nursery for a kaleidoscope of exotic epiphytes.

Jared and Chris decided to stop to stretch their legs. As they stepped out of the vehicle they were unnerved by the sensation that all eyes had locked on to them. Chris suddenly remembered a news story he had read back in Boulder. Some time ago, a group of Japanese tourists had been hacked to death in a Maya market. The villagers had thought the tourists were there to steal their children. Chris motioned for Jared to get back in the truck but both of them got distracted by a murmur coming from the chapel. Curiosity trumped their unease and they stepped toward the building. An unusual cross dominated the chapel façade. Flowery embellishments decorated its arms and vines twisted up its sides.

"Check that out," Chris whispered, pointing.

"The cross?"

"Yeah. That's amazing. You know the ancient Maya worshipped a cross too? It represented their World Tree, the center of their universe, and it looked a whole lot like that."

They stepped closer and peered inside the chapel's double doorway. An intricate arrangement of candles cast forth a dancing light and a fragrant carpet of pine needles covered the floor. Statues only vaguely reminiscent of Christianity sat on the altar. These included a dark-skinned Christ on a crucifix surrounded by flames as well as a number of other figures, perhaps meant to represent the saints. As Jared and Chris's eyes adjusted to the light, they realized these other statues barely even looked human. Their stylized forms could just as easily have represented animals or nature motifs. A group of women kneeled before the altar. They chanted and prayed as one of them dripped blood from a chicken into an urn of burning incense. The head of the animal lay beside her, its blank eyes staring into the abyss.

Jared and Chris stood transfixed. Perhaps they stayed a moment too long to be respectful, or perhaps they weren't supposed to be there at all. In any event, before they realized what was happening they were surrounded by an irate mob. Many villagers had rocks in their hands, others machetes. "What are you doing here?" they demanded in almost unintelligible Spanish. "You are disturbing the ritual! You are upsetting the saints!"

Jared and Chris backed away quickly, apologizing. When they reached their truck they almost tripped over themselves getting in. Jared fumbled with the keys for precious seconds and finally started the vehicle. He saw the villagers wave their blades in anger through his rear view mirror as he and Chris roared out of town.

It took some time to process the event. Eventually Jared spoke. "More syncretism?" he asked.

"I'd say so," Chris replied. "That looked like a Catholic church, but that cross was so bizarre, and I'm pretty sure chicken decapitation isn't a common Christian sacrament."

Chris's hope sank with the sun as the last

vestiges of daylight gave way to a starry night. What a shame it would be to come so close to Dr. Conroy's speech and miss it! Still, they had a shot, and Chris, now at the wheel, felt more in control of the situation. Snoozing to his side, Jared woke with a start once they started their descent from the highlands to Lake Atitlán. The road angled so severely that they were literally hanging forward in their seats. Their view beckoned them. Below, a lake shimmered in moonlight while all around loomed the silhouettes of giant volcanoes framed by the universe.

Lake Atitlán had long been considered a spiritual place, and it was thus fitting that their destination, the Circulos y Cuadrados Retreat, would be built on its shores. The logo of the retreat, a square embedded within a circle, captured the essence of the place. For many cultures, the circle represented spirituality and wholeness while the square invoked the physical, the mundane. Chris smiled as he thought about how clever the logo was, capturing the essence of an entire metaphysics in a simple geometric combination.

They arrived at the normally sleepy village of San Marcos to encounter a Tetris of parked cars. Squeezing Sherpa into what must have been the one remaining parking place was like fitting a middle-aged woman into her high-school prom dress. A good ten minutes of grunting and rearranging later, they locked up the truck, and jogged toward a constellation of lights twinkling by the shore. A wooden sign carved in the shape of a square inscribed in a circle announced their arrival to the retreat. Beneath it, a poster advertised the evening's event. It read, *"Tonight, anthropologist Jason Conroy, PhD, discusses the Awakening of December 21."*

They made their way to an enormous spherical structure, which they assumed was the main meeting house. Body heat and the fragrant scent of incense wafted out of the building as they opened its large double doors. The inside of the structure was rectangular, *the square within the circle*, mused Chris. Several hundred men and women sat listening with rapt attention to a speaker who Chris instantly recognized as Dr. Conroy. A dazzling blue butterfly the size of a small bird fluttered above the congregation, buffeted by the vortices of heat rising from the bodies below. Chris and Jared spied two open seats and made their way through the aisle.

Dr. Conroy was a slender man with knowing eyes and tousled hair that reached out frenetically toward the walls around him. He nodded almost imperceptibly as the newcomers sat and continued talking. "So we must wonder" he said, his prominent Adam's apple keeping time with the patient rhythm of his words, "how a butterfly such as this can possibly navigate through the same three-dimensional world that we inhabit with a brain only a tiny fraction as large our own. How can the butterfly find food and mates and avoid predators and do all of the other things necessary for its reproduction using only that miniscule processor in what must seem to it to be such an overwhelmingly complex environment?"

"The answer is simple, it filters and focuses. Although it physically inhabits the same space as us, it does not perceive this world in the same way that we do. From the potentially bewildering onslaught of its sensory inputs, it manages by focusing selectively on just those few things that are most important to its survival. For instance, it remains sensitive to brilliant colors because they might mean flowers and potential mates. It notices swiftly moving shadows because they might mean predators, and it registers shimmering lights because they might indicate the presence of water. To a butterfly, the rest of the intricate details of our world would effectively not even exist.

"And yet here is the point that is relevant to

tonight's topic. We are just butterflies as well. While our brains are much more powerful than an insect's, we are similarly limited by our own perceptional focusing and filtering and by the processing power of our nervous systems. What we think we are seeing as the actual world around us is just an imperfect model of that world that we have created within our own heads. The real 'it' out there is vast and we can be reasonably confident that we know no more of it than a butterfly knows of our world.

"And now," continued Dr. Conroy, "we reach our main topic of the evening, the Awakening of December 21."

The crowd murmured excitedly. Heads moved back and forth between neighbors in ripples of anticipation.

"You may have heard news," Dr. Conroy began grandiloquently, stretching his arms upward for dramatic effect, "of a Maya prophesy of impending destruction due to cosmic alignments, magnetic pole shifts, alien abductions, and any number of other fantastical incarnations of doom."

The crowd held its breath as one.

"While it is true," the speaker continued, lowering his arms and placing his hands firmly on the podium, "that this phase of Maya Long Count calendar will indeed end just days from today, and that the Maya did generally ascribe substantial importance to such calendrical transitions, it does not appear that they made any of the apocalyptic predictions related to this event that many have attributed to them. In fact, as far as any of our scholars can tell, the Maya were completely mum about what they believed would occur, if anything, at the end of this cycle of their Long Count.

"But this does not mean that the Maya Long Count calendar is irrelevant. It just means that its true importance may not necessarily lie in literal prophecy. I would like to suggest another way of understanding the role of the Maya and their calendar and the significance of the ending of this cycle of the Long Count. You see, in my view, we are indeed hurtling towards an 'apocalypse,' but only in the old sense of the word, as a revelation: We are hurtling toward the truth. I believe the Maya have simply provided us with a focal point to help us get there.

"What is this 'truth' that I speak of? First, let us acknowledge that our world is in a sad state. We continue to engage in old-style military brinkmanship but with new-style weaponry, our environments are under siege, our rich legacy of biological diversity is dwindling, our climate is changing, we are depleting our fossil fuels, and huge numbers of us are veritably drowning in voids of alienation.

"That much is clear. What may not be so obvious is what I believe to be one of the root causes of our sorry condition, and that is that we have become unbalanced by the embrace of a singularly powerful worldview at the exclusion of all others. As a result, we have boxed in our potential and have forced the dark projections of our collective psyche onto the material world.

"This worldview that I speak of is known as 'empirical rationalism'. It is the idea that nothing important exists beyond the realm of the measurable, the testable, and verifiable. It is the erroneous assumption that the world as we perceive it is the world as it truly is. It is the underpinning of our modern material-centric paradigm, and it is the epistemological basis of our sciences.

"I do not wish to deny the benefits that we have accrued by embracing this natural philosophy. As a result of its exploitation we have banished some of our more patently absurd superstitions and have created remarkable technologies, thus vastly improving our material comfort. But, unfortunately, in the process we have also lost the sacred and we have forgotten our true power as co-creators of our realities.

"By reducing nature to nothing more than ostensibly objective facts obtained through the cold gaze of the detached scientist, we have degraded the inherent value of all things. Through this lens, the majestic tree has become nothing more than a store of timber, the noble animal nothing more than a source of meat, and the kindly neighbor nothing more than a potential customer. By allowing ourselves to believe in an essentially valueless material world, we have helped to usher in the endless-pursuit-of-everything culture that so defines our modern market-based societies.

"Rationality, Efficiency, and Material Well-Being. These are the gods of our modern mythos, and these gods demand offerings like all others. In fact, we devote our entire lives to their worship. Our jobs are our good works, our shopping malls our temples, our shopping sprees our holy rituals, and the McDonald's Cheeseburger our holy sacrament of communion. The good news is that our intense devotion to these new idols has produced wealth beyond measure in many parts of the world. The bad news is that we have left a scorched wake of destruction behind us on our way to the Promised Land of Material Splendor.

"What's worse is that The Church of Empirical Rationality, like all religions, does not tolerate views outside of its accepted paradigm and punishes heretics with excommunication. Thus, our material-centric worldview has been self-perpetuating and self-limiting. Free-thinking academics have been routinely denied tenure. Independent scholars have gone unfunded and unpublished. Anyone thinking outside of the box has typically been labeled insane, or worse yet, 'irrational.' It is incredible to me and very telling of our closed mindset that instead of letting our modern day spiritual seekers follow the consciousness-expanding paths of the ancients by using traditional sacraments of plants and fungi, we have outlawed these natural substances and have instead condoned the use of only highly synthesized, corporate anodynes such as Prozac, the Twinkie of Modern McMedicine.

"This vicious cycle of self-imposed ignorance is unfortunate because, as Einstein is said to have noted, we cannot solve problems by using the same kind of thinking we used when we created them. The result is that it has been difficult to imagine a way out of our predicament. Yet there is hope. Thankfully, as Carl Jung once said, 'God enters through the wound'. In other words, suffering invites the sacred, and clearly we have long suffered. I believe that from deep within the morass of our spiritual, theological, and teleological theories and from the hard-won insights of our visionary philosophers, seekers, prophets, scholars and scientists, a new paradigm is self-organizing and now sits teetering on the cusp of our collective consciousness, poised to emerge fully formed in the near future. This new consciousness represents a synthesis of the rational and the sacred, a merging into unity of cutting edge rationalistic theories with indigenous mystical knowledge.

"What synthesis of thought am I referring to? What wisdom could the archaic beliefs of indigenous cultures possibly have to contribute to our atom-splitting, genome-mapping, wonder-drug producing, seemingly omnipotent worldview? I would like to suggest several examples of how our dominant paradigm is lurching inexorably towards integration with the sacred myths of the ancients. Given that we are here discussing this topic directly as a result of the Classic Maya, I will use their culture as my primary model.

"First, it is becoming clear that there are multiple ways of knowing. Rationalistic views of knowledge acquisition stress deductive reasoning and material discovery. But there is another way of accessing the truth, that which mystics have called 'revelation.' The Classic Maya believed that they could call 'vision serpents' into existence from the plumes of smoke swirling upwards from their smoldering religious offerings. They believed that they could communicate through this mist with the spirit world and thus divine the future. In fact, almost all traditional cultures have analogs to this belief. At various times in various civilizations through history we have seen mystics attempt divination using the amorphous shapes that appear in crystal balls, entrails, flocks of birds and so on.

"Modern science has shown us that most of what happens in our minds is not accessible to direct reflection. We are not aware of most of the processing that happens at the 'subconscious' level in our brains. Science has also shown that variation exists in our abilities to make predictions of all kinds, whether of the behavior of the stock market, the course of the weather, or what will happen on the next episode of our favorite television show. And finally, science has very clearly shown that 'pattern recognition' is an important aspect of perception.

"I suggest that we are talking about the same thing using different languages. I invite you to consider that perhaps all the methods I just mentioned by which traditional societies made their mystical predictions acted as sort of Rorschach ink blot tests to access the awesome pattern recognition capabilities inherent in the subconscious minds of the diviners. In other words, those gifted in divination are those gifted at pattern recognition. Some patterns may be so complex and diffuse that they remain forever out of the grasp of most people, and yet some remarkable individuals may be able to connect the dots, to see the forms through the chaos, and to intuit what to others may seem, or what for all intents may well be, miraculous revelations.

"The second example I'd like to offer involves views on what lies beyond the curtain of directly observable natural phenomena. Visit any Maya or other indigenous village and you will see people living in worlds rich with ritual. To these people, every aspect of the material world has a 'spirit' essence and all spirits are intimately interconnected. It is the transcendental interactions of these incorporeal entities that manifest themselves as our material world. Because of this tightly coupled nature of spiritual and material existence, all things and all events are considered to be sacred and deeply meaningful.

"Now we are seeing our rational empirical viewpoint move towards unity with this idea of connection and transcendence, though again it has been doing so using a different language. In our effort to understand our physical universe, we have been delving deeper and deeper into the atomic and sub-atomic realms in the search for the 'fundamental' units of reality. First we discovered the atom and thought that we had found the basic level of existence. Then we discovered subatomic particles - protons, neutrons and electrons - and were sure there were no levels of existence below them. Then we found that protons were actually made of quarks and leptons, and then we found hundreds of other even smaller particles, or maybe they were waves, or perhaps 'wavicles' was a better term. These 'objects' were so strange we couldn't even describe them adequately using language. But the telling thing is that as we continued to explore fundamental physics, we found that we could not even ascertain the existence of many of these exotic entities directly. Rather, we have had to use particle accelerators to hurl subatomic wavicles at each other in order shatter or combine them. Only by studying their interactions during such collisions have we been able to glean information about their nature.

"But what have these experiments shown? Despite the veneer of recondite mathematics surrounding their measurements, we have simply discovered that at its most basic nature, the physical universe is made of nothing more than connections. The reason that it has been so hard to describe our subatomic particles is that they are not really 'things' at all, they are just ephemeral patterns of flowing information and energy. What this means is that, as we try to envision the world as it really is from a scientific perspective, we end up with a view uncannily similar to those posited by the ritual-performing, spirit-believing ancients. We envision a plane of interaction from which the phenomena of material existence emanate. Whether we refer to this plane through the rational constructs of string theory or hyper-dimensional space or through the mystical view of 'spirits' and Oneness the end result is that we have gone full circle back to the beginning. We have found what the ancients have always known, that there is no such thing as true randomness, and that because all things are related, all things have meaning and value.

"My third example involves the modern fallacy of objectivity. In the Maya creation myth, the narrative begins with an empty world. The action gets underway only when the gods begin to engage in dialogue. As they talk of the sea, so it is created, and as they talk of the mountains, so do they rise. In other words, the thoughts and the words of the gods bring the world into being.

"Again we see a parallel with modern rationalistic thinking. Quantum physics has informed us that it is not possible to take the observer out of the equation, that subatomic particles 'collapse' into one of multiple probabilistic configurations as soon as someone attempts to measure their existence. This should not be surprising. As an integral part of a connected universe, we co-create our realities just as the Maya Gods did. We 'make' our world perceptually by creating models of it in our heads, interactively through our actions, and in mysterious ways simply through being. We are only beginning to understand just how intimately linked we are with our environments and how powerful even the most seemingly inconsequential acts, or even thoughts, may be as they ripple through waves of connection to the rest of the world.

"These are just a few examples of many of the emerging synthesis of empirical rationalism and sacred aboriginal knowledge. I will mention just one more. The Classic Maya were known for their intense devotion to sacrificial rites. Some of these rites may seem gruesome to us now, but the lesson is clear: In order to progress, we must sacrifice. In this case, it is our unidimensional view of existence that we are in the process of letting go, or to be more accurate, that we are modifying. Perhaps paradoxically, we are re-embracing ancient wisdom in order to move forward.

"We are realizing the limitations of our perceptions and beginning to accept that there are multiple, legitimate ways of knowing. We are recognizing the intricate connectedness of the world and our place firmly within that matrix of relationships. We are realizing that in an intimately connected world, all things are important, and we are remembering our power to create our own realities. I'm hesitant to put forth utopian visions, but I would like you to imagine a world of supreme technological ability tempered by appreciation and respect for all things, aided by expanded views of the possible, and guided by a secure knowledge that we are in charge of our futures. Perhaps this promising new world will simply be the result of a new mind. Perhaps the 'Second Coming' will simply be a return of the sacred.

"It could be a coincidence that this cycle of Maya Long Count calendar is set to expire and a new cycle set to begin just as we seem to be on the precipice of the death of one worldview and the birth of another, or it could be that this is all part of some grand cosmic plan, the pattern of which is too obscure for us to recognize. What is clear is that because of the Maya we have tuned in and discussed the topic. For that, we must thank them."

Jared and Chris finished pitching their tents by the shore and took a break to soak in the tranquility of their surroundings. From their vantage atop a small forested promontory, they saw a sky full of stars reflected in the glassy water below. They let their exhaustion unwind with them and fended off the brisk night air with a small campfire and mugs of steaming hot tea.

Chris wriggled to get comfortable in the cushion of leaves under his rear. He probably would have started purring if he were a cat. He turned to face Jared, who was staring into the fire. Jared had been silent since the lecture. Chris thought he must have been either disappointed or deep in thought. "So what did you think of the talk?" he ventured.

Jared took a sip and released a long sigh. "It was a Zeitgeist" he said finally. "I think the guy captured something profound brewing in a lot of people's minds."

Chris smiled proudly. "Zeitgeist." he repeated. "That's the word I was looking for."

"That said," Jared continued, "there was something that bothered me about his position."

Chris shifted his weight. "What's that?"

"Maybe I'm biased since I was trained as a scientist, but I don't think it's so much that science has lessened the value of things, it's just that it can't say anything at all about what's right or wrong, or beautiful or ugly. It deals only in facts. It can only tell us how things are, or at best why our brains might have evolved to prefer this or that. It can't touch how things *ought* to be."

"Yeah, but that's kind of the point. There used to be a time when we put knowledge of aesthetics and morality on par with knowledge of physical nature. But we've become unbalanced – we've focused almost entirely on rational objective thought. As a result we've gotten ridiculously good at producing technology and wealth, but have neglected the rest. I don't think we've made any progress on right or wrong since the ancient Greeks. Our wisdom hasn't kept up with our power. We're like babies with bazookas."

Jared nearly snorted his tea laughing. "Hah, true, but here's the thing – if we let go of objective rationality as a guide and embrace the values of the past, whose past do we embrace? With so many options and no objective way of knowing what's really right and really wrong it just seems like guesswork. We'll end up with a syncretic blend alright, but of what? Maybe we need to re-embrace the sacred, but it's not clear whose sacred we should be hugging."

Chris cleared his throat. He had to admit, before spending time with Jared, he thought of trees as merely timber and certainly would not have noticed the magic of an anthill or the complexity of plant behavior. Jared had opened his eyes to the wonder of things, and Chris was thankful for it. "Your approach seems like a good start," he said, "just trying to get people to appreciate the fragile beauty of their surroundings. It's a path to valuing things that we've historically taken for granted or never even noticed. I know I'll certainly be less likely to step on an ant for laughs after what I've learned."

"I appreciate that, but sometimes I wonder. Maybe I go too far. Maybe I don't go far enough. It's just so hard to tell. Conroy put a positive spin on a really hard situation. Once we recognize the limits of rationality as a guide, it's a murky world of options out there."

Chapter 6

Cave Worship

The large man glances at the date on the sheet of paper and feels glad. The time is approaching. He moves the small glass vial aside and studies the information his men have left for him.

He starts with a pile of photographs, each image an awe-inspiring representation of nature in the raw. His eyes wander over the verdant valleys of the Hetch Hetchy Valley, the splendorous forests of Haiti, the sleek lines of a marsupial wolf, the drama of a million Passenger Pigeons in flight. His heart wells with longing. If only he could see these sights in person and know that the creatures and lands of the earth were safe. But he knows these images are just ghosts of things long dead and gone.

He moves on to examine photos of the present, of the Amazon rainforests retreating under the assault of plow and hoe, of the disemboweled mountains of North America ravaged for their coal, of doomed sea turtle hatchlings stumbling toward city lights. His hands tremble as his face contorts with resolve. He would think nothing of detonating his own body into a billion bits of flaming flesh in order to further his cause. Nothing exists for him beyond the importance of carrying forth his mission. He sees only one path. He has no doubt about what is right. There is still hope.

***

Jared woke with a smile to sweet bird song. He was glad that he and Chris hadn't been able to find a camping spot closer to town - this was ideal. He sat upright in his sleeping bag and yawned peacefully. Though the sun itself was only just waking, the temperature had already soared. Jared took off his sweatshirt, put a kettle on the camp stove, and walked to the edge of the promontory for a glorious morning stretch.

The giant volcanoes surrounding the lake embraced a baby blue sky. There was something comforting about the looming peaks, silhouetted in the morning light, like they were the shadows of caregivers overlooking the precious child of Lake Atitlán. Jared searched for the perfect view. He found his spot. He was surveying the landscape contentedly when a motion caught his attention. In the distance, a young woman - nude, glistening, and gorgeous - skipped away along the water's edge. Her body seemed athletic enough to escape the fastest predator and voluptuous enough to nourish a small army of babies. Her honey-hued hair fell in sun-kissed waves to the small of her back and her legs went on forever. Jared struggled to breathe as his loins galloped to attention.

The woman turned and started back toward Jared. He took in her salacious curves and felt weak. The kettle began to whine. Jared looked away. This wasn't right. As he shifted his gaze, he noticed a bundle of clothing below the promontory. An object within it looked familiar, a green kerchief. The kettle whistled more insistently. Jared turned back to the woman. She drew closer. *It couldn't be her, could it?* He heard a clanging back at camp. Chris must have been rummaging through the truck. Jared's rational mind demanded an audience but he was so filled with primal energy he barely paid any notice. He wanted to run to the girl, nay, knucklewalk to her, grab her by the hair and…

The kettle shifted tones like a race car. Any second now it would begin to wail.

Jared was kissing the back of the woman's neck,

running his hands along her thighs…

It's her, Jared! blurted his mind. *Shut up,* growled his libido.

"Jared?" Chris yelled.

Jared turned. "Hush!" he whispered.

"Jared, where are you?" Chris yelled again. He must not have heard.

The girl was very close now, blocked from view by the trees.

The kettle screamed at full volume. "Jared?" yelled Chris, loud as ever, as he appeared from behind a thicket. "Oh there you are. Do you know where the –"

A branch cracked. Both men turned to see the woman standing before them, a towel barely covering her spilling fertility.

"-tea is?" Chris finished meekly.

"Jared," the woman said.

"Sybil Lee," he replied.

The three of them shared breakfast, though Jared only half engaged in the conversation. His mind kept jumping frenetically between past and present. How was this possible? What were the chances of running into Sybil Lee here? There was no chance. No chance at all. In fact, this was impossible. But there she sat, with her penetrating eyes alight and her lustrous hair wrapped in its usual green kerchief. Jared supposed he shouldn't have been too surprised to have run into her. He knew she was in the area. She was "fighting the good fight with Earth Might," organizing protests to protect the environment in Mexico. Apparently, she'd hitched a ride to Guatemala to catch Dr. Conroy's lecture. "Something big is going to happen on the 21st," she said, "a lot bigger than anything Conroy talked about."

Sybil Lee Renée. Her name resonated through

Jared's mind as a tsunami of emotions overtook him. She was a badass, a naturalist, a poet, and an activist with enough soul to light up a city and enough conviction to fuel a penal system. Jared remembered when they had first met. It was in a place much like this, a retreat from the modern world. They had both been stationed at a biological research station in Belize where they had signed up for a summer of volunteer work. They would wake before the morning dawn to hike through the rainforest where they would spend their days studying the habits of the Scarlet Macaw. When they weren't working they would play guitar and sing, try to capture the majesty of their surroundings in watercolor, have long conversations, and otherwise frolic in the splendor around them. They couldn't tell where the fun ended and work began.

Jared remembered the exact moment when Sybil Lee had captured his heart. They'd made the trip to town to rent a video shortly after they'd met. At that point Jared had thought his new colleague was an impressive person with noble goals but hadn't really considered her romantically. With her unflattering field clothes and frumpy safari hat she hadn't exactly been the picture of desire. The thing that did it, and Jared laughed to himself as he remembered, was the video that she chose. She had come bounding over, excited as ever, to hand Jared a nature documentary about tropical frogs.

Now people fall in love for many reasons, thought Jared. Sometimes they are attracted by physical beauty, sometimes by personality, sometimes by money, and then other times, very rarely, they are smitten by the fact that a person can be so quirky and self-assured and so in tune with nature that that person would actually consider renting a video on frogs. Once under Sybil Lee's spell, Jared was helpless. Her infectious personality and gorgeous physique only pulled him in further. Her sense of wonder and the fact that she shared almost all of Jared's passions further cemented his feelings. He had poured his heart out to her. He had told her that he finally understood how the birds that they were studying could pair bond for life and what the phrase "madly in love" really meant. He was crazy for Sybil Lee.

That summer had been supernova of molten perfection; Jared's every day with Sybil Lee an ecstasy of existence. She'd ravaged his heart shortly thereafter. It had started promisingly enough. They had kept in touch and Jared had made plans to visit Sybil Lee in Berkeley, where she was finishing her degree. In retrospect, she had seemed distant once she'd moved to the city. Jared should have known. She waited for him to visit to give him the news. She had looked awful. Jared knew something was wrong. After giving a few hints, she dropped the bomb – Sybil Lee had met another man. What's worse, apparently the guy wasn't even treating her well. He'd made promises but delivered nothing but heartache. Jared's happiness died in agony like a slug under a mountain of salt.

They kept in touch for a time but it was too painful. Jared was terrified by the hold Sybil Lee had on him and knew he needed to forget her as best he could. But it was useless. Her memories tormented him like a cat toying with a mouse. His attempts to date other women were disasters. He always seemed to end up with vapid women who disgusted him. They cared for nothing but status and the acquisition of shiny objects and made Jared feel like a freak for his indifference to such things. He'd never felt that way with Sybil Lee. She was real. She made him feel connected like nobody ever had.

Several years went by and they met again in the forests of Oregon. At this point, Jared had achieved some notoriety as an environmental activist and was staging a tree sit-in to raise awareness for an old-growth grove threatened with destruction. He had intended to stay in the tree for only a week but his cause received so much attention that he extended his stay repeatedly. One day, Jared noticed a woman with long, dirty-blond hair talking with fellow protestors on the ground far below. He told himself that it couldn't be her, that there were millions of blondes in the U.S. and that the probabilities were negligible. But he knew it was Sybil Lee from the start. She climbed up the tall tree and into his arms. She told him that she admired what he was doing. She said he was a hero. They made love in the cool forest air and spoke of saving the universe together.

She came to visit him often. It was difficult carrying on a relationship under the circumstances, but every time Jared suggested he end his vigil, Sybil Lee implored him to continue. The cause was too important, she had said. Jared was happy to do whatever he had to in order to keep her by his side. He was in heaven once again, locked in the loving embrace of nature and the woman of his dreams.

She had left unexpectedly. Her mother had fallen sick and Sybil Lee had moved to New York to take care of her. At first she wrote Jared often. Then her ebullient river of letters slowed to a morose trickle. Her mood seemed to be deteriorating dramatically. At first Jared attributed this change to her mother's sickness, but in fact her mother had made a strong recovery. It was living in the city, he realized, that was tearing Sybil Lee down. She hated cities with zeal, thought they were nothing but asphalt tombs for the raw nature she so treasured. Jared asked her to hold on, told her that soon they could be together again. He shared with her an epiphany that he'd had while contemplating the forest around him. He'd gained a profound understanding of the underlying harmony of the land and seen such beautiful sights. He wanted to try to capture this beauty and harmony on film and share it with others. In this way, he believed he could increase appreciation for our beleaguered natural environments and thus promote their protection. He had been surprised by Sybil Lee's reaction. "It's not enough," she wrote him sternly, "You have too much faith in people." "Where was the old Jared, the one who knew what needed to be done?" "You're going soft." "You're as bad as them." And then he received her last letter.

"Something wrong?" Chris asked. Jared looked up from his food and realized he hadn't said a word since they'd started eating. He cleared his throat, mumbled something about getting something in his eye, and excused himself from the campsite. He walked a short distance to the shore and quickly fell back into his reverie.

Of course Sybil Lee had met someone else in New York. Some douche bag working in the city. And of course that guy had turned out to be a jerk as well, manipulative, always after something. Or so Sybil Lee had said later. And so went Jared's relationship with Sybil Lee. Every so often she would make a tantalizing appearance in his life but whenever he tried to reach out and grab her he found another man in the way. His tender feelings for her became just a giant emotional meat hook attached to his heart that she would yank on painfully at her whim. Connected, yes, but to what end? When she was good to him, she was so good, but she could be merciless. He knew it was unhealthy. He knew he should try to date other women and try to be closer to other people, but he could not break his addiction. And now here she was again, just a few yards away, her entire being virtually screaming for him to embrace her, but he already knew how this would end. Jared closed his eyes and sighed like he never wanted to take in another breath again.

Chris and Sybil Lee smiled at Jared conspiratorially when he arrived back at camp.

"What?" he asked.

"Well, now that we've been lucky enough to run into each other again I don't want to let you go," Sybil Lee said cheerfully.

"Sybil Lee had a great idea!" Chris added.

"What's that?"

"For you two to join me on a tour today," Sybil Lee said, "to see millions of bats fly out of a cave."

"And to see artifacts," Chris added. "The Maya used to use the cave for rituals."

The word 'No' came to Jared's mind, loudly and forcefully. For one thing, he wanted to hurry up and get to the Petén to start capturing the footage they'd come for. For another, his heart was already one big ball of scar tissue. Jared was as surprised as anyone to hear his answer. "I suppose that might be worth filming. When does the tour leave?"

An hour later they were on the road, sharing the ratty bench seat of an old pickup with its driver, a lean Guatemalan man with short dark hair and a once white t-shirt now mottled with memories of the outdoors. A waterproof shell containing Jared's most rugged camera equipment bounced on his lap as they drove. The bouncing was innocuous for the first hour or two, but by the time they reached their destination Jared's beaten legs ached like he'd run for miles.

The entrance of the cave was a nondescript gash in the earth covered with tangled vines and hanging mosses. They slipped inside and walked until the light of day dissipated and their path was blocked by a swiftly moving stream. By boat, they then glided through the darkest dark any of them had ever seen. Their headlamps provided only enough illumination to highlight the surrealness of their surroundings. As they traveled through a glistening tube of organically shaped rock, they felt as though they were passing through the slimy bowels of a monstrous earthen creature.

Eventually they stopped in front of a thick rope dangling from above. "*Vamonos*," said the guide, clambering up expertly. "A shortcut." Jared, Chris and Sybil Lee gave each other quizzical looks. Were they going to have to scale the wall? Shouldn't they wear safety gear, or maybe full body armor? Chris climbed first, slowly at first, then faster as he got the hang of it. Sybil Lee followed. The tanned skin of her athletic legs glistened like the walls around her as she climbed. Jared caught himself. He fiddled with his headlamp, as though a malfunction had caused it to shine directly on her rear.

They scrambled over ledges and crawled through tunnels, waded through frigid waters and squeezed through narrow crevasses. Eventually, they knew they had reached a large chamber when they were enveloped by an echoey roar and could no longer see the sides of the cave. Their guide flipped on a halogen spotlight and introduced them to a new world. They were tiny pebbles in an epic universe of swirling rock and eerie sound. Mighty limestone pillars heaved under the weight of the Earth. Throngs of bats swarmed through the air. A broad lake drank the ground and terrifying daggers of stalactites threatened to plummet from above.

Jared paused to set up his camera equipment. This was a natural wonder if he'd ever seen one, and would become even more dramatic later that evening when a million bats took flight. He took some time to record other fascinating sights - the eyeless fish and translucent crustaceans that swam through the water, the grubs and worms that burrowed through mounds of bat guano, and the foot-long centipedes that weaved their bodies through the air menacingly, fishing for flying sustenance.

When it came time to continue their tour, the guide asked that everyone turn off their headlamps. From this point, respect demanded that they use only candles. The guide led them to an edge of the cavern and across a flaxen bridge hovering precariously over a chasm of indeterminable depth. From there, they entered a chamber cast in pallid glow. A galaxy of tiny pinpricks of light seemed to poke through the walls, an underground cosmos in miniature.

"Glowworms!" Sybil Lee marveled.

"Coooool," oozed Chris and Jared in unison.

As they walked, they passed the shattered remains of ceramic jars, wrapped in the embrace of calcium carbonate arms deposited by the moist environment.

"Offerings," the guide explained.

"So amazing," Chris bubbled, "I've read about this kind of ritual. The Maya believed all objects had spirits. They would bring these jars here filled with precious offerings, and smash them to bits to release the spirits of their contents. They were always feeding their gods."

They turned a corner to enter a field of whitish debris. All at once they understood what they were looking at.

"*Sacrificios humanos,*" the guide said.

Before them lay the grizzly remains of human sacrifice, fossilized skeletons. The group knelt over the bodies. Each displayed obvious signs of trauma. Some had their chests split open, others holes in their skulls, and still others held arrowheads in their rib cages. One small skeleton gave no obvious indication of how its owner had met his or her end. Judging by its pelvis and the pristine condition of its teeth, this skeleton must have belonged to a young woman.

"I wonder how they killed her," Chris said.

The guide pointed to her lower back. "There."

Just above her sacrum, her spine had been split in two.

"What a way to go," Sybil Lee said.

"*Los* Mayas believed the more suffering, the more good the offering," explained the guide. "Sometimes, they tortured many years before they killed."

Jared looked with pity at the young sacrificial victim and imagined what her last days must have been like. Her back broken, she would have been unable to walk. She would have lain in the darkness for what must have seemed an eternity, shivering in the cold with pain her only companion, a glorious offering to a bloodthirsty pantheon. How could anyone be so obsessed with anything that they would discount human pain like this? Jared wondered. His eyes moved to Sybil Lee, breathtaking in the candlelight, and he felt comforted. He loved her so much. He looked back to the skeleton. No beliefs were worth it, he thought, no obsession worth that level of heartlessness.

Jared snoozed on the way back to Atitlán. He had strapped his camera equipment in the back this time and the ride was now much more comfortable. Chris's enthusiasm brought him back to semi-consciousness. He was talking about how much power the ancient Maya had ascribed to caves. To the Maya, caves represented links to the Underworld, where the greatest spiritual battles were fought. There was evidence that some of their most important temples had been built over cave systems where people had been worshipping for thousands of years. Chris couldn't wait for the next leg of their trip. He dreamed of discovering a Maya temple with its very own portal to the Underworld.

Sybil Lee mumbled something softly. Through his haze, Jared couldn't quite make out her words.

"Yeah, to the Petén," Chris replied, "but I think we've got one more stop first."

Sybil Lee muttered something else. She must have asked another question. Chris's next words hit Jared like a methamphetamine jolt. "I'm pretty sure we've got room," he said, "but you'd have to ask Jared about that yourself."

Chapter 7

Cities

The large man unfurls a poster-sized satellite image of the earth at night, its surface a luminescent web of human habitation. He retrieves a table of airline routes, a printed spreadsheet, and a series of photographic cityscapes. Comparing documents, he makes notations, paying particular attention to the brightest city lights. He growls to himself as he examines scenes of people enjoying the fruits of urban life. Can they not see the hollowness of their existence? Can they not see the futility of stuffing their insatiable emptiness with the health of their planet? He will help them to see, and the truth will set them free.

The large man finishes his task. Gazing at the skein of lines and numbers he has marked, he nods, pleased. He sets aside his documents, reaches for the glass vial and holds it, almost affectionately, in his hand. It is a simple laboratory test tube, stopped at one end with cotton. A winged insect flutters inside. The creature settles and looks directly at the man. They gaze peacefully at one another for some time.

Someone knocks respectfully at the door. Two men bearing heavy assault rifles enter, pulling behind them a lighter skinned man by a rope. "What the hell is going on here?" the captive grumbles. His guards look at him fearfully, shocked at his impertinence. "Who do you think---" the prisoner continues, but as the large man waves his hand, the captive suddenly seems at a loss for words. He tries to speak but succeeds only in stuttering. The large man turns to face his guest. "Have a seat, Verderber," he says flatly, motioning to the empty dentist chair. "I'll be with you in a moment."

***

The next day, Sherpa roared like a monster as she clawed her way out of the steep Atitlán valley. The terrain leading to their next stop, Antigua, was more forgiving, though it seemed like Guatemalans had no concept of building roads around mountains instead of directly over them.

It hadn't taken Sybil Lee long to convince Jared to let her come along. Among other things, she pointed out that she could help carry gear once they were in the field and that she could use her experience as a naturalist to scout shots for Jared's documentary. Her pitch was irrelevant. The previous night they'd spent together by the shores of the lake may as well have been a needle full of Sybil Lee crack injected straight into Jared's jugular. He was a junkie all over again.

As they drove, Jared's trepidation grew. He was more than a little concerned about bringing Sybil Lee into the city. Granted, as far as cities went, Antigua was supposedly quite beautiful. Its legacy as the one-time capital of most of Central America meant it boasted a rich architecture and its location in the highlands meant it enjoyed a pleasant climate. But Sybil Lee's distaste for cities dwarfed even Jared's and she always seemed to act differently in their midst - distant, aggressive. Nevertheless, Jared had promised his childhood friend, Vadia, that they would stop by on their way to the Petén.

In truth, Jared had barely anything to say to Vadia these days. They'd been close once, but she'd taken a different track in life. She was a businesswoman now, dedicated to shepherding rivers of gold into her purse. This, it seemed, was a family specialty. Vadia's uncle, Roger, had also managed to tame the money dragon and the two of them had recently joined forces to slay it. It was to Roger's downtown estate that Jared and company were now headed. That night, Vadia and Roger were hosting what was to be the first of a series of "end of the world" parties in honor of the Maya prophecy. The thought of a cacophony of phonies made Jared cringe. He longed instead to take Sybil Lee far into the countryside and sleep with her under the stars.

Yet Antigua did turn out to be quite attractive. Traditional Spanish architecture lay bathed in pigments of mustard and ochre beside well maintained cobblestone streets and sprawling tree-lined plazas. Magnificent cathedrals vied for aerial supremacy with giant volcanoes looming in the distance while trendy shops offered colorful wares to crowds of smartly dressed pedestrians. Provincial hamlets, thought Jared, dreamed of growing up to be a royal Camelot like Antigua.

Vadia, elegant and refined, greeted the travelers at the door and escorted them inside what must have been the most palatial residence in the city. From a marbled antechamber, they walked across a courtyard boiling over with flowers and art and passed one lavishly appointed room after another. The courtyard was so vast that by the time they reached its other end they had managed detailed introductions and an in-depth review of Jared and Chris's recent adventures. Eventually, they reached a grand hall where a jazz band played for the pleasure of a large crowd of well-dressed guests. Men wearing trendy horned-rim glasses and women wearing stiletto heels held their daringly designed martini glasses with pinkies outstretched and threw their heads back in self-satisfied laughter. From this cultured crux emerged a smiling gentleman holding a glass of wine in one hand and a beautiful woman on the other.

"Well hello, Vadia!" he said. "These must be your guests." He was the type of man that nature had not made overly attractive but experience had refined into the very embodiment of pleasure and good will. His almost too large eyes beamed forth a peaceful sense of accomplishment and his curly salt and pepper (mostly salt) hair gave him a boyish charm unusual for a man of his age.

"Yes, this is Jared Foster and his friend Chris Burgeis and, I'm sorry, what was your name again, love?"

For a moment Jared feared that Sybil Lee' hand was reaching for Vadia's throat, but in the end it veered toward Roger.

"Sybil Lee Renée" she said, "Nice to meet you."

"Pleased to meet you all," Roger replied. "This is Gabrielle. Isn't she just gorgeous?" Roger playfully kissed the woman's neck, almost spilling his wine in the process. She giggled and pulled away. Another woman poked her head around his side.

"Hola Roger!" she said.

"Hola Baby!" Roger put his other arm around the new arrival. "And this is Maria Natalia." He leaned over and gave her a sloppy kiss on the cheek. "Am I a lucky man or what?"

Roger's smile could have given faith to the damned. His warmth was unprecedented. Jared and Chris could only stare at him in awe.

Vadia led the group to their room. She and her uncle were hosting over a hundred houseguests over the coming days and so quarters were tight. The room was set up for four. Apparently they would be sharing it with one more guest.

They took some time to clean up. The shower was piping hot and its water pressure could have sufficed to put out a good sized residential blaze. Jared removed his clothes and invited Sybil Lee to join him – he couldn't possibly get enough of her - but he wasn't overly surprised when she refused. Her mood had already darkened visibly.

Fresh and clean, the group rejoined the party. Vadia was mingling with the other guests by the courtyard. She looked at home, a round peg in a round hole of high society. Roger laughed heartily, the shoulders of his sports coat dancing as his chest heaved in merriment.

"This is really nice," Chris commented.

Sybil Lee glowered. "I can think of a thousand better things to do with all this money."

Jared chewed his lip. On the one hand he wished Sybil Lee would lighten up. On the other, well, she was right, wasn't she?

Roger motioned for the group to come over. "So how's it going, gang?" he asked. "What brings you to Guatemala?"

"We're heading to the Petén," Jared replied, "to do some filming for a nature documentary."

"Say again?"

"We're heading to the Petén to film."

"Well, normally I'd say that's a fantastic idea, lots of ruins up there, lots of wildlife, but you know there's been trouble in that area recently. Course it's hard to tell what's truth or fiction with any of these government reports, but as near as I can tell we've got a revolution brewing. Also, it's the tail end of the rainy season so that whole region is going to be a mud pit. If it's nature you want, you should head down to Costa Rica. Beautiful there, absolutely beautiful. I remember one time…"

Roger was interrupted by Maria Natalia whispering in his ear. He laughed as he put his arm around her thin waist and turned back to his guests. "We're going to be finishing up here soon, gang. Then we'll head to my restaurant for a feast. Maria here is getting hungry. She needs to feed these things!" He growled as he buried his head in his girlfriend's provocatively exposed cleavage.

"Roger owns the premiere hotel in Antigua, *La Goutte*," Vadia explained. "The hotel restaurant is famous. The chef is French and cares for nothing but food."

"Probably why the bastard weighs three hundred pounds," Roger said, "bless his blubbery soul."

The party exited Roger's home to enter Antigua's impossible poetry of early evening. The setting sun painted the picturesque world around them in its most flattering of palettes, coaxing the deepest hues from the city's rustic buildings. The hotel entrance was majestic, as was every other minute detail of the place. A small army of porters greeted the group as they ascended the marble steps to the lobby. It was clear that Roger was king here. He made his way across the hotel courtyard like a slow motion comet followed by its tapering trail of entourage and staff.

The restaurant's Classic French décor featured dazzling chandeliers hanging from the frescoed ceiling and ornately carved, red velour furniture. Intricately embroidered tapestries graced the walls while a palpable aroma of fine wines and rich sauces permeated the air. The culinary parade began almost the moment the group was seated. Appetizers of succulent *foie gras*, creamy *champignons* and savory *escargots a l'Alsacienne* preceded entrées of prime meats and delicately braised vegetable side dishes, while bottles of rich Malbec and Shiraz served in sparkling crystal provided the perfect liquid complement to the feast.

Discretely, Jared asked if anyone knew where the meats had come from. He would partake in them only if he knew the animals had been raised humanely. Sybil Lee overheard his question and interjected. "There's no such thing as humane murder," she said. A brief look of shock ran across the faces of several guests. Jared grimaced. There she goes again, he thought. He probably would have been more upset with her if he didn't think that she had a very good point. Vadia had to finish swallowing her *foie gras* to answer Jared's question – clearly she had no such dietary complications. No, she said, she had no idea about the origin of the food they were eating.

Across the table, Roger seemed serene sipping his wine. In quick glimpses, however, Jared thought he saw a distinct look of sadness cross the man's face, as though he couldn't decide what mood to be in.

"Is your uncle okay?" he asked Vadia.

She leaned closer. "He's been struggling with a condition; the doctors can't figure it out. He doesn't have long, you see, and he loves his life so much."

"The condition is called *mortality*," Sybil Lee said sharply, picking past the meat in the serving tray in front of her for the few vegetables hidden underneath. "It's why we all need to find something to live for besides eating helpless animals and drowning our angst in wine."

"Sybil!" Jared couldn't hide his exasperation. Why did she have to be so damn righteous? And so damn right? "I'm sorry, Vadia, we should probably go."

"No, no," Vadia insisted. She shot Sybil Lee that condescending look which forms the bread and butter of daytime soap operas. "Your friend here just has her own views, that's all. You all must join us after dinner – we're continuing the party at *La Cara Bonita*."

La Cara Bonita, a brisk walk across town, was a candlelit, Bohemian refuge.   Inside, a diverse crowd gathered around a pony-tailed Latin man strumming a guitar and a fleet fingered gringo mixing colorful cocktails behind the bar. Jared and Chris eased into an opening to order drinks for the group. To Jared's side sat a much older man, perhaps in his seventies. To Chris's stood a chubby young woman.

The old man turned to Jared and started talking. His accent gave him away instantly as an American. "New to Guatemala?" he asked.

"Yes, just arrived yesterday."

"I'm here all the time these days. I take care of these people, you see."

That's kind, thought Jared.

The man's pockmarked nose and furry ears were all out of proportion to his face. He took a long sip of scotch and smacked his lips. "Been looking after this young Guatemalan girl for a couple of years now. Tiny little thing. She just turned fourteen last week."

Jared winced. He didn't like where this was going.

"Damn sweet brown skin." The man grinned as he elbowed Jared playfully in the ribs. "Glad I brought a suitcase full of blue pills!"

Jared's dinner lurched and almost made an unexpected reappearance. He forced a smile and turned his focus to the bartender.

Meanwhile, Chris was making friends with the young lovely beside him. "Hi, I'm Chris," he said.

"Carly, nice to meet you."

"Where are you from?"

"Cleveland, how about you?"

"Boston originally, but I'm in grad school in Colorado now. What brings you to Guatemala?"

"I'm in the Peace Corps."

"Cool! I have some friends in the Peace Corps." The woman's perfume was nice. Chris shuffled a bit closer. "What kind of project are you working on?"

"We're developing ways to provide micro-loans to the indigenous communities in the highlands."

"What's a micro-loan?"

"It's a just a small loan designed to help families develop marketable crafts so they can participate in the economy. They're so poor, they need as much help as we can give them."

Chris smiled. At this point he found himself in a

conundrum. He disagreed with the entire concept of encouraging indigenous communities to join the free market. The fact was that the Maya throughout Central America had been able to maintain their identity and way of life precisely because they had *avoided* the market economy. They supported themselves in the ancient tradition; they grew their income in the soil. Chris didn't dare mention any of this. He didn't want to upset his new friend. She had a really pretty face.

"That's so wonderful," he said. "Can I buy you a drink?"

At that point, the bartender rang a bell. Apparently the VIP room, offering only the rarest liquors, was now open for business. Vadia and Roger waved their group over and everyone made their way through the crowd to enter a room of glossed hardwoods and rich leathers. A sturdy bar of burled walnut and ivory dominated the room. On its back shelves stood ten or twenty hand-made bottles, each carefully labeled in pencil and illuminated by a small votive candle.

Roger himself poured the first shots. Though Jared seldom drank alcohol, his last conversation called for the sweet smother of liquor. Soon, he found himself getting caught up in the good cheer around him and joining toast after toast. Chris was right there with him, and even Sybil Lee tried a glass or two. Five bottles were empty, then ten, and then the bar owner had to wheel in another case of the stuff. Guests grew boisterous and started smashing their glasses in the fireplace after every cheer. At one point, the owner of *La Cara Bonita* joined others behind the bar to pour shots. He recounted the dramatic tale of his acquisition of the potent brew everyone was enjoying. He'd had to sneak it over the border, across rivers and jungles and past customs and pirates, all for this moment of pleasure.

Sybil Lee was the first to ask, though it had

probably crossed the minds of many - "What makes this liquor so valuable, and hard to procure?"

"Oh, it's made from a very rare cactus," replied the bar owner. "I think it may even be protected. The Indians have gathered the plant for centuries for their rituals, but now others have caught on. Those poor Indian bastards probably can't even afford it now."

"It's absolutely rare and wonderful and god awfully expensive stuff," Roger added as he jovially raised his cup. "Nothing is too dear for you, my dears! It's the end of the world, let's live it up!"

Sybil's Lee face went black. Suddenly, Jared didn't feel well. How much had he drunk anyway? Couldn't someone have someone told him that the liquor he'd been pouring down his gullet represented the demise of a rare species and the crushed dreams of a culture? He vomited violently into the fireplace. It was time to go home.

Back at Roger's, the three travelers hesitated before opening the door to their bedroom. Someone inside seemed to be giving someone else a pep talk, saying things like "Good one. Oh, yes, cutting my man, cutting."

The reaction was instant once they opened the door.

"Sybil Lee?" exclaimed a man in boxer shorts standing before a mirror. His accent sounded almost British.

"Alan! What are you doing here? Jared, Chris, this is Alan Hotchworth. We met in Mexico just last week!"

Jared swallowed an annoyed expression as he forced a smile. Chris waved his hand in greeting.

Alan was a well-built, unusually handsome blond guy with a chiseled jaw and supercilious demeanor. "Hullo," he said. There was that accent again, not so much British as just vaguely affected. "Well, as I might have mentioned previously, I'm here on behalf of my family's foundation." He spoke as though he were giving a presentation and his audience cared deeply about what he had to say. He faced Sybil Lee, but judging by the volume of his voice his words were for everyone's benefit. "We're looking at the possibility of accelerated modernization of Third World nations such as Guatemala. We've created some fascinating strategies for Win-Win-Win situations between the Indians, the Ladinos, and foreigners. I expect we'll be awarded some prestigious prize or another when everything is said and done. Anyway, since I was in the neighborhood I thought I'd stop in on my old family friend, the Rodgster, but I'm afraid I've missed the party."

Jared hated him instantly. It wasn't just his tone, it was everything about him. It was the fact that he was half naked, showing off his perfectly cut physique in a shared room. It was the way his perfectly formed lips pouted, as though ready to disdain anything that his condescending eyes encountered at a moment's notice. Above all, it was the way he flexed when he spoke to Sybil Lee.

"Oh Alan!" Sybil Lee said breathlessly. "I'm so happy to have run into you again. We have to catch up!"

Was it Jared's imagination or was she posing now too? With her back arched, she cut a devastating figure.

"Why don't we step outside," she suggested alluringly, "and let these guys get some rest?"

"Sure thing!" Alan replied. He moved with panache, as though repaying the Earth for creating itself in preparation for his presence. He followed Sybil Lee outside, the muscles of his shirtless back rippling in fusillades with each step, and slammed the door shut behind him.

Jared's eyes were cemented shut, his breath shallow, and his head a pounding reminder of the previous night's overindulgence. This was hereby his worst hangover ever. He put his pillow over his head to block the light that kept burrowing its way through his eyelids and cursed himself. Thirty-two years of experience and apparently he still hadn't learned that this was the inevitable consequence of a night of heavy drinking. He tried to tally the number of cocktails he had consumed. The act was somnolent, like counting sheep. He groaned as he fell back into a dreamless sleep.

Sometime later he woke again. With a start, he remembered Sybil Lee. He turned to see her sleeping peacefully next to him. Chris and Alan snored across the room. He eased out of bed and to the kitchen to make coffee. His every motion was a reminder of his stupidity the previous night, his every step a small revenge of his conscience. His first attempt at making coffee was a disaster. Coffee grounds and water littered the countertop. His second was a success and Jared carefully poured himself a cup of the precious liquid. Two servings later he had accomplished nothing but making himself more alert to the discomfort of his body. He took a handful of aspirin and drank another cup.

A short while later, Sybil Lee emerged, radiant after a hot shower. She bounded over and sat next to Jared. Smiling, she grabbed his coffee mug and took a sip.

"Alan and I talked forever last night," she said.

"Uh huh," Jared grunted. He didn't know what to think.

"I told him all about what we're doing and

116

convinced him to come along."

Sybil Lee's words were a well swung baseball bat to Jared's throbbing head. "What?" he choked. "No way!"

"Let me finish. You see, Alan's family is filthy rich. I don't mean just run of the mill wealthy, like Roger, I mean there's an entire region complete with ancestral castles named after them in England. Haven't you ever heard of the Hotchworth Fund?"

"*The* Hotchworth Fund? The one that just bequeathed all that money to the U.N.?"

"Yes, that one. Alan's grandfather started The Fund and Alan is its Director of Strategic Giving."

"What are you getting at?"

"If Alan comes along and likes what he sees in the Petén, he could protect the entire area with a wave of his pinkie."

Confusion and disgust canonballed into the pool of nausea already inhabiting Jared's gut. He wanted to end this conversation yesterday. "What the hell would he want to come along for? I'm guessing he's got about as much love for the environment as a lawn mower."

"Maybe he wants to greenwash his foundation. I don't know, I don't care, what does it matter?"

"I don't want to be responsible for anybody else."

"Oh, don't worry, I told him about the rumors Roger mentioned. He said he wasn't scared. Apparently he's been taking martial arts since he could stand and he's a champion athlete. He also said he's had a lot of outdoors experience."

"And you believe him?"

Sybil Lee paused. "I believe he's rich. And that we can use him."

Jared wanted badly to say "No!" one more time, loudly, and be done with it, but here he was faced with a moral quandary. The fact was that Alan probably did come from significant money and that he would almost assuredly be willing to donate some of that wealth in exchange for accolades and recognition. That was the way the conservation game was played and it would have been selfish of Jared to let his personal feelings get in the way of a real chance to protect the environment. Sybil Lee's smile worked at him, loosening his resolve. He hated her. He hated him. He hated everything.

"Fine, but I swear if he gets in the way in the slightest he's going to have a very hard time walking back with my boot up his ass."

They emerged from Roger's house to dismal weather. Jared and Chris didn't speak much as they drove out of town. Jared found himself virtually babbling every time he opened his mouth and Chris needed to focus his equally stunted mental capacities on deciphering the maps spread before him. Alan and Sybil Lee chatted in the back. Jared still didn't understand their dynamic. As far as he could tell, Alan represented everything Sybil Lee despised, yet there she was giggling at all his inane self-congratulations. Apparently he'd made his first million at twenty-one. Could that have been because his daddy had given him nine hundred ninety-nine thousand, nine hundred and ninety-nine dollars to start with?

According to Chris, the highway to the Petén passed directly through the sprawl of the nation's capital, Guatemala City. This would not have been so disconcerting in and of itself, but for the fact that it looked as though they would have to negotiate a series of exchanges and their maps gave no clear indication how to do so. Furthermore, signs had been virtually non-existent throughout Mexico and Guatemala and so it was likely that they would be left guessing what street was what. In their weakened states, Jared and Chris found the entire prospect of navigating through the monstrous city daunting.

Traffic congealed to a gooey mass as they approached the capital. The refurbished school buses that served as Guatemala's public transports belched thick grey plumes as they wrestled with the slopes. The entire atmosphere smelled like diesel fuel and mangos. As they passed a bend, they saw the entire city splayed across the vast expanse below. Like a ravenous fungus from a B-movie nightmare, it had probed the mountains and plains with its tendrils of development, extracting every bit of nutrition and sustenance that it could from the virgin land before extruding its body on top of the spaces permanently. It seemed to breathe in the fresh air around it and exude a noxious soup of airborne waste in return. Jared and Chris looked on in horrified wonder.

"Oh, that's one of the Rodgster's developments on the plains there," mentioned Alan. "Quite impressive, I must say."

Eventually they descended far enough to penetrate the lingering miasma that hung over the city. Jared and Chris, already struggling to overcome the toxins of the previous evening, found this new insult almost too much to bear. They hacked and wheezed as glistening tears formed in their eyes. Closing their windows helped only momentarily. After a short time, the foulness of the air inside the truck equalized to that outside and they resumed their fits of misery. Sybil Lee had stopped talking. If she had been pretending to be in a good mood her ability to do so had been tapped. Alan continued to marvel at the rapid modernization of the country, in between coughs.

It was in this disoriented state that they encountered a sign for the first highway interchange. The sign did not bother to mention where the various routes led, it just indicated that an interchange was imminent. Chris scrambled to make sense of it on his map.

"Shit, I don't know," he said.

"That's not very helpful," Jared replied.

"Sorry, I think that's it. That might be it."

Jared turned into a gigantic freeway tangle of concrete confusion. The signs were useless and the travelers soon found themselves funneled on to a one-way street from which they could find no exit. Eventually, they were dumped unceremoniously in the middle of an extraordinarily unattractive neighborhood. Aggressive weeds attacked crumbling buildings. Litter clogged the streets and even the pedestrians looked dirty and unkempt. Grease stained mechanics in the shops along the road glanced up from their decrepit automobiles to watch the travelers drive by.

Chris struggled to find their location on the map but, as feared, street signs were nonexistent. Reluctant to stop for directions in such a seedy area, Jared drove in widening circles hoping to find a main thoroughfare.

Just when they thought they must have seen the ugliest part of the city, they drove into an even more appalling area. Before them, lay an endless train of "*llanta*" workshops, all specializing in the re-treading of old tires. The cutting smell of burned rubber invaded the lungs of the group as they marveled at stacks of tires two stories high. They continued past the street, becoming more and more anxious as they drove unwittingly into the fetid bowels of the town.

And then they came upon what must surely have been the most wretched of neighborhoods that existed anywhere in the world. Here there were no shops. There was nothing but trash and despair. Men lay passed out in their own vomit and feces. Others stumbled along the sidewalks in drunken stupors, stopping occasionally to piss upon the sides of the ruined buildings. Sad dogs rummaged through large piles of debris. The air was so foul that its putrid essence could be tasted on the tongue. Jared drove around these varied obstacles in a perverse and desperate slalom.

He slammed on the brakes. An enormous hole in the ground had swallowed the road ahead. Incongruously, it was surrounded by wreaths of flowers. Jared recognized an opportunity. He opened his door and walked into the rank air outside, retrieved a video camera from Sherpa's cargo area, and started filming. The others followed him outside hesitantly. Jared focused on the hole. Wet earth extended two hundred feet below its asphalt crust. At its bottom, swarms of flies covered a mass of slime flowing between the gaping maws of two shattered drains. A sewer main must have burst, they realized, and swallowed a city block. The group put their shirts to their noses to cover the stench. But they hadn't seen the worst of it. Among the writhing worms and trash below, half buried in the filthy morass, lay a pair of sandals. Next to them was a baseball cap and a little further away the torn remains of a blouse. The flowers suddenly made sense. They were funeral wreathes. The hole had swallowed more than just buildings. Some unfortunate souls had met their grisly ends in the pit of human waste below.

Chapter 8

Planning the Expedition

The highway meandered over sparse and mountainous terrain. Jared and Chris took turns driving, letting the widening spaces and greening countryside wash away the city sins of the previous day. The group didn't talk much. There seemed to be a strong correlation between the frequency with which Alan opened his mouth and the volume of the music. As the day wore on, Sherpa transformed into a virtual dance club, the thumping beats of her stereo pounding back any talk of leveraged buyouts or genetic prowess.

The setting sun celebrated their approach to the city of Flores, the last Maya capital to have fallen to the Spanish, with an ooze of fiery crimson. They could see the city set on an island in the middle of Lake Petén Itzá from its sister city of Santa Elena on the shore. As they drove across the causeway they were giddy with excitement. They were approaching the limits of modern civilization. Beyond Flores lay only primordial wilderness dotted with mysterious ruins.

The group debated their lodging options. Alan suggested they stay at a fine hotel. His back was "achey," he claimed, and he could have really used a feather bed. He was overruled in favor of a hostel, which seemed a better bet for the purposes of organizing an adventure. Navigating through the narrow streets of Flores proved a challenge but the city was tiny and a short time later they reached their chosen destination. They walked through the nondescript doors of the *Hostel de la Selva* to enter what was clearly an epicenter of the backpacker universe. Cozy lounges strewn with sofas and hammocks surrounded a luxuriant ornamental garden. Candlelight danced off richly hued tapestries. Calming jazz music filled the air. Throughout these comfortable nooks and crannies milled a small army of world travelers, alternately talking, playing chess, reading, and otherwise unwinding from the rigors of the road.

A registration clerk greeted the group. They booked a couple of rooms and Jared asked about hiring a guide. "You will want to speak with Koenrad, the co-owner of the hostel," the clerk said, pointing to an earnest looking man setting dining tables across the room. "Since leaving Holland, he has spent much of his time exploring the jungles north of town. He will know best."

Koenrad had closely cropped hair, round spectacles, and most curiously, a small parrot perched on his head. Unfortunately, he was busy preparing for the dinner rush so the travelers would have to wait. They sank into well-worn sofas and took the opportunity to chat with other guests. Each person they met seemed eager to share his or her opinions about the best things to see and do in the area, and in the world for that matter. One interesting thing the group discovered was that no one appeared to be venturing into the Petén. Even Tikal, the famous ruined city at the edge of the rainforest, now required military escort for every visit.

Finally, his chores completed, Koenrad approached the group and introduced himself. "I understand you intend to explore the Petén," he said. "Shall we have dinner and discuss your plans?" His parrot, Pito, had now migrated to his shoulder and nibbled his ear affectionately. The group took their places before heaping plates of spaghetti. "So," Koenrad began, "tell me."

Jared took a deep breath. "We're here to film the most majestic places we can find in the Petén rainforests. We hope to use this footage to raise awareness of the special status of this region and thus gain support for its protection. We would also like to explore some of the ruins spread throughout jungle. My assistant here, Chris, studies the Maya and would appreciate an opportunity to see their old cities firsthand." Jared pulled a series of documents from his pack. These included topological maps, giant satellite printouts, and a number of articles and magazine clippings describing the area. "So the question is," he continued, "where can we find the most spectacular flora, fauna, and archeological sites in the Petén?"

Koenrad chewed his food pensively. He turned to his bird, as though trying to ascertain what it thought of the proposed mission. Pito released a nervous squawk and Koenrad shook his head sadly from side to side. "This is a noble and ambitious project. I wish I had better news for you, but I must tell you that it would be very foolish for you to continue."

Chris was the first to reply. "We have to continue!" he said. "We just drove all the way down from the States!"

Koenrad blinked. "You drove?"

"I have a truck specifically designed for these kinds of expeditions," Jared explained.

Koenrad took a moment to consider this new information. "Under normal circumstances," he said, "such a vehicle might be helpful, but the entire area is unsafe now. No one goes there. It is far too dangerous."

"What kind of dangerous?" Jared asked.

"And if that's true, why are people considering its development?" Sybil Lee added.

Koenrad looked around and leaned closer. "It is only recently," he said quietly, "...that people started...disappearing."

The four travelers exchanged concerned expressions. Pito extended his wings in a flourish of red and blue.

"Disappearing?"

"Yes. First, it was just a few hunters, then some loggers, and now it seems a group of businessmen has vanished along with their entire military escort. No bodies have been found, and that was not for lack of looking."

Jared squinted his eyes. "Well, there has to be some rational explanation."

"I am sure. The government blames guerrillas, but nobody believes that. Otherwise, there would have been demands for ransom."

"What else could it be?"

"Perhaps it is a conspiracy meant to create fear, to increase military authority. Or perhaps narco-traffickers are trying to hide their activities." Koenrad lowered his voice. "Or perhaps, as the locals believe, the jungle itself is to blame. They say the 'Guardians of the Forests' have reawoken and are now taking their revenge on humanity."

Jared sighed. This was already due to be a challenging enough expedition without the added worry of guerrillas, drug smugglers, or man-eating forest bogeys. Nevertheless, unless Koenrad offered some concrete danger he was not willing to give up. "Look, I really appreciate the advice, but we have to do this." Jared paused and looked at the others. "Or at least...I do."

Chris swallowed hard and nodded his head vigorously in the affirmative. "We do," he said. "We've come too far and this is too important."

"Puleease," Alan erupted with bravado. "Guardians of the Forest! As if we'd be scared off by angry monkeys. We'll bring some bananas."

Sybil Lee was inscrutable. If she were frightened she didn't let on, but neither did she voice support for the trip.

"I cannot stop you from going," said Koenrad, "but I cannot stress enough how much I would prefer that you did not. It is not only for your own safety that I am concerned, but also for the economy of this area. Every tourist that vanishes means a thousand more that will not come. If anybody hears that you stayed at this hostel and never came back from your trip, we will be ruined."

Sybil Lee broke her silence with vigor. "This is bigger than the economy of this region or the future of this hostel. We're willing to risk everything to protect the environment and all you can think about is dollars. You walk around with that little parrot on your head like you're one with nature and yet you're willing to let that rainforest die the grisly death of greed. I don't understand you."

Koenrad and Pito looked taken aback. They regained their composure and Koenrad sat for a moment, deliberating. He lifted his wine to his lips and downed it in one gulp. "You are right," he said, setting his glass down roughly, as though pounding a gavel. "I love this hostel and I hope that this area continues to thrive economically, but I love the rainforest more than any of these material concerns. I tell you this for your own good though. The disappearances are true. Beyond this, you are walking into a swamp pit. The rainy season is only just ending, and quicksand does not just exist in the movies. The bugs you will encounter are voracious and even the trees in the *bajos* are dangerous. They are covered with thorns and defensive chemicals. This is not to even mention the snakes or jaguars."

"None of us are expecting a walk in the park," Jared said, "and we're prepared for just about any contingency." He pushed the maps closer to Koenrad and pulled a pen from his pocket. From another pocket he produced a stack of Guatemalan currency as thick as a fist. "Now if you'll kindly tell us where we may be able to find the highest concentration of wildlife and ruins we would certainly appreciate it."

Koenrad stared at the money. "This is not necessary," he said finally, pushing it away. "I will help you."

He went on to explain in detail how to reach what he described as a hidden land of enchantment set deep within the farthest reaches of the forest. He drew unmarked roads on Jared's maps as well as potential hazards. He highlighted what he suspected were overgrown ruins and wrote phrases such as, "Turn east at the tree stump that looks like a skull" and "Watch for vipers here." At the end of a long series of scribbled notes, he circled a small portion of the map. "This is 'The Spot,'" he said.

It sounded too good to be true. There, claimed Koenrad, existed such profusion of animal life that even he agreed it did not seem possible. In one day of wandering about the area he had seen sixteen Resplendent Quetzals, two Harpy Eagles, seven sloths, a dozen troops of monkeys and a sky full of parrots. The trees in the area grew to gargantuan proportions and flowers covered virtually every square inch.

Sybil Lee, having specialized in birds in her earlier career, was skeptical. "Aren't Quetzals known to live only at high altitudes?"

"I am only telling you what I saw," said Koenrad. "I have no reason to exaggerate. Quetzals are unmistakable."

Jared couldn't have hoped for better news. The Resplendent Quetzal, Guatemala's national bird, namesake of its currency, and a sacred symbol of the Maya, was a spectacular creature, with iridescent, green feathers that hung a half meter from its body. Unfortunately, these elegant birds had become as rare in

Central America as vultures had become common. Evidence of a previously unknown population in the Petén lowlands would have greatly aided in Jared's fight against development. Beyond that, footage of the other animals in their towering forest environment would make for compelling viewing. Harpy Eagles were the largest birds of prey in the Americas, sloths were unabashedly cute, and monkeys, parrots, and all the rest would round out Jared's documentary into a balanced work of natural art. He nearly levitated out of his chair in anticipation as he reviewed Koenrad's notes.

Chris stared at the pile of cash lying on the table and looked to Jared for approval as he slid it toward Koenrad. "Maybe you could come with us as a guide?" he suggested.

"I am sorry," Koenrad replied, pushing the cash back again, "I would love to but I must tend to my hostel. My partner and his wife are going back to Holland for the holidays and the day-to-day operations of this place will fall on me. I'm afraid you will have a very hard time finding anyone to guide you. I would not waste your time trying to do so."

"I think we'll be fine on our own with these maps," Jared said. "Thank you, Koenrad. I don't know how to repay you."

"Bring back some good photos...and don't disappear."

Jared, Chris, and Sybil Lee finished their dinner and headed across the causeway to Santa Elena to purchase last minute gear and supplies. Alan stayed behind. Apparently he had "portfolio concerns" and could not spare the time. Disturbingly, when Jared had tried to clarify what camping equipment Alan already owned, the heir had dismissed his question and asked that the group just get him whatever they were buying for themselves. He had then disappeared in a rush to get to the Internet nook. Jared wondered with concern whether the champion of all that is winnable was avoiding their shopping foray in order to hide his ignorance of the outdoors.

The group talked as they drove out of town. All expressed trepidation regarding Koenrad's warnings, though none were scared enough to back out. They agreed they would have to be vigilant and stick together. If things got uncomfortable they would simply turn around. If things got really uncomfortable, they could use Sherpa's onboard communication system to send a distress call. They also discussed the possibility of purchasing a gun but realized how futile that would be. First of all, if it was true that entire squads of military personnel had gone missing, it wasn't clear what carrying around a little pea shooter would accomplish. Second, gun ownership by foreigners in Guatemala was illegal, and the thought of a Central American jail was scarier than anything they were likely to encounter during their trip.

They reached Santa Elena to find a swarm of markets bustling with patrons. They went on to collect their supplies, which included four hammocks, six days' worth of dry foods, two bottles of rum, a packet of re-hydration tablets, a box of chocolate, and at Jared's suggestion, what seemed an unreasonable amount of bug spray. They also purchased a cheap tent and sleeping bag for Alan, not because they were being stingy but because quality outdoor goods were not available. They had brought everything else they would need from the States.

Back at the hostel, Jared and Sybil Lee double-checked gear while Alan swooned over financials and Chris, anticipating an extended Internet absence, filled his psychic tank with sporting news. Excitement and trepidation made sleep that night an elusive target for all, for the next day they would embark for the emerald unknown.

Chapter 9
Adventures in Mud

They beat the sun to be the first up. Sherpa sat bloated with cargo, but as with a bursting belly at a feast, there always seemed to be room for one more little thing. Jared eased in the last of their supplies and everyone hopped in the truck. With a turn of the ignition, Sherpa roared to life. They were off!

The sky and roads did not share their good cheer. Clouds smothered the air and the gravel track below them quickly deteriorated into a sloppy mess. Within half an hour they were gliding over pure mud. Sherpa so vaguely obeyed the direction of her steering wheel that Jared felt like he was piloting a boat.

Alan peered out his window into the gloom. "Oh Gawd!" he lamented, "I hope you all had the foresight to purchase me a quality rain slicker."

"Sorry, Alan," Jared replied. "We looked. Guatemalans are small. Even their extra large jackets wouldn't have fit you. We have some plastic bags. We can make you a poncho."

Chris sniggered and then coughed to cover it up. What a treat it would be to see the blueblood pretender in the back sporting the latest in trash bag attire!

Eventually the swelling sky could stand it no longer and decanted, pouring down an almost solid rain. Sherpa sunk deeper into the road. By the time the group reached the town of Carmelita, the malevolent weather had so choked the sun that it may as well have been nighttime.

Alan's stomach grumbled until his mouth expressed its desires. "I'm afraid in our rush I neglected to provide myself with sufficient alimentation. Perhaps we could stop to pick up a snack?"

"We could..." Jared said as he studied the buildings beside the road, "but I'm afraid this place doesn't look too lively."

Indeed, despite the stormy darkness of the day, no lights were visible in any of the windows. Nobody walked the streets, no dogs roamed the alleys, and no livestock filled the fields, all unusual absences for a Central American settlement. When, a few moments later, they reached the town square, they saw its buildings too were darkened.

"Maybe it's a holiday," Sybil Lee offered absently.

"Maybe," Jared said, with little conviction. He pulled in front of what looked like a store.

"There must be somebody around," Alan insisted. "Listen, sport," he added to Chris, handing over a wad of cash, "why don't you run inside and take a look? I'm starving and don't have proper weather gear like you do."

Chris turned to Jared, rolled his eyes, and flicked his head toward the outside. Jared nodded. He and Chris slipped into ponchos and stepped out. The building had definitely been a market at some point. Coca Cola signs and advertisements for batteries hung on its walls and racks of empty bottles lay neatly stacked just outside its entryway. They peeked inside a broken window. Dust and debris covered every surface. Empty coolers lay toppled on the floor. Though they called to see if anyone was around, the only response they received came from a pair of bats hanging from the ceiling. The animals voiced their displeasure at the intrusion with a petulant squeak.

Turning back to the truck, they caught a glimpse of a faint light across the street. Something was happening in the chapel. The building's tall double doors were open at odd angles and shadows bounced around its interior. "Hang on a second," Jared said. Chris followed him. Pine needles crunched under their feet as they walked through the entryway. Once they got a clear look inside, they each shuffled back a step.

A forest of candles set on an altar at the opposite end of the building illuminated an unnerving scene. Pews clumped in heaps on the sides of the room, jagged chunks of ceramic littered the floor, and a bloodied blade impaled the altar. Jared and Chris's senses went on high alert. They took a few steps closer and suddenly understood the origin of the ceramic shards. A statue of Christ had been thrown down. In its place hung a wooden cross carved with gnarly vines and monstrous animals forms.

"Whoa," Chris said under his breath. He and Jared crept toward the cross. Chris extended his hand to touch it. "Whoa!" he repeated, recoiling. The entire length of the object glistened with crimson. At that moment, their hearts nearly leapt out of their chests and sprinted out the door when they were startled by an obnoxiously loud noise. They peered out the chapel entry to see Alan stretching from the back seat to reach Sherpa's steering wheel.

Chris released a nervous sigh and shook his head in exasperation. "You think they nursed him on shit? I mean, you are what you eat and all."

"Sorry. I didn't want to let him come along, it's just..." Jared looked back at the cross. "What do you think it is?"

"It's a Maya World Cross. It represents their tree of life, the center of their universe."

"I mean the red stuff."

"Blood? Chicken blood?"

"Yeah, chicken blood." Jared rubbed his cheek. Koenrad wasn't kidding. Something very weird was going on. "Do you think we should turn around?"

"I don't know. No, I don't. I think I should get

my camera and take a picture."

Sherpa's horn blared once more. Jared and Chris nodded to each other and walked briskly back to the truck.

"What took you so long?" Alan demanded. "Did you bring me back anything to eat?"

"Store's closed," Chris said.

Jared pressed the accelerator and Sherpa lurched out of town. A tidal wave of dense vegetation loomed before them. They dove in quickly, as if to avoid the frothing chaos that would ensue if the wave crashed. Burrowing through the foliage, they drove through darkness so pervasive Jared had to flip on the headlights.

Chris studied his maps. "So we follow this road for a few miles and then turn onto a seasonal track."

"I don't know if I'd even call this a road," Alan sniffed from the back. "If we have to turn onto an even more primitive thoroughfare, we're sure to get stuck."

"We're prepared for that," Jared said. "You've got a strong back, right?"

Alan bristled. "Jared. I will remind you that I am your guest here. If, as Sybil Lee has informed me, you are really interested in a Hotchworth grant then I hope for your sake that you are joking."

Jared bit his tongue, hard. He concentrated on the road ahead.

Eventually they found their turnoff. They tore through a veil of vegetation to enter a path barely wide enough for Sherpa. Indeed, branches and twigs clawed at her sides. Large bumps alternated with watery craters to cover the whole of the track. Within minutes, Sherpa had floundered to a stop.

"You see, this is absolutely ridiculous!" Alan

exclaimed.

"Is this the eject button?" Chris whispered as he pointed to a switch on the dash.

"No, unfortunately. Crank the music please."

Jared slipped Sherpa into her 4-Low gear. This channeled the entire force of her powerful engine into a range so limited that maximum RPMs translated to only about one mile an hour. One gentle press on the accelerator and the truck shot violently out of the muck.

They continued along the track as it slithered through the undergrowth. With time, the rain eased and a fine mist enveloped the rainforest. Jared's eyes tired from their ceaseless efforts to detect hazards in such low visibility. At one point, he would have surely crashed into the remnants of a fallen tree were it not for a string of fluorescent ribbon strewn about the debris. Gaping ruts in the surrounding mud provided evidence that someone had tried to drive around the blockage. Chris poked his head out to read the writing on the ribbon. "'*Ejército de Guatemala. Prohibida la entrada*,'" he said. "Check my Spanish but seems the Guatemalan army would rather we stay out."

Jared pulled closer. A large chunk of the fallen tree's trunk had been excised. As they eased through the opening, Alan cleared his throat conspicuously. "So I take it we are going to disregard the Guatemalan military's *direct* orders not to proceed into this swamp pit?"

Jared slowed Sherpa to a stop. He looked expectedly at the others.

"The tape's been cut," Chris noted. "Someone's already passed through."

"Plus it's half buried," Sybil Lee added. "Whatever happened here is old news."

"Alan?" Jared asked.

"It does seem others have passed, as has any immediate danger, but I am having an *increasingly* hard time believing anything worthwhile lies ahead...unless it's mud you treasure."

"Koenrad mentioned that The Spot is on higher ground," Chris said, "and should be drier."

"There's only one way to find out," Jared said.

"Well then," Alan harrumphed, thrusting his chin forward imperiously.

Jared slipped Sherpa back in gear. Her engine revved rhythmically as he negotiated one jutting protrusion after another. If they had closed their eyes, they could well have been sailing in tumultuous seas.

It wasn't long before they reached the next road blockage.

"Is that the top of a car?" Chris asked incredulously.

They stepped outside into mud to their ankles. As they trudged closer to the blockage, they realized that it was, in fact, the remains of a vehicle. Only an arm's length of roof protruded from the ground. The rest had been swallowed by wet earth.

"Now that's stuck," Jared noted dryly.

They circled the car. Several of its windows were shattered. Guatemalan army tape peaked from the surrounding mud.

"You'd think they would have removed this hunk of junk from the road," Alan quipped.

"Now what do we do?" Chris wondered aloud.

"I'm thinking," Jared replied. He peered inside the wreck. Brown sludge speckled with shards of glass filled the interior. "Hey, look at that," he said, fishing out an object the size of a book. As ooze dripped from its sides, he realized what it was - a walkie-talkie. He wiped his prize clean with his hands and showed it to the others.

"Looks like a nice one," Sybil Lee said. "Shame about the moisture."

"Yeah, it's probably hosed," Chris concurred, poking a stick in the car in search of more buried treasure.

"Might be good for parts anyway." Jared hated to throw anything valuable away. He placed the radio in Sherpa's cargo area.

"Well?" Alan demanded. "How do you propose we pass this obstacle?"

Jared looked back and forth between the sunken vehicle and Sherpa's oversized tires. He motioned for the others to get back in the truck as he climbed into the driver's seat. "4-Low," he replied simply.

With the exception of a river crossing and the precarious passage over a disturbingly rotten bridge, the rest of the day passed in a blur of mud and mist. The road didn't so much end as peter out. Vegetation growing within its bounds steadily proliferated until the track ahead became indistinguishable from the jungle around and they could drive no further. The group shook out their legs and set camp on the driest patch of earth they could find. Jared, Sybil Lee, and Chris strung up hammocks, careful to drape mosquito nets over their tops, while Alan opted to sleep in a tent. They tied a large plastic tarp over their camp to protect them from the rain, ate a hearty meal, and nestled into the arms of a well-earned slumber.

A million leaves conspired to prevent even a hint of moonlight from penetrating the thick forest canopy. Jared woke to such darkness that his view remained unchanged with eyes opened or closed. He lay for some time in his hammock, listening. Shrill insect calls intertwined with eerie wails and rhythmic groans. One call in particular rose above the rest. It sounded like a party whistle as it blared in time with the rest of the natural music. A few flashing lights, thought Jared, and this could be a vampire disco.

Eventually Jared stepped to the moist ground below. He followed the light of his headlamp to where he thought he had parked Sherpa and, for a moment, panicked. It took him a few seconds to realize the vehicle stood directly ahead, camouflaged in viscous mud. Jared opened the tailgate and filled his water bottle. Taking a long drink, he noticed the two-way radio he'd found the previous morning tucked in a corner, still filthy. He picked up a towel and examined the device as he cleaned it. The radio was heavy, of seemingly high quality. A steel plate on its side held an engraving, "*Propriedad del Ejercito de Guatemala.*" No wonder the radio was so sturdy, it was military. If that was the case, thought Jared, then it was almost certainly water resistant. He plugged the radio into a universal charger and it burst to life.

Jared fumbled to turn down the volume. He didn't want to wake the others. He eased the volume back up and pressed the radio against his ear. He thought he'd heard something unusual. Indeed, from a swelter of crackles and pops emerged what sounded like the occasional word, but as hard as Jared strained, he couldn't understand a thing. It sounded like gibberish, or the ramblings of a lunatic. The transmission stopped abruptly. Spooked, Jared whipped around. All was darkness. He scanned his environment. He saw trees, lots and lots of trees, but not much else. Walking back to his hammock, he kept looking over his shoulder. He crawled under his blanket and lay there for a long while, eyes wide open in the darkness, listening.

"Oh Gawd!" Alan bellowed. Everyone woke with a start. Jared leapt out of his hammock and ran to Alan's tent where he found him yanking on the entrance zipper. He helped him open the flaps and then laughed at what he saw. Alan's soaked clothes clung to his body and his sleeping bag squished with every movement. A pool of filthy water covered the floor. He must have slept so hard that he hadn't even noticed being waterlogged until just now. "Where's the plastic tarp I gave you?" Jared asked.

"On top of the tent, dummy, where else did you think I would put it?"

Sure enough, there was it was, neatly laid on top of the tent. Jared laughed harder. They had already covered the camping area with a larger tarp. "I'm sorry, maybe I should have been more clear. Your tarp was supposed to go *underneath* the tent. What about the shovel I gave you, didn't you dig a drainage ditch?"

Alan charged out of the tent with a growl.

In the dripping dawn of a jungle that seemed to loath direct light, the group broke camp and prepared for their day. Chris noticed the radio humming in the cargo area. "This thing still works, huh?" he asked. Jared considered sharing his earlier experience with the strange transmission. He still wasn't sure whether he had imagined the voices. Better not to unnecessarily scare the others, he thought. "Yeah," he said simply.

After unloading Sherpa, everyone laid their supplies on tarps for sorting and packing. Jared carefully secured his camera gear and electronics in water tight cases. He was clicking his OnePod's encasement shut when he noticed the device showed only partial battery charge. Confused, he checked the charger connection to its socket. Sure enough, it was loose. This wasn't good. They needed the device as a navigation backup. Jared asked the others for a status on their smart phones. Chris's OnePod held even less charge, Sybil Lee traveled without any phone at all, and Alan's WonderPod was optimized for city use – its navigation features only worked within range of cell phone towers. The group hadn't seen one of those since Flores.

"Alright, it's not a big deal." Jared said. "We should be fine as long as we don't use any functions besides GPS." He registered their coordinates, activated tracking, and clicked his OnePod's protective cover shut. As he started to put the device into his front pocket, he thought better of it. He'd sewn a special waterproof sleeve inside the waist band of his pants. He slipped the slim device inside - safe as can be.

The group finished packing and changed into their expedition wear. Jared, Chris, and Sybil Lee put on quick-drying nylon pants and shirts, stepped into heavy-duty hiking boots, and pulled over heavy ponchos - backpacker models with extra lengths of material. Alan looked at them with their well considered attire and mumbled. He wore khakis, a polo shirt, and an old pair of sneakers.

"Alan, is that all you have to wear?" Jared asked with concern. "We could have bought you proper gear in Santa Elena."

"Apparently that's a moot point given the size selection there."

Jared shook his head. Chris hadn't had much outdoors experience but had admitted as much and had asked Jared what equipment he needed. Alan had bluffed and blustered and now there he stood, ill-equipped and ill-prepared. He may as well have worn a big sponge. His cotton clothing would drink the humid air and his sneakers would be water-logged within seconds of stepping in the muck. And then there was the issue of rain gear. Jared went to work on a couple of trash bags. A few cuts and a shoe lace later, he handed his creation to Alan.

Alan hesitantly put on the makeshift poncho and cap. "Thanks," he said half-heartedly. His vaguely

British accent seemed to have disappeared for the moment. Chris muffled a chuckle. What a transformation! From Pompous Ass to Refuse Smurf in less than a minute.

As a last order of business, Jared secured his truck. After unhooking the main battery, he engaged a hood lock. Next, he installed an anti-theft steering wheel bar and bolted the safe console shut. Moving to the rear of the vehicle, he carefully placed all loose items into two large, lockable boxes. Between the cargo barrier mounted behind the rear seats and the steel bars welded across the rear window frames, it would be nearly impossible for anyone to steal anything from the area. Finally, Jared locked all the doors and clamped a padlock between the tail-gate at the rear lift-gate.

"Wow," Chris remarked.

"We need Sherpa to be here when we get back."

Within minutes of starting their walk the group knew they were in trouble. The deep mud beneath their feet sucked the wind from their lungs and hop from their step, while the jungle lashed at them mercilessly with spiny vines and branches. They cursed as they sank into the muck, then cursed even louder when they reflexively grabbed branches for support and thus impaled their palms. Legions of ants existed for the sole purpose of stinging them ferociously on the most delicate of body parts, while clouds of ravenous mosquitoes proved the fallacy of a benevolent god. Jared watched in awe as a mosquito landed next to an ant stinging him on his hand. As the ant pumped away like the star of some sadistic porn nightmare, the mosquito slurped his blood like a vorpal pig. Insect repellent proved useless as the sweat pouring from their pores washed it away as quickly as it was applied. No number of desperate machete swings could match the ferocity of a jungle that clearly resented their existence.

As they walked, their vocabulary regressed. Primitive grunts met every uncomfortable insult. Their only relief came in the form of torrential downpours. At least during these times, the insect attacks abated. It was in the middle of one such drenching that Alan uttered the first non-curse words anyone had spoken in hours.

"Oh Gawd!" he wailed. "How much longer do we have to carry on like this?"

"You're building character," Sybil Lee replied.

"I don't need any more character!" Alan slipped into a particularly deep spot of mud. "Damn this place to hell!"

"Relax, Alan," Jared said. "We'll be there soon enough."

"How much longer?" Alan demanded, his voice cracking in frustration.

Chris checked his maps against Jared's OnePod. "Umm, we've got a ways to go. We've moved about a knuckle on the map and have another hand to go."

"Oh Gaaaawd!!!"

If they had looked up they might have noticed wildlife or the dark beauty of the forest around them, but they were too busy staring at the mud beneath their feet lest they fall into it. Their sensory worlds narrowed to the limited inputs of pain, discomfort, and liquid earth. They focused on movement: Right foot forward, extract left foot, slap bug, left foot forward, extract right foot, slap bug, repeat, again, and again, and again.

Chris made the mistake of looking at his watch. "Time crawls when you're not having fun."

"Does that mean the secret to a long life is to be miserable?" Sybil Lee asked.

"We'll live forever in this shithole," Alan grumbled.

Suddenly, the monotonous rhythm of machete whacks and step slurps was interrupted by a crumpling sound. Sybil Lee turned to see Alan finishing a packet of candy. He threw the plastic wrapper behind him. She stopped. "What are you *doing*?" she asked in a tone severe enough to make a small child pee.

"I'm hungry," Alan mumbled, chewing.

"You can't throw litter like that!" Sybil Lee struggled to the empty wrapper and put it in her pocket. "We're packing out our trash!"

Alan shrugged, nonchalantly threw a gum wrapper on the ground when Sybil Lee turned her head, and continued walking.

Time crawled at the anguished pace of their slow-motion footsteps. Seconds ticked interminably into minutes and minutes added grudgingly to hours. The dim light in the forest began to fade. Then, happily, the incessant drizzle eased and the clouds began to dissipate. For the first time in what seemed like days they could see the sun's location in the sky. It probed the leaves and branches of the forest in search of a clear path to the ground, casting checkerboard rays through the deep green undergrowth. Wisps of mist danced from the forest floor and embraced the rays like an old friend. The trail expanded and the puddles diminished. They were climbing toward drier ground.

Beside them, they noticed raised mounds of earth, each the size of a garden shed. Many had tunnels burrowed into their sides.

"What do you think they are?" Jared asked.

"The little hills?" Chris replied. "I'm guessing Maya burial mounds."

"And the tunnels?"

"Tomb raiders, I imagine." Chris examined his map intently and smiled. "We're getting very close to the main ruins at the edge of The Spot."

As their excitement grew, they hastened their pace. A short time later the mud beneath their feet hardened to solid earth and they found themselves virtually trotting along dry land. They were weightless as they bounced along the easily passable trail. The sun soon abandoned its attempts to illuminate their path. Light transmuted to sound as the deep emerald hues around them shifted to dull grey and the forest creatures began to sing their evening songs with gusto. The volume and intensity of this natural music pulsed and swelled until finally reaching a crescendo just as the trail broadened and the group walked into a wide clearing.

Chapter 10

The Spot

They threw down their packs and gaped at the site of a jungle reaching for the stars. Colossal mountains of vegetation jutted from the ground at angles too severe to be natural. Chris looked back and forth between the massive mounds and his map. Suddenly his expression changed from puzzlement to bliss. He looked like a child who had just discovered birthday cake for the first time. "We're here," he said breathlessly.

"So those are..." Sybil Lee started.

"Temples."

The group stood in a broad clearing surrounded by the one-sided outcome of a thousand-year battle between plants and mortar. Trees with trunks the widths of elephants marched up the sides of the abandoned structures, their twisting roots penetrating the ancient stones, their great branches extended in a show of victory. Chris wasted no time. He walked to the nearest temple and climbed. Exhausted though he was, Jared followed. Sybil Lee hesitated. She looked expectedly at Alan.

"What?" he huffed incredulously. "Go up there?" He sat heavily on his pack. "I couldn't walk another step if my life depending on it!"

Sybil Lee turned and ran toward the others. They scrambled on all fours, heaving themselves up using vines and branches. It was an ambitious task given what they had just been through, but they were fueled by excitement. They gasped for air as they climbed, then gasped in wonder when they reached the summit. An immensity of stars greeted them, casting the landscape in an otherworldly pale. Soft strokes of the darkest green flowed in every direction with nothing save an occasional blemish to disturb the limpid sea of leaves.

"Hey Chris," Jared said, peering at the bumps in the distance, "do you think those are other temples?"

Chris nodded. "Definitely. Those would have been central temples of neighboring city states. We're in the old heartland of the Maya."

"It's so magical!" Sybil Lee gushed, as she twirled with arms outspread.

They sat to catch their breaths and admire their surroundings. It was incredible to think what a different place the Petén would have been a thousand years earlier and what a challenge it must have been to eke out a living in its unforgiving environment. But as Chris explained, the Maya didn't just eke out a living there, they thrived, creating one of ancient world's most sophisticated civilizations. They had advanced architectural, astronomical, and agricultural technologies, their institutions of government and kingship were efficient and long lasting, and their art inspired and amazed to this day. As Jared and Sybil Lee listened to Chris's ruminations, they pictured the area as it had once been, full of glorious pyramids and monuments, all painted blood red. Then Chris's grist for their imaginations stopped. He had shifted his attention. They followed his gaze to a sky that so throbbed with celestial bodies it seemed alive. Shooting stars sacrificed themselves high in the atmosphere in exchange for one dazzling last dance. Distant galaxies hurled waves of light across the universe.

"Look, there's Seven Macaw!" Chris said excitedly, pointing upwards.

"Is that a constellation?" Jared asked.

"Yeah, a Maya one. Our Big Dipper was their Seven Macaw, a really important figure in their creation myth. I think one of the most interesting things about the Maya was the way their astronomy meshed with their cosmology."

"What do you mean?"

"I mean they got to watch a movie of their creation story play out night after night in the stars. One part of the story involved an epic battle between a false god named Seven Macaw, who was a vainglorious pretender to the sun, and two deities known as the Hero Twins. If you watched the constellation of Seven Macaw cross the sky over the course of the night you'd see the battle unfold. And look, there's the Maize God, on his way to the Place of Creation. Keep watching that constellation and you'll see his death at one end of the sky and resurrection at the other."

"Fascinating," Sybil Lee remarked. She sat on her knees staring at Chris, as though he had become as intriguing and mysterious as the night sky.

"The crazy thing," Chris continued, "is how the Maya could be so sophisticated and yet so bloodthirsty at the same time. I can't believe we're here now, sitting where this city's ajaws must have come to open their sacrificial Portals to the Otherworld."

Jared and Sybil Lee looked at Chris in confusion. He'd switched to speaking pure anthropology, a language with which neither of them was particular familiar. "You're going to have to explain that one," Jared said. "What's an ajaw? And a portal to what?"

"Oh sorry, I guess those terms wouldn't make sense without background. We live in a world where we define physical reality in terms of science and relegate spiritual reality to religion. To the Maya, these were interpenetrated aspects of the same whole. As a result, they believed that their mundane actions rippled through layers of connectedness to affect the welfare of supernatural beings, and vice versa. It was the job of the ajaws, or kings, to act as divine shamans. Through the power of their sacrificial rites, they would open portals to

147

the Otherworld to communicate with the spirits there. It was up to the shamans to keep the universe in balance. Their actions determined the fate of everything."

Jared couldn't tell which woke him first, the exuberant bird song or the cackling monkeys. He opened his eyes and blinked. Above, a steely pre-dawn light illuminated a cloudless sky. To his side perched an avian gem, shimmering with iridescence. It wore a curious crown of feathers and a long, tapering tail. Jared recognized the species immediately. It was a Resplendent Quetzal, the sacred bird of the Maya.

The bird cocked its head and cooed. "Stay right there," Jared whispered. Ever so slowly, he positioned a video camera on his shoulder. The quetzal hopped higher on its perch. "Smile," Jared whispered as he pressed the record button. The quetzal fluffed into a ball, cooed again, and leapt into the air. In as smooth a motion as possible, Jared panned his camera to follow the bird as it flew over his head. Suddenly another quetzal joined the first in midair and, together, they flew to the pyramid the group had climbed the night before. Ascending the steep face of the temple, they were like little jade tears falling in reverse.

Jared hadn't even realized he'd been holding his breath. He shuddered as he exhaled. Awake all of two minutes, he had already captured dream footage. He now had evidence that the elusive Resplendent Quetzal lived in this rainforest. He danced a little dance of joy as he roused the others. "Rise and shine!" he trumpeted. "It's 5:30am and the sun is about to rise and shine!"

Chris and Sybil Lee launched out of their hammocks as though propelled by unseen springs. Their eyes gleamed with excitement as they observed their surroundings in daylight for the first time. This wasn't just a pleasant rainforest setting, this was an archetypal Eden. The remarkably lush foliage before them boasted copious smatterings of flowers and sang songs of fertility. The crisp air they breathed soothed like menthol and their every turn revealed a fairy tale grove yearning to be explored. They threw on their hiking boots and bounded over to Jared.

Alan's nylon sleeping bag rustled within his tent. "Ugh, it's early!" he grumbled. Moments later he was snoring.

"We'll wake him when we come back," Jared said, beaming. "Come on, let's get to the summit to catch the sunrise!" He handed Chris and Sybil Lee an armful each of camera gear and walked briskly to the ruins.

It was as though they had climbed a different temple the previous evening. The view from its summit now in the early morning light extended to the ends of the Earth. A shroud of mist hung above the forest canopy. The sky had become an epic stage for the drama of its favorite star. As the sun peeked over the horizon, intense beams of oranges and yellows ignited the landscape in a flush of impressionistic glory.

Jared placed one camera on a tripod to capture the sunrise, and with another panned their surroundings. Toucans and macaws flew in cacophonous flocks over towering trees. Branches swayed in the distance as armies of arboreal creatures began their days foraging. A chorus of unrivaled complexity emanated from deep within the trees. The temple mounds in the distance were clearer now. They stood as silent witness to the grandeur unfolding around them.

Jared continued to arc his camera until he inadvertently captured Sybil Lee in its frame. He started to pull away, then changed his mind and held fast. Her honeyed caramel curls glowed in the rising sun like halo around her face. With full lips parted, she looked as though she were about to give the rainforest a kiss. "Ohhh, it's so beautiful!" she purred in the most rapturous of tones. "Yeah," Jared replied, with equal yearning, "beautiful." If only moments could be frozen, he would have happily chosen this slice of now as the eternal forever.

With great reluctance, he continued panning his camera. A large pyramid came into view. Jared pulled his eyes from the viewfinder to get a broader perspective. The temple was of a similar size and shape to the one they were on. Jared peered back into his viewfinder to examine the twin structure more closely and noticed something unusual. "Hey, check it out. That temple has stairs."

Chris used his hand as a visor to block the sun's glare. "Really, I don't see any."

Jared glanced back and forth between the actual temple and the image in his viewfinder. The stairs were barely visible to the naked eye - it was the camera's magnification that made them obvious. He motioned for Chris to take a peek.

"That's crazy! You're absolutely right. But how could those stairs have avoided the overgrowth?"

"I don't know. I suppose they must have been excavated."

"But these ruins weren't on any of the archeological maps. Koenrad was the one who highlighted them."

"That reminds me," Sybil Lee said. "I've been wondering about all the cleared space below us. I mean, why hasn't that been covered with trees like everything else?"

Chris scratched his ear, as though trying to remove some impediment to brain function. "That is weird. Maybe the trees had a hard time growing through the old plaster that covered the plaza."

Sybil Lee shook her head doubtfully. "Wouldn't the temples have been covered in plaster too?"

"I tell you what," Jared suggested, "we've got a lot of filming to do today. Tonight we can take a closer look and try to figure out what's going on. Okay?"

Chris and Sybil Lee nodded their approval. The group took in an already nostalgic eyeful of their surroundings and clambered back down to camp.

Alan was awake when they returned, sitting on a hammock examining his bare feet.

"Good morning," Chris chirped.

"Look at these," Alan replied forlornly. His feet were covered heel to toe in puss-filled blisters.

"Oh man, sorry."

Jared looked on with concern. "I'll grab the medical kit. Would you two mind packing lunches for us?"

Sybil Lee glanced at Alan's festering feet. "Should we pack one for everyone?"

Alan's accent returned with a vengeance. "If you are asking if I plan to walk one more step today the answer is no."

Koenrad's warnings echoed in Jared's mind. He tried to view the area around him in a dark light, but could see nothing sinister in the sunshine and birdsong surrounding him. Nevertheless, he felt uneasy about leaving Alan behind. "We should really stick together," he said.

"Puleeease, Jared. Are you seriously concerned with the boogey monkeys? I will be fine, I assure you. I am quite capable of defending myself."

They argued briefly, but Alan did have a point – if he walked on his blisters now he would only exacerbate his injuries. He could stay, Jared relented, as long as he did not wander out of camp.

A short time later, Alan's wounds were covered in bandages and the group's daypacks stuffed with gear. Jared dug out his OnePod and registered their coordinates.

"How's the battery level?" Chris asked.

Jared slipped the unit back into his waist pocket. "We're good."

They slung their packs across their shoulders and marched happily into the trees. They knew that wildlife might be elusive so their plan was to first scout promising locations to set up blinds. As it turned out, there was no need to hide to find the animals. Life saturated the forest as fruit weighs the branches of orchard trees in autumn. Howler and spider monkeys leapt acrobatically through the air, furry agoutis rambled along branches, and spectacularly plumed curassows and turkeys gobbled and squawked through the undergrowth. A bewildering variety of song birds fluttered about, and the group even saw evidence, beneath a carpet of blue morpho butterflies, of fresh jaguar tracks.

Jared had Chris and Sybil Lee film him as he remarked on the wonders of the rainforest and described some of its more curious biological phenomena. He explained the foraging behavior of army ants, whose simple interactions between workers combined to produce devastating colony-level efficiencies. He interpreted cleared areas around various species of plants as dramatic examples of subterranean chemical warfare between roots, and he described the curious practice of clay eating in parrots, thought to help buffer the animals against various toxins in their diets.

At one point the group recorded a caterpillar out of whose ruined body they saw emerging two distinct species of wasps. This unfortunate creature had been doubly parasitized, explained Jared. Interestingly, one wasp species was a hyper-parasatoid of the other, which meant that it parasitized the caterpillar's first parasite. Thus, one wasp larvae went about eating its host while the other went about eating it.

"Coooool," said Chris and Sybil Lee, poking at the remains of the poor creature.

They were so engaged with their task and so busy marveling at the rainforest's wonders that they barely noticed their hunger. By the time they stopped to eat it was already late in the afternoon. They sat on the moss carpet of an old log and pulled out their packed lunches.

"I can't get over how amazing this place is," Chris said, munching happily.

"Soooo much nicer than the swamp we had to cross," Sybil Lee agreed, "but worth every step." She closed her eyes and leaned back to soak in the sun. Her smile evaporated when she looked up. "Uh Oh."

"What Oh?" Chris asked. "Oh."

Dark clouds were gathering once again.

Jared too gazed up, but he noticed something other than the shifting weather. "Chris, could you hand me that camera please?"

"What do you see?"

"A sloth, I think. Eleven o'clock, thirty feet off the ground."

"Oh, how cute!" Sybil Lee said.

Everyone stared at the camera's LCD screen for a better view. With tufts of fur above its puppy dog face, the sloth was indeed cute. It climbed the tree in no particular hurry. It couldn't have hurried even if it had wanted to, explained Jared. Sloths dealt with the poor nutritional value of the leaves that they ate by moving with extreme lethargy.

"So how do they avoid predators?" Chris asked.

"They're pretty well camouflaged," Jared replied. "Algae grow on their backs so they look a lot like the trees they climb. Plus, they move so slowly that they rarely attract attention. The thing is once a sloth is discov-_"

Jared's jaw fell mid-sentence. Sybil Lee gasped, and Chris just kind of gurgled. A raptor with a wingspan as wide as a car swooped from the trees and plucked the sloth from its perch. With a sickening crunch, the bird dispatched its prey and disappeared into the forest.

"Did you get that?" Chris asked, his eyes bulging in excitement.

"Yes! That's the shot of the century! Harpy Eagles are so rare, I can't believe that just happened. I can't believe it!"

"Poor little sloth!" Sybil Lee lamented. It was always that way witnessing nature in its rawest form. There was respect for the predator, and sympathy for the prey.

"It's like I was saying," Jared said, shaking his head, "once discovered, a sloth doesn't have a chance."

Back at the ruins, Alan was nowhere to be found. The group called and whistled for him loudly to no response. Jared might have been more concerned were he not so annoyed. He'd specifically asked Captain Conceited not wander out of camp. Nevertheless, it was already dark and nobody liked the idea of Alan in the rainforest alone. Chris and Sybil Lee agreed to search around the plaza while Jared started on dinner. It would take some time to cook their meal and Jared would join the others once he put the stew on heat, if Alan hadn't already turned up.

After putting a pot of water on the stove, Jared

set up a camera to review footage while he chopped vegetables. He first watched the sloth shot, unable to get over the shock of the capture. Despite the intensity of the footage, Jared knew it would make excellent fodder for his documentary. Nothing drew people in like the hunt. He rewound to the start of the day. In the camera's LCD display, the sun was rising once again. He shook his head at the glory of the images. There were simply no words to describe the poetry of what he was seeing. If a picture said a thousand words, a high definition video said it all. Sybil Lee's face came into view and Jared swooned. He was so happy with her, here, in this magical place. Watching the video, his entire being resonated like a tuning fork set to yes.

Jared froze mid chop. He realized he had not heard Sybil Lee or Chris call for some time. He looked around but could not see the arcs of their flashlights. A pang of panic welled in his gut. He had not intended for them to wander outside the clearing. An image change in the camera's display caught his eye. The second twin temple had come into focus, its improbably excavated stairs clearly visible. Jared glanced ever so briefly at the screen and did a double take. Something looked odd. He studied the screen intently. What was that? He expanded a small portion of the image. His disbelief increased. He zoomed in again. Impossible. One more time. Absolutely impossible, but clear as day. How could he have missed this? Mounted on top of the pyramid, tucked between a bush and a tree, was what appeared to be a large satellite dish.

An explosive flash of lightning and thunder introduced a torrent of rain. Jared whipped his head around. He thought he'd heard a woman's scream within the tumult. His stomach dropped as he launched to his feet and scanned his surroundings. The darkness was impenetrable. He switched his headlamp to its highest setting and held it in his hand in front of him, like a flashlight. He strained his ears but heard only the heavy roar of rain. Then, something rustled beside him. He swung his flashlight about violently. Its beam of light raced over the stove and backpacks and around the hammocks, and then stopped. Jared leaned closer. It couldn't be. He touched the objects to make sure they were real. How could he have missed this as well? Under a hammock, the whole time Jared had been preparing dinner, had been Alan's only pair of shoes.

Now the scream was unmistakable. Jared bolted upright. "Sybil?!" He heard another call, followed by a clambering in the distance. Jared leapt to his pack and ripped his machete from its holster, then sprinted in the direction of the noise.

He stopped at the edge of the clearing and struggled to hear above his heaving breaths. Shining his headlamp into the dark forest, he recoiled violently. A hundred eyes greeted him. He struggled not to panic. The eyes were too small to be those of major predators, he reasoned, and human retinas don't reflect light that way. Choking the handle of his machete, he approached the animals. Soon he stood just a few body lengths away. Still he could not make out their forms. He walked closer still and suddenly an immense whoosh of birds scattered into the air around him.

Jared chuckled nervously and placed his hands on his knees to catch his breath. Then he heard a familiar call. Chris was screaming from deep within the jungle. Jared bolted into the undergrowth, slashing his way forward with all his might. Thorns tore at his skin as he leapt over shrubs and fallen trees. Vines entangled his feet. He felt as though the undergrowth itself was purposely slowing his mad dash. Still, the calls continued. Jared barreled onward as fast as the ferocious terrain would allow. The voices grew louder. Jared grew closer.

Then he heard a new call. "Oh God!" someone screamed just ahead. *Alan.* Jared took a few more steps and slowed to a crawl. He flipped off his headlamp. It was time for stealth. He crept along slowly, silently cursing the treacherous leaves below his feet for their sonic betrayals. Ahead lay a solid wall of vegetation. He felt his way through using his hands. He heard more calls, muffled now. They were close, wretched in their desperation. Jared flattened to his stomach and slithered like a snake. Men whispered amidst flickering lights. Jared's heart galloped as stabs of terror impaled his thoughts. And then he was surrounded by staccato voices and heavy footsteps. Leaves and branches thrashed around him. A swift shadow brought searing pain, and Jared's world went black.

Chapter 11
The Prisoner's Chamber

Each drip had its own periodicity. One ticked off every few seconds, another every minute or so, and still others took five minutes or more to contribute their reverberating little plops to the chorus. Murmurs echoed within murmurs like reflections in a funhouse. Something cold and damp touched a sore spot and Jared lurched to consciousness.

It took a moment for his vision to adjust to his new reality. Sybil Lee came into focus in the dim light. She was a dream of comfort as she leaned closer to sop his brow with a rag. Her silken hair caressed his skin while her familiar scent whispered of home. "Hold still," she soothed, "you're bleeding." Chris shuffled over. They both looked terrible, pasted with muck and tiger stripped with wounds. Chris seemed strangely exposed without his well-worn baseball cap. Only tangles of detritus now covered his head.

Jared struggled to his elbows. The group sat in an expansive chamber lit by the trembling filament of a single bulb. Rounded protrusions bulged from dark walls and moisture dripped from the ceiling. Several dozen men and women lay in torpid poses about the room, some with heads in their hands, others staring blankly into space, all silently screaming in despair.

"Where are we?" Jared rasped.

"Dunno," Chris replied, "but I think we figured out where everyone went when they disappeared."

Jared's probed his wound gingerly and stretched his jaw to rediscover his speech muscles. He studied the other prisoners. "And Alan?"

Chris nodded toward a man rocking himself. A nausea of guilt welled in Jared's gut. Alan's proud lion had become a trembling kitten, its dank fur clinging to its surprisingly skinny body. He'd gotten more than he'd bargained for, Jared lamented. They all had. He continued his survey of the room. A mortared partition with a single barred opening bisected the chamber. Something was moving on the other side.

"That's where they keep the really unlucky ones," said a soft voice. Jared turned to see a young woman. She might have been pretty, though it was difficult to tell past her tattered clothes and begrimed skin. She certainly had pretty eyes, diffident stars peeking past chestnut bangs. Her round face claimed no ethnicity, and with her torn apparel, she looked as though she had just returned from a five-year hike through a thorn bush.

"Thanks for the cheer, Krystal," Sybil Lee said in a dismissive tone. Jared didn't know if that meant he wasn't supposed to like the new entrant into the conversation.

"That's Katy," the woman corrected.

"Oh, sorry," Sybil Lee apologized. "That's right, Katy, the *architect*." She pronounced the word "architect" like it was a scatological term.

"Nice to meet you," Jared said, attempting to soothe the awkwardness with formality.

Katy's mouth tried to smile. The stars behind her flowing bangs blinked.

"How long have you been here?" Jared asked. "What is this place?

"Ten days, I think. I'm afraid I don't know any more than you about where we are." The young woman's eyes moved to Jared's wound. "Are you alright?"

"I'm more worried about what happens next."

Katy glanced around her. "The guards haven't treated us too badly...at least not the people on this side of the room." She looked nervously past the barred windows of the partition. "Those poor others though."

"Why? What's happened to them?"

The woman shifted her gaze down.

"What is it?" Jared insisted. "What's happened to the others?"

Katy turned to Chris and Sybil Lee for guidance. They nodded. She turned back and took a deep breath. "They've been tortured," she said finally.

"Oh... What, um, what kind of tortured?"

"I shouldn't say. I don't want to scare you any more than you already are."

"I'm the idiot that got us here. Scare me, I deserve it."

Katy's lips quivered. "A man lectures them..."

"And?"

"He cuts off..."

"Tell me."

"Pieces."

"Oh, dear."

Tears obscured Katy's eyes. "Oh god, I'm so sorry! I shouldn't have said anything."

"No, that's fine, I asked. What kind of lectures? About what?"

"I don't know, he's insane! He talks about vengeful spirits and thinks he's a king."

Jared digested the information and sighed. "So nothing like that is happening to people on this side?"

"Sometimes they'll take one of us, but all they do is perform a ritual with an insect. I wish I knew more but people are so scared when it happens, I don't think they have any idea what's going on." Katy composed herself, shaking the look of anxiety from her face. She turned to Chris and took a deliberate step from the dark edge of the conversation. "So that was Boston, right? You said you were from Boston?"

Jared looked at his new friend with curiosity.

Despite her worries, there was something reassuring about her, something warm in those soulful eyes. The four prisoners continued to talk for some time, dancing around the horror of their situation by focusing on more mundane subjects – jobs, hobbies, pets. It turned out that Katy hailed from Evergreen, Colorado, not far from where Jared and Chris lived. She was an "organic architect," dedicated to designing structures that meshed with their environments in as aesthetic and functionally low impact a way as possible. She'd come to Guatemala to study the Maya ruins, as they displayed such a textbook harmony of masonry and Mother Nature. She'd been captured while visiting one such ruin.

As the group talked, other prisoners shuffled over to introduce themselves. It seemed that they too had been captured in similar situations, exploring ruins or remote wildernesses. They came from around the world, and some had even been kidnapped in their home countries. Their theories regarding the motives of their captor were as varied and bedraggled as the rags of clothing on their backs. Nobody really had any clue what was happening, and their confusion fed their anxiety.

A thunderous rumble of footsteps in the distance abruptly silenced the group. It sounded as though an army were approaching. Whispers erupted on the other side of the partition. "Is it you today?" someone asked. "I...I don't know!" The footsteps drew closer, ferocious war drums, beating their way to battle. They stopped, just outside the chamber. A swarm of heavily armed men burst into the room. They lined up neatly on two sides of the entrance and stood at attention. Tense seconds passed and a giant extruded itself through the doorway.

It was hard to gauge the man's true height given his towering headdress of jade, but he was a bear among dogs in proportion to the others. His immense chest would have made a gladiator hang his head in shame and his pendulous hands looked as though they could have popped off heads like bottle caps. As the man eased his gaze toward his captives, he revealed a face as fearsome as the predators carved into his headdress. His strong jaw and aquiline nose spoke of a ruthless efficiency while his burning eyes and down-turned lips boasted of an indomitable wrath. In his overwhelming stature and regal demeanor, the man appeared before the prisoners like a mythical figure. He looked, in fact, like a god.

The giant uttered something severe in an unintelligible tongue and motioned toward the prisoners spread about the room. Heads ducked before the wave of his hand. One of his troops broke ranks to kneel before him and then raced to the door. He returned with another man who carried a small pack. Jared suddenly realized what the two men had begun to retrieve from the bag. ID cards. Reflexively, he checked his pockets. His wallet was gone, as were his keys.

The men scanned through the cards, lifting each in order to compare it with the prisoners. One after another, individuals were bound and escorted out of the room. Soon, a large group of prisoners had been taken away. Jared glanced at Chris and Sybil Lee. They watched the proceedings tensely. He caught Katy's eye and she shrugged. Apparently, she too didn't understand what was happening.

The giant walked to the partition with two henchmen in tow. He opened the reinforced door and stepped inside. "Ooooh noooo! Pleeeeease!" croaked someone from the other side. A booming voice with a pronounced accent replied. "Relax, Dr. Delgado. This is not your day to suffer or die." Footsteps pounded to meet a startled squeal. "Unfortunately for this despicable little piggy, it is his day for both!"

Hysterical pleading and a buzz saw of ripping cloth filled the air. "No, no, no!" wailed a man. "I egg oh ou! Leese! Nooooo!" Two soldiers emerged from the partition yanking on a flaxen rope. As they pulled, the bloodied and bound hands of a light-skinned man appeared, followed by his fleshy arms and corpulent body. He was a grotesque slug being hauled across the floor. His head was bald but for a few dark wisps of hair, his body blubbery and nude, and his face a horror show of protuberant eyeballs and chattering teeth. He tried to speak but his words were garbled. The reason was now clear. Between his prominent jowls, where his lips should have been, lay nothing but a red, meaty hole.

The giant hulked over the sobbing creature. He lifted an enormous leg and flattened the man against the ground. Then, with a hideous crunch, he kicked him halfway across the room. "Make haste, Sloan!" he seethed. "The Gods tire of their blood snacks. With you, their feast begins!"

A deathly quiet reigned until the footsteps had receded. Then a raucous chorus burst forth. "Why did the guards use identification cards this time?" "What was with the leader's new headdress?" "And with stripping Sloan?" "What did that mean about him providing the feast?"

Theories were positing and fears expressed but throughout the entire hubbub Chris sat silent and pensive. It wasn't until the room had quieted that he spoke and it became apparent that he had just been dredging his mind for a memory. "I've seen that scene before," he said. "I recognize that scene."

"What scene?" Jared asked. In the room's newfound stillness everyone could hear their conversation.

"Of a giant with one leg over a nude prisoner who had been disfigured in a similar way."

"Where?"

"It's a famous Maya mural. It represents a king dominating a vanquished rival. Supposedly, the captive was tortured for years before being killed. The Maya only bothered to sacrifice their most prized prisoners." Chris looked at the barred window to the partition. "I wonder if that's the VIP room," he said ominously.

"There is a doctor in there," mentioned one eavesdropper.

"And a rich developer," added another.

"And a government official, and a Catholic priest," added a third.

"Well," Jared observed, "if the guy is trying to emulate past rulers that might explain his behavior."

"Yeah, here's the other crazy thing," Chris said. "I recognize that guy too."

"Who? The 'king'?" Jared asked.

"Yes...the 'king'," Chris replied, lost in thought once more.

"From another mural?" Sybil Lee suggested.

"No, not from another mural. From..." Chris shook his head and chuckled. "...from a photo in one of my dad's old magazines of a guy riding a tidal wave like he owned it. I spent hours looking at that picture. That's Xavier del Rojo Reino, world champion surfboarder back when my dad was in college."

"Oh Gaawd! You've *got* to be kidding!" Alan was alive.

"No, I'm completely serious. Rojo Reino was just a kid then. He's probably got another hundred pounds of muscle on him now, but his face is unmistakable. He has two different colored eyes, didn't you see? And that crooked nose and those humongous hands. It's the same guy, I'm telling you. Rojo Reino burst on the surfing scene one year, won all the major championships, and then disappeared from the sporting world."

"Yeah, but this guy uses a different name," Katy said. "It's Kaul or Cool or something."

Chris looked at her intently. "K'uhul?"

"That sounds right, but there's more to it."

"K'uhul Ajaw?"

"Yeah, and then something else."

"'K'uhul Ajaw,'" Chris explained, "was the title that the Classic Maya used for their divine God Kings."

"It's 'Kab'," said a wavering voice from the other side of the partition. Everyone looked in the direction of the new participant, a wan man peering past the barred window. His face was a scrabble of thought lines. "Kab is the last part of his name."

Chris turned to face his friends but looked right through them as he spoke. "K'uhul Ajaw Kab," he said, his words crackling with amazement, "means The Divine Earth Lord."

Alan hobbled closer to the group. "So, you're saying our captor is a world championship surfer who thinks he's an earth god?"

Chris shrugged. "I mean, I could be wrong, but it certainly wouldn't be the first big ego to come out of the sporting world. Besides, how many Guatemalan world surfing champs have there been who happen to look exactly like a younger version of that guy?"

"Why not?" Alan sniffed. "As if any of this makes sense."

The little man on the other side of the partition craned his head out further. "Did I hear you correctly? That name, that other name you mentioned just a minute ago, was that 'Rojo Reino'?"

"Yes, why?"

"But it can't be the same person."

"What is it, Delgado?" a gruff voice asked from behind the partition.

"Well it's just, we read books by a Rojo Reino in

medical school, you see, parasitology texts. I distinctly remember them as I was specializing on the topic." Delgado paused for a moment. "He was an unusual intellect who made contributions to a number of fields. He wrote one famous paper on toxicology, another on the genetic modification of gene leader sequences, and then a third –"

"Speak English!" the gruff voice scoffed. "What the hell does that mean?"

Delgado shook his head. "It doesn't matter. It doesn't matter anyway. It can't possibly be the same person. The Rojo Reino I'm thinking of must have been an American because he did his research at the AMRIID bioweapons lab."

"Delgado, I'm sure you're a fine doctor, but you don't know squat about business. If it's cheaper to outsource labor, people will a find a way. It's called globalization."

Delgado chuckled mirthlessly. "Then maybe we shouldn't be making all our decisions based on economics." He pulled his head back into the partition. "I just hope it's not the same man, because I hate to think what someone that talented and insane might be capable of."

Chapter 12
Glimmers of Hope

Dejection and despair descended on the captives. Things appeared to be escalating dramatically. Usually K'uhul and his men picked only one or two prisoners a day for their rituals but today they had picked ten. Further, they had displayed a new ferocity in humiliating Sloan. As hours passed and no one returned, anxiety gnawed mercilessly at the prisoners' thoughts.

Katy motioned to Jared's watch. "Do you know what time it is?" she asked.

Jared glanced at the remains of his timepiece. With its crystal shattered and innards rent, it now served as nothing more than a questionable fashion statement. In any case, his OnePod would have the time, he thought, as he patted his waist pocket. He caught himself and shook his head - of course it wouldn't be there, the guards would have…wait a minute. Even he could hardly tell the slim device was there but, sure enough, there it was. Evidently his specially sewn pocket had protected his OnePod from more than just moisture. He clicked the unit's cover open and touched its screen. Its backlight flashed on, illuminating his face in the dim chamber. On its display were the last GPS coordinates he had entered. Clearly, no satellite signal had been available for some time to provide updates. Jared noted the time and informed Katy.

"They never keep them this long," she worried.

Fatigue eventually overcame anxiety. As the first prisoners fell asleep, their peaceful snores combined with the room's ever present drips to create an irresistible beacon to the dream world. One by one, the group drifted into unconsciousness. Jared, unfortunately, could not find slumber. He felt like his head was being alternately squeezed by a hand and beaten by a hammer. As he lay in his cloud of pain, he stared at the minutes ticking by on his OnePod. Unexpectedly, an icon blinked on the screen. His heart stuttered. It was the wireless signal indicator - the OnePod had detected a connection. With a trembling finger, he touched the 'Connect' button. The screen changed.

'Please Enter Password' it read.

It couldn't have been that easy. But who knew, maybe they could figure out the password? Then, if they could just get some clue as to where the hell they were, they would be a quick email away from rescue. Jared looked at the power indicator on his OnePod. It held at forty percent. He turned the unit off to conserve battery charge and carefully hid it under a pile of debris. His mind somersaulted through a rush of emotions as he tried to fall asleep. As desperate as their situation was, he'd found a tiny glimmer of hope.

The prisoners sighed as they woke to another day of captivity. There was still no sign of their companions. Everyone's mood improved dramatically, however, after the guards left with the last of their breakfast dishes and Jared explained what he had found. A massive brainstorming session commenced to determine the wireless password. Maybe it had to do with surfing, or parasitology? Maybe it was a derivation of the name of one of the local ruins, or of an important Maya deity?

Hours passed with no breakthroughs but at least the blanket of gloom had lifted. Amid the brainstorming, a semblance of normality emerged. People began to engage in discussions that had nothing to do with their sorry situation. Jared happily noted that Alan was capable of forming sentences that did not involve bragging or complaining. Chris and he discussed memorable surfing championships over the past several decades.

The password suggestions continued, but to no avail. Chris and Alan moved on to naming all-time football greats. Now frustration set in. Four hours of attempted hacking and the prisoners had managed only to wear the OnePod's batteries down further. Still, Chris and Alan continued to chat. Chris was rhapsodizing on the music of nature. He went into detail about the various melodies, rhythms, and harmonies created by the natural world. To Jared's surprise, Alan seemed to be enjoying Chris's ruminations. It must have been comforting to hear about beauty and life while trapped in such a dismal environment.

The rest of the day was devoted to more hacking, but Jared decided to keep his OnePod off until they could come up with some really promising password suggestions. At one point, he was brainstorming with Katy when their discussion evolved into a nice conversation about how she had gotten interested in architecture. Growing up surrounded by spectacular scenery and wildlife in Colorado, she had become fascinated by how animals built their homes. Termite mounds and beaver huts, fox burrows and spider webs, all were made of natural materials and blended perfectly into their environments. If they caused damage, it was of a benign sort that contributed to the landscape rather than dominated it. Katy had watched the city sprawl of Denver eat away at some of her favorite hiking areas and determined that there had to be a better way. She'd become an architect to learn how to build homes sustainably and beautifully, like the animals in nature that she so admired.

"It's a matter of respect," she said. "We used to make slaves of people, and then at some point realized the tribesmen next door were as human as we were and were entitled to a similar level of respect, if not full equality. Seems to me, once we get over our narcissistic love of our own species, we're going to realize the same thing about other living things. Maybe we won't grant them full status as equals, but we'll recognize their intrinsic value and right to exist. The types of buildings I design are the least I can do."

Jared loved Katy's take. It seemed that the values he was trying to impart through his films already figured prominently in her mental makeup. When he looked into the stars of her eyes, he saw hope. She'd been lucky, though, to grow up in a state like Colorado, where nature lived strong. Unfortunately, there were billions of less fortunate city dwellers who wouldn't know the fragile majesty of an ecosystem from a Vegas hooker playing bingo. The only values they recognized were the values people put on things. Their worlds revolved around the staples of sex, money, and politics, spiced, perhaps, with a dash of sports and a smidgen of art. To Jared, these things represented but a pauperized slice of an infinitely fascinating universe. If only he could light up others eyes like Katy's, and turn more people on to the wonders of nature. In his mind, there were ten million other species as deserving of our love, attention, and respect as our own.

Sybil Lee joined the conversation uninvited. She was having none of Katy's eco-crap. "The only good *architecture* is trees," she said bitingly. "Your 'organic' building is a joke."

That put a quick end to that discussion. Jared didn't understand Sybil Lee's aggression. Maybe she really thought Katy wasn't going far enough in her work, that we should be rolling back development altogether. He was certainly sympathetic to that view. There was no such thing as half a murder after all. Or maybe Sybil Lee just didn't like the fact that he really seemed to be enjoying his conversation with his new friend.

Eventually, the prisoners began to drift into the comforting oblivion of slumber. A smoldering ache had replaced Jared's inferno of head pain and he was finally able to relax. As he lay down, he overheard Chris and Alan heatedly debating the intelligence of a small bug they had found crawling across the chamber floor. He laughed to himself as he heard his own words come out of Chris's mouth in defense of the powers of the little bug's brain. Something was comforting about the fact that his friend would have taken such a strong interest in a topic he had initially found so boring. Even more comforting was the fact that Alan was so clearly engaged in the conversation. Maybe there was hope for the man after all. With that thought, Jared closed his eyes and found rest.

Chapter 13
Sacrifice

There was no sun to wake to, nor the singing of birds. Only drips of water marked the time. But just as the dawn wakes through its steadily rising light, the rain of moisture that night grew ever louder until everyone had stirred. It was only when the drips from the ceiling had reached an echoey roar that it became clear to all that what they had really been hearing were the thunderous footsteps of K'uhul's army approaching.

Everyone peered nervously at the door. Their trepidation was richly rewarded with yet another explosive and carefully choreographed entry. Pandemonium ensued as the guards removed a large group of prisoners. This time, Jared, Chris, Sybil Lee, Alan, and Katy were among them.

Outside the chamber, the group found themselves in a dimly lit tunnel. They gave each other nervous looks of reassurance as they heard the telltale sounds of K'uhul's soldiers rounding up partition prisoners and stripping them of their dignity. They watched horrified as the captives clawed at the ground to avoid being pulled out the door. The doctor, Delgado, struggled before them, as did a much older man. A third captive, broad shouldered and surly tongued, lashed at K'uhul with vitriol. "Sick fuck!" he yelled. "You'll pay for this! Mark my words, you'll –"

The bottom of K'uhul's fist might have been a bass drum for the cavernous tone it produced as it hit its target. "No, Verderber," he said to the crumpled heap before him, "I'm afraid you're the one who is not well and owes a debt."

Terror grew from embryo to snarling dragon as the guards prodded the prisoners onward with bayonets.

K'uhul led the macabre march, followed by his henchmen and captives. Darkness swam around their steps, retreating only occasionally in the face of proletariat light fixtures mounted along the tunnel wall. The group shivered in the dank air as they snaked past eerie rumbles and whirs. Eventually, they reached a stairway of hewn stone and climbed to enter a broad passageway. Bright lights illuminated an expansive hallway bejeweled with stainless steel doors. Earnest men in lab coats nodded solemnly as the prisoners shuffled past.

The group halted in front of a massive vault. Two guards labored to spin a bezel the size of a frigate's steering wheel. As the structure heaved open, a wall of flowing water inched its way into view. The guards jabbed the prisoners with bayonets. Fearing death by drowning, the group resisted until the blades dug deep. In an instant, they stood opposite what they now realized was a waterfall tumbling from high above. Torchlight illuminated throngs of bats flying in wide arcs. Streams dripped from colossal stalactites. All at once, the captives understood that the entire complex they had just traversed lay deep within the heart of a cave.

The guards harried the prisoners across the cavern to enter a steeply pitched passageway. They ascended until their lungs burned and thighs ached. A dim light appeared ahead. A few more steps and the group emerged into a dazzling night sky.

They stood on a stone terrace high above the forest canopy. Flickering torchlight hinted at stern faces amidst a series of enormous urns. Stairs descended to meet a clearing that swarmed with shadowy figures. A temple thick with vegetation loomed nearby. More men stood in torchlight at its summit. In the distance, bright specks hovered above the horizon.

Suddenly Jared realized where they were. Sure enough, beyond the tangled branches of a bush next to

173

him lay the satellite dish he knew would be there. They were on top of the twin pyramid. He, Chris, and Sybil Lee had gazed at the stars from the adjacent structure just days before. Staring into the distance, Jared realized that the glimmers of light hovering above the forest canopy were emanating from the peaks of other ruined temples. The entire Petén basin teemed.

The guards split the prisoners into groups. The five friends and several others were to remain where they were. The partition captives were led to a lower terrace where they were ordered to kneel. The remaining prisoners were escorted to another platform, promptly stripped naked, and washed with rags soaked in steaming water. Meanwhile, a group of soldiers laid out neat piles of clothing. As the prisoners changed into the garments, K'uhul spoke. He gestured to the sky and the rainforest around them and bowed courteously before motioning for his guards to take the captives away.

Jared glanced at Katy for a hint as to what might be happening. She shook her head. He watched as the prisoners were herded down the steps to the clearing below, through the crowd of shadows, and into the forest. Were they lambs on their way to sacrifice? Were they being freed? Turning to Chris to ask for his thoughts, Jared was surprised to see his friend staring at the heavens. He looked up. The constellation of Seven Macaw glowed brightly above all else, while the Maize God lay drowning in a sidereal sea.

K'uhul began to chant, followed by his guards and the stern-faced figures on the terrace. The crowd below soon joined, as did the men standing on the summit of the adjacent temple. A drum roll introduced a hypnotic rhythm as the inhabitants of the distant temples added their own tiny voices to the chorus. With time, the chanters adapted their songs to respond to the chirps and wails of the rainforest around them. Wild interweaving human and animal calls tumbled and swelled over waves of rumbling drums to reach breathtaking levels of intensity. Just as this epic consonance reached a climactic point, a group of men wearing flowing headdresses skipped from the cave passageway to the terrace. They weaved about in time with the music, stopping briefly to light the contents of gaping ceramic vessels spread about platform. Geysers of fragrant smoke billowed from the pots. Still the wild chorus grew ever more intense. The dancers thrashed about in an orgy of bodily drama. Now the chorus achieved an unbearable power. It seemed as though the entire Earth were bellowing forth a song of mourning. The dancers fluttered to the lower platform. With one motion, they pulled free an enormous tapestry to reveal a stone altar surrounded by grotesque animalistic statuettes.

Another group emerged from the dark passageway, their steps reverberating in time with the throbbing canticle around them. Masks of carved jaguars and serpents obscured their faces and their bodies glistened with crimson in the torchlight. They promenaded down the steps to the lower platform and hopped and spun to the high status prisoners huddled in a corner. Dr. Delgado reared back in terror as they cut him free from his ropes. They nudged him ever closer to the altar. Through the grace of their movements, his desperate attempts at resistance were transformed into flowing parody of struggle. In panic, he dashed between them. They caught him, lifted him horizontally, and eased him on to the stone slab.

Delgado screamed for reason and mercy as the masked men grabbed his limbs to immobilize him. The feathered dancers leapt to K'uhul. They were tiny before him, insects fluttering about a mighty oak. They beckoned him to the center of the platform and he followed them slowly, regally. Reflected torchlight swirled in whirlpools along his towering headdress of jade as he reached the side of the altar and gazed at his victim. All at once the resounding chorus of Earth and Sky stopped. The dancers prostrated themselves flat against the ground. Only the occasional cricket or frog dared croak in the distance.

K'uhul swept his arms for emphasis as he spoke quietly to Delgado. With each word, his voice grew harsher and his movements more severe until, finally, he stood foaming in fury. He retrieved an enormous blade from his side and lifted it high above his head. With a sickening rip, Delgado's piercing screams were rendered into pathetic gurgles.

The chorus of chanting and wailing exploded anew. K'uhul raised Delgado's still beating heart and roared. He gently placed the organ into a smoldering urn, knelt before the statues that ringed the altar, and dabbed the mouths of each with blood. Delgado's lifeless body was cast down the temple steps. K'uhul rose to his feet with the wrath of god burning in his eyes as the dancers hopped and skipped to retrieve their next victim.

"Why?" Jared whispered to Katy. "Why would they kill a doctor?"

"I don't know" she answered, "but now they're untying the priest."

The same tragic scene unfolded for K'uhul's next victim. He was pinned, scolded, and executed, his torn body cast down the temple stairs and his blood offered to the grotesque statues perched around the altar. The last of the high status prisoners, Verderber, resisted mightily. Given his size, the dancers struggled to keep his abduction graceful. Eventually he too was subdued and laid prostrate across the altar. K'uhul seethed and raved as he plunged his knife deep into Verderber's chest. He tore him open with the savagery of a wild animal. The prisoners gagged and choked as Verderber's body was thrown, in disjointed chunks, to the clearing below.

The chanting burst forth once again as the dancers skipped up the stairs to the upper platform. Jared bucked violently as they cut him free from his ropes and dragged him from the group. Sybil Lee and Chris screamed in horror while Katy and Alan quivered in speechless desperation. As the masked men cinched Jared's limbs across the cold stone slab, a tornado of emotions and images engulfed his mind. His breaths were a chaos of pants. Terror and nostalgia tore at his gut as images whizzed by too quickly to process. He saw the forest that had been his world for three months, then Sybil Lee's face, beatific in the rising sun. He saw the sprawl of Guatemala City, and the corpses of those who had died there in their own filth. And then he saw the gaping chest cavities of the men he had just witnessed meet the most hideous of fates. He had too much left to do. He couldn't die, not this way, not now!

The images screeched to a halt as the thunderous chorus of chanting and wailing fell silent. K'uhul loomed above, an otherworldly giant framed by an infinite expanse of stars.

"You are American?" he asked softly.

Jared nodded yes.

"Then I will speak in English for you. Know this. It is through the pain that we inflict that we will turn the world to tears, and it is these nourishing rains of sacrifice that will awaken our world to its glorious renewal. Your death will not be in vain."

Jared distinctly heard the words "pain" and "death." His every muscle harnessed every drop of three and a half billion years' worth of evolutionary survival instinct to pull free from his captors. The bulging veins of his neck threatened to burst in the intensity of his struggle. But he was easily restrained. K'uhul reached for his blade. With eyes brimming with fear and sadness,

Jared glanced at his companions. Judging by their expressions, they may as well have been on the altar with him.

He looked back at K'uhul. To surprise, his executioner had retrieved a small glass vial instead of a knife. An insect inside buzzed angrily. K'uhul moved the vial closer, removed its cap, and set its open end against Jared's arm. The insect quieted and scurried down the side of the container.

"What the hell is that?" Jared glurped.

K'uhul blinked and leaned closer. "What did you say?"

The insect probed Jared's exposed skin. "I said what the hell *is* that?"

K'uhul looked intently at his victim. "Say 'Here we see nature in its unspoiled grandeur,'" he ordered.

"What?" Jared's confusion was almost trumping his terror.

"Say it! 'Here we see nature in its unspoiled grandeur.'"

Jared repeated the words. He'd said them many times before.

K'uhul's face softened. He locked the insect back in its glass prison. "But you're the famous nature filmmaker, Jared Foster," he laughed. "I've seen all of your shows!"

Jared stared up, thunderstruck. Of all the scenarios that had played out in his mind, this one had not occurred to him as a possibility.

"You look like hell," K'uhul added solemnly. "I didn't recognize you until I heard your voice." He motioned to the masked men to release their captive and helped Jared off of the table. "You and I are one, Jared Foster, we are brothers! We'll talk more later." With that, he ordered his dancers to select a different victim.

Chapter 14

Lights and Shadows

In the swirling purgatory between sleep and wakefulness, Jared struggled to understand where he was. The warm embrace of his blankets reminded him of home. Was he there now? Had he just been having a ghastly nightmare? His fantasy of comfort vanished the moment he opened his eyes. The sickly glow of a fluorescent light above illuminated a windowless cube of stark white walls and concrete. He was in the same private room where he had gone to bed.

The horrors of the previous evening came hurtling to the fore of his mind. He heard the epic chorus of death and saw the stars and smoke and grisly murders of men. Then he was there himself, splayed on the cold, hard stone, awaiting his own unspeakable demise. And yet he had been spared. The others had survived as well. K'uhul had simply allowed a bug to bite or sting them. Curiously, Sybil Lee had avoided even that. Like Jared, she had been lain across the stone, but subsequently helped back up unscathed. Jared winced as he remembered the way the giant's eyes had feasted upon her body as she writhed on the altar. Her tattered clothes had only accentuated the sensuality of her tan skin and ample curves. Had that been lust in K'uhul's eyes? Or tenderness? Or obsession? Jared didn't know and shook his head violently to clear the images from his mind. He fast-forwarded his memory. They had all been escorted back to the cave after the ceremony. He and Sybil Lee had clutched desperately to one another as the guards tore them apart. Where had they taken her? Where was Jared now? What *was* all this?

Jared hopped out of bed and paced like a caged lion. He pulled mightily at the reinforced steel door but its heavy lock mocked his efforts. Then he noticed a flash of movement, something tiny running in frantic circles on the ground. Jared crouched over the creature. "Oh man, you are *lost* aren't you, buddy?" he asked as he let an ant crawl up his hand. It was a relatively big ant, the size of a honeybee, rust in color, with two rounded humps on the back of its head. He recognized the species immediately; it was a leafcutter, *Atta cephelotes*. His identification was made all the easier by the fact that the insect still held a sliver of plant matter in its mandibles.

Jared wondered what was going though its tiny mind. Fright, perhaps, or at least as close to that emotion as an insect could get. Leafcutter colonies were huge, often reaching millions of individuals. It wasn't surprising that an ant would lose its way, and a lost ant usually meant a dead ant. Assuming that the animal's nest was not in his barren room, Jared shepherded his charge out of the bottom of the door. "Good luck," he said with a gentle push.

He hadn't even stood back up when he heard keys jingling outside the door. Two guards entered. In mangled Spanish they told him he was being summoned. He dressed and followed the men into the dimly lit tunnel outside.

As they walked, Jared heard the same rumbles and whirs that the group had noticed on their way to the sacrificial mount the previous evening. The sounds reminded him of Sherpa, though at that moment he couldn't understand why. As the guards led him past an open door, Jared glanced inside and understood. A man wearing grease-stained overalls poured motor oil into a nozzle at the top of a grumbling machine. It was an enormous engine, a diesel like Sherpa's. Most likely, it served as the power generator for this complex. Strange that they would put a generator inside a cave, thought Jared, given the danger of noxious fumes. Perhaps that represented an attempt at secrecy. He stopped abruptly outside the room. Something had caught his attention. His guards quickly nudged him forward, but he'd had enough time to register what he'd seen. His little ant friend was making a mad dash underneath the mechanic's legs to the opposite end of the generator.

The guards escorted Jared to the next level of the complex, through the hallway bejewled with stainless steel, to stop in front of a heavily guarded door. Jared's confusion roared forth in a hail of blather when he saw what lay on the other side. Batteries of lights illuminated a scene straight out of a research university recruitment brochure. Men in white lab coats labored over high work benches overflowing with test tubes, pipettes, and flasks. Computer workstations and deep freezers lined the walls, along with PCR thermocyclers, centrifuges, and other implements of modern genetics research. Huge whiteboards lay scribbled with diagrams. A group of men gathered around one such board, paying rapt attention to a speaker as he explained a series of unusual notations. The man towered over his listeners like a mountain over pebbles. Even without his headdress, K'uhul was unmistakable.

By the time the guards had escorted Jared across the room, K'uhul had closed his lecture and dismissed his audience. Lab workers looked on curiously as their leader smiled broadly in greeting. "Good morning, Jared Foster!" he said.

Though unmistakable by his girth, K'uhul seemed a different person than the daemon of the previous evening. Gone were his usual trappings of jade and stone and his fearsome expression. Now he wore just a plain t-shirt, light expedition pants, and a weather-beaten pair of hiking boots. His face was calm, almost cheerful. He looked like an unusually fit professor.

"Please, sit down," he said, motioning to an open

chair. He snapped his fingers at an assistant, said something in Mayan, and sat down himself.

Jared studied the notes K'uhul had been discussing on the white board. He saw abstruse equations and calculations, as well as several dozen seemingly random marks spread across a map of the Earth's continents.

"Allow me to formally introduce myself," K'uhul said, extending his hand. "I am K'uhul Ajaw Kab, Divine God King of the Maya, two hundred and sixth direct descendent in the line of Dark Jaguar, and previously your jailor."

"I'm Jared Foster. I make nature movies, and you're still my jailor."

"Of course I know who you are. I mean you no harm, but," K'uhul glanced at his empty hand, "I recommend you do not antagonize me."

With that, Jared extended his arm and they clasped palms.

"I have seen all your programs," K'uhul effused as he earnestly shook Jared's hand, "and it is clear to me that you have reached a level of understanding of the natural world second, perhaps, only to my own. We share the same spirit. We speak the same language of reverence. We have both heard the desperate cries of our Earth Mother and have devoted our lives to her protection. You and I, Jared, we are One."

With that K'uhul leaned back in his seat and smiled once again. "I am your jailor no longer. I am your host!"

A worker placed a tray of fragrant coffee and assorted pastries in front of the two men and swiftly retreated.

"Unfortunately," K'uhul continued, "I cannot release you just yet, but I can assure you that you are in no danger."

It's a very strange world, Jared thought. "Why are you keeping us here?" he asked guardedly. "What have you done with Sybil Lee?"

"Please, Jared, we will have plenty of time to talk. Right now, have some breakfast. That's a shade grown bean, a premium Guatemalan roast. It's a beautiful day outside the confines of these subterranean quarters. When you are done eating, we will go for a walk." With that, K'uhul patted Jared on the back and left him to his food.

Jared stared at the steam rising from the carafe. He wasn't hungry but thought food might give him strength. He poured himself a cup of coffee and took a bite from a sweet corn wafer. His mind tried to process his situation as his mouth worked on his food. He wondered what these people were up to, in this strange oasis of modernity in the middle of a cave in the middle of a wilderness. What did this operation have to do with the rituals of the previous evening? Jared continued his survey of the room. Men were going in and out of a door with a window at its center at the other end of the lab. Perhaps that led to an ancillary laboratory. On a shelf adjacent to the door lay several dozen glass vials, similar to those K'uhul had used in his ceremony. Jared couldn't tell at a distance, but it looked like insects were fluttering about inside. His mind failed to find answers but his mouth enjoyed more success. Before he knew it, he had eaten four pastries and finished two cups of coffee. K'uhul noticed that Jared had finished his breakfast and walked over. "Shall we get some fresh air?" he suggested.

Moments later the enormous vault doors were heaving open. Two escorts, stretching on their toes, used umbrellas to shield K'uhul and Jared as they passed through the waterfall to the cavern beyond. The group proceeded in silence across the dank chamber and up the long passageway to the top of the temple. They emerged, blinking, to see the rainforest at its early morning peak of glory. The air pulsed with animal calls as rainbows of vibrantly plumed birds painted the sky. The sun was brilliant in its early morning poses and the clouds floated by like ephemeral works of art.

"You have seen the abundant wildlife of this area?" K'uhul asked, as he led the group to the clearing below.

"Yes, I've never seen anything quite like it."

"That is because virtually everywhere else on this planet people hunt or otherwise 'control' animal populations. We let this area find its own balance. The spirits of the wild are strong here." They reached the bottom of the temple. "Come," K'uhul continued, "today we will visit our howler monkey friends." With that he took off at a brisk clip into the rainforest.

Jared had difficulty keeping up. K'uhul seemed completely unencumbered by the tangled vines and patches of mud on the trail. Whereas he would step through puddles without losing momentum, Jared repeatedly found himself getting bogged down.

"You are not yet attuned to this forest," K'uhul noticed.

Jared's frustration was somewhat allayed when he heard someone curse behind him and turned to see one his escorts hung up on a thorny branch. The man's clothes were pricked with tears and slathered in mud. *At least I'm doing better than that guy,* Jared thought.

Despite the challenging terrain, the scenery was that of a proud Mother Nature showing off what she could do. Mountains of trees sheltered a parade of animal splendor. K'uhul stopped frequently to listen. Initially, Jared heard nothing unusual during these pauses, though eventually he was just able to make out a rustling in the distance. Soon, a steady rumble of grunts and snorts joined the commotion. A short time later they walked amidst a large troop of howlers. Doe-eyed babies followed their mothers to perilous perches to retrieve ripe fruits while juveniles played gymnastic games of pursuit. A big male patriarch at the center of the troop simply glared at the world in perpetual suspicion.

The guards unfolded two small chairs which they proceeded to set up in a prime viewing area for the wildlife show. K'uhul motioned for Jared to sit and then reposed himself. "Our version of television," he offered. Jared couldn't help but admire the tranquil simian scene before him, wondering at how lucky these animals were to have such a pristine environment to live out their lives. More pressingly, however, he also wondered what to say to K'uhul. Although his jailor was now acting as a benevolent, if obligatory, host, Jared remained aware that his temperament could change without warning. He had to be careful, but more than that, he had to know.

"Why did you kill those men?" he asked.

"Jared, you must understand, I did not kill those men last night for joy or malice, I sacrificed them. While death is often a part of sacrifice, it is not the goal. It is a means to an end."

"What end then?"

K'uhul's eyes descended to the ground. Jared followed his gaze to meet a column of army ants swarming over a small bird. The doomed animal flapped one of its wings pathetically, as if waving goodbye to the world of the living.

"The end is balance," K'uhul said finally. "You do realize that behind every light there is a shadow?"

"I'm not sure what you mean."

"I mean any change for the good will result in an equal and opposite negative effect."

Jared paused. If he could understand K'uhul's

rationale, he might be better able to reason with him. "I don't know, what would be the negative impact of a cure for cancer?"

"I am surprised that you in particular would say that. A cure for cancer might seem beneficial on the surface - suffering of the afflicted would be reduced - but the dark side is obvious. Cure a disease and you increase the population. Increase the population and you increase a wide variety of ills – more competition and warfare, higher rates of disease and famine, and last but certainly not least, an increased strain on our already beleaguered ecosystems."

"I suppose I can't argue with that." Jared looked for an exception to K'uhul's statement. "What about technological progress?" he said, though he knew it was a bad example as soon as the words left his mouth.

"I hope you are not trying to tell me that the invention of the automobile was net positive gain. It has led to the burning of fossil fuels, increased urban sprawl, and global climate change. More generally, technological innovation has led to the collapse of traditional societies and has left billions of people living vapid lives devoid of meaning."

"I'm beginning to see your point." Jared tried hard to think of an example of something indisputably good that could not possibly have any ill effects. "What about the cessation of pain?" he offered. "What if someone could invent a pill that cured all the misery in the world?"

K'uhul shook his head sadly. "Imagine life without pain. You would not know when you were being burned. You would not know when you were being bit or when you were sick. You would be dead before you knew it. There is no escape from the truth of what I have said." K'uhul continued, staring at the weak struggles of the dying bird as he spoke. "But this truism works both ways. There is a balance of light and dark forces in the world and so, just as there is a shadow behind every light, there is also a light behind every shadow. Consider this place. It thrives only because we have guarded it so vigorously. It is the darkness associated with our acts that has led directly to the light of this forest's health. Consider that bird. It is dying a gruesome death, but in its death it will contribute sustenance to its predator. The darkness of its fate will be balanced by the light of its gift of energy. More generally, every meal that we eat represents the demise of another living entity. There is no life without death as there is no light without darkness. There is only balance."

Jared considered K'uhul words. There was a logic to his point. "I can't argue with what you've said, but I'm not sure what it has to do with my initial question. Why did you kill those men? What were the ends you were trying to achieve through their sacrifice?"

"The ends should be obvious by now. Through the darkness of their deaths I brought forth light into the world."

Jared leaned back in his chair. He'd listened to K'uhul's argument closely and agreed with it on some philosophical level, but when it came time to apply the lesson to the gruesome murders of the previous evening he could not make the connection. "I understand that you are very concerned with the state of the natural world," he said, "as am I, and as such you might consider the sacrifice of a developer to be a good thing, but why a doctor, and a priest? They were just trying to help."

"In the case of the doctor, I will only say that too much of anything invites the negative. Even good, clean water is toxic in excess. Behind the light of every life that the doctor saved was the darkness of one more person who would continue to defile the Earth. The doctor needed to die for the sake of balance.

"As far as the priest goes, the spirits have been begging me for the blood of a Catholic prelate since they first began to speak to me. You see, the Catholic Church is guilty of two major sins. The first is that its gospel has displaced countless pagan faiths that were much more in tune with nature. It has taught these new converts that they are not one with the Web of Life, but masters of it. The Church's second major sin has been its insistence on rampant procreation. It is this combination of swelling throngs of humanity and diminished respect for the environment that has led to our current state of ruin.

"My own ancestors were killed and their sacred books burned to dust under the auspices of this very same Church which now preaches forgiveness and light, but it is precisely this light that has cast its dark shadow across the farthest reaches of the Earth."

"You can't blame a single church for all our environmental ills," Jared said carefully.

"Of course not, the Catholic Church is just one of the worst transgressors. Even my own Maya ancestors, with all of their spiritual ties to the forests, were not immune to self-inflicted environmental degradation. In fact, our classical civilization fell largely as a result of soil erosion due to deforestation. The sacrifice of the priest and the others was just a drop in the bucket of necessary offerings. It was just a start. You see, my ancestors sacrificed diligently, but it was not enough. If they had only stepped up their efforts and poured blood into the mouths of the gods then they would not have exhausted our lands and would have been able to maintain their civilization for many more years.

"I have been summoned to this world by the wild spirits of nature to correct these wrongs. I am here to restore balance. I intend to perform the ultimate sacrifice. Blood will flow like rivers into the heavens, and through the unimaginable darkness of my offering, I will drown the world in beauty and light."

"What is it that you plan to do?" Jared asked. His voice implied curiosity, but his eyes belied his fear and distrust.

"Do not worry, Jared. You will not be affected, of that I am sure. You will only approve of the results. But come, it is time for me to return to my labors. We can continue this discussion this evening."

A short time later Jared found himself locked back in his private room. Although he was now theoretically a "guest," his freedom was still severely curtailed. Set before him lay a lavish lunch as well as a couple of books K'uhul had lent him to ease his boredom. Jared picked at his food as he perused his reading selection. It was limited, to say the least, comprising two technical tomes. One text was entitled "Advanced Principles of Recombinant DNA", and the other "The Hygiene Hypothesis: Using Parasites as a Therapeutic Agent."

Jared had read books on genetics as a student, but he'd never heard of the "Hygiene Hypothesis." With nothing better to do, he browsed the pages of the parasite text. Apparently the Hygiene Hypothesis stated that modern societies had gone too far in their ceaseless pursuit of cleanliness and sanitation. As a result, the immune systems of many First World inhabitants were confused. The fact is throughout millions of years of evolution, humans and their ancestors had always carried heavy loads of parasites. Tapeworms, pinworms, hookworms, and many others were a constant and inevitable part of life and an entire branch of the human immune system had evolved specifically to deal with these unwelcome cohabitants. Now that we humans had effectively cleansed our environments to the point that these historic parasites were no longer common, this branch of our immune system did not know what to do with itself. It began to turn on itself and to attack innocuous foreign substances in the environment – pollen, foods, dander and any number of other harmless proteins. In other words, it started to create allergies for its owners.

A shadow behind every light, Jared mused.

As evidence, the textbook discussed the fact that allergies simply did not exist before the advent of our modern, ultra-hygienic societies and were still unknown in cultures that lived more primitively. Furthermore, purposely infecting a person who had a great deal of allergies with even a minimal load of parasites seemed to redirect the immune system back to its traditional target. The allergies disappeared.

A light behind every shadow, Jared thought.

He fought the urge to validate the madman's words, but here was a clear example of their truth. Oddly enough, balance was maintained in this particular system by a parasite.

Jared set down the book and fell back into his concerns. He thought of his friends in their dark chamber and worried if they were okay. He seemed to have K'uhul's attention. He might be able to influence the man's actions. In the midst of his reverie, Jared was roused by the sound of people talking outside his room. He rushed to press his ear against the door. He heard a man with a deep voice speaking with a woman. The man was definitely K'uhul and the woman…the woman was Sybil Lee! Jared could not hear their words and his mind tangled in knots trying to understand what they were talking about. He hoped his love was alright. She sounded calm. His ear stayed locked against the door until long after the voices receded into the distance.

Chapter 15
Greek Gods

Jared had managed just one page of the genetics text before following the lure of his exhaustion to a fitful sleep. He awoke to the smell of warm food. Two guards waited patiently while he finished his dinner and then walked him back to the lab. He tried to make conversation with them but they were stony faced. K'uhul, on the other hand, was still smiling.

"Hello Jared! Did you enjoy the texts?" he asked laughing.

"Nothing like a little light reading."

"Well, I am sorry for the limited selection. I have collected a few more books for you if you are interested."

"Sure, thank you."

"Come, the sun is due to set shortly. Let us view it from the sacred temple."

With that, they once again climbed to the top of the twin pyramid. They emerged from the cave to a world of pastels. The guards quickly produced chairs and Jared and K'uhul sat to watch the dramatic grand finale of the day.

"Tell me," K'uhul said earnestly, "is it true that you and your associates managed to rewire all of the traffic lights in Denver to stay green for an entire day?"

Jared wasn't particularly proud of his eco-prankster days, but there was no reason to be coy. "Yes," he replied. "I liked the symbolism but felt bad afterward when I heard there were some serious crashes."

"Bah! Anyone living in the fetid city hells should expect to attract nothing but misery to themselves. And of course you were responsible for the Smoke Stack Attacks?"

"Yeah, that was tricky, but we managed to

reroute a good slug of smog right back to the onsite corporate offices. That was the first time I truly got the shit beat out me. Those company goons were not happy."

"I love it. I've followed your career closely, as you can tell. You have been an inspiration."

Normally Jared would find such approbation encouraging. This time it made him nauseous. "Thank you," he said uncomfortably. "Can I ask you a couple questions?"

"Please."

"My friend, Chris, said he recognized you as a championship surfer. He said you burst on the scene one year, won every major competition, and then disappeared."

K'uhul shook laughing. "Oh ho! Yes, that is true, but I have to admit, I did cheat a bit."

Cheat? How could someone cheat surfing? Hesitant to delve into what must have been a massive delusion on K'uhul's part, Jared moved to his next question. "Is it true you're a medical doctor? Dr. Delgado --" Jared stumbled over the graphic images of the previous night. "-- Dr. Delgado thought you were the same person who wrote some texts he had read."

"I do have a medical degree, but let's just say I did not study medicine for the usual reasons."

"What does that mean?"

"It means I am a healer, but not a healer of men. I suppose you could say I took the Hippocratic Oath backwards. You see, I am here to heal the Earth of its human disease."

Jared caught his jaw dropping and pretended he was just opening his mouth to speak. "Yes, of course," he said, in as respectful a tone as he could muster.

"It took me a long time to understand my purpose, my destiny," K'uhul continued. "I had always been attuned to the natural world and this connection only increased with time. Eventually, I could feel the pain of the felled trees as though my own limbs had been sawn off and the screams of the animals were like those of my own children. The spirits were pleading with me, Jared, begging me for relief from the privations of our rapacious species."

"So," Jared asked hesitatingly, "the spirits 'talk' to you?"

K'uhul laughed. "Yes, they 'talk' to me, but only in a metaphorical way. I am not crazy. It is like when a plant droops its leaves and 'tells' you that it needs water."

Jared gazed into the sunset and said nothing for some time. "But you do believe in spirits?" he asked at last.

"Of course, but probably not in the same way as most people. Spirits are not supernatural, nor are they beyond comprehension. They are a rational extension of our world. They are the epiphenomena of our existence, and we of theirs."

Jared was shocked to hear such a rational explanation coming from K'uhul's lips. Then again, the man was apparently a trained and accomplished scientist. "Epiphenomena?" he asked. "Isn't that just an old-school way of saying 'emergent properties,'? Like when flocks of birds display cohesive behaviors even though no particular bird is in charge? Or like when ant colonies make decisions or brains make thoughts? It's the whole that comes from the interactions of the parts."

"Something like that, yes."

"I've been leaning toward a similar explanation," Jared said, reflecting on his earlier conversation with Chris at the Southwestern Research Station. "I've begun to think of spirits as disembodied intelligences akin to the life cycles of organisms, where you have perception, intention, and mood without the need for bodies or brains. So the 'spirit' of a virus would be like an emergent property of its lifecycle."

"I believe you are on the right track, but I can tell you with certainty that the phenomenon is much more general than that."

"How so?"

"Spirits are the emergent properties of existence across an infinite number of organizational levels. We are just the result of interactions of lower levels of organization and other entities are the emergent properties of our level. It is the interactions across these various levels that affect us in mysterious ways that we then interpret as the actions of the spirits."

"I'm not sure I understand."

"I will give you an example. Imagine for a moment that you are an atom. We'll make you a uranium atom just for the sake of argument. You are very special uranium atom in that you are conscious of your surroundings. Even so, your experience of your world would be quite limited to your level of organization. You would see other atoms around you quite easily but you would need some sort of a microscope to see subatomic particles and a telescope to see the larger molecules in what would be your equivalent of outer space.

"The interactions of matter at your level of organization would be quite simple. Atoms would bump into each other and react in predictable ways, always reaching for the most energetically stable configurations. Looking into the equivalent of your heavens, however, you would have a harder time explaining the behavior of distant molecules. Although these would be composed of nothing more than combinations of interacting atoms, they would behave in difficult to comprehend ways due to the added complexities of their intricate structures.

"Eventually, some scientifically minded atoms might come up with a theory to explain the movements of the heavenly bodies. They might even be able to make accurate predictions regarding these movements and to develop an entire astronomy, but they would have an exceedingly hard time perceiving the next level up of organization. They would probably never realize that some of the molecules in the distance had become the constituents of life: proteins, fats, carbohydrates, and nucleic acids, and that these were interacting to create the tissues of living organisms. This would be such a distant, different, and bewilderingly complex level of organization from their standpoint as atoms that it would forever be out of their realm of comprehension, completely out of scale with their world, though intimately related to it.

"Eventually one of these celestial organisms might evolve into a human capable of developing a nuclear bomb. You, as a uranium atom, would most likely never realize that such a bomb had been detonated even if you had been inside its warhead, but you might notice when a number of your neighboring atoms suddenly split in two in a flash of released energy. You would be mystified as to what had caused this strange phenomenon. It would be so out of step with the normal workings of your world that you could only ascribe the action to some supernatural power. You would assume it was the work of the spirits and you might beg them to spare you the same fate.

"Of course, this sudden splitting of atoms would not have been the work of supernatural forces, but rather, could be better understood as the direct result of feedback between your level of existence and the emergent properties of higher levels; in this case, feedback from the world of warring humans. Nothing magical here, nothing mystical, just the rational result of interactions across scales.

"It would be the same thing for an ant wondering

how its own colony was making decisions. It would appear to such a creature that some spirit of the colony were in operation. It would be the same with a dollar bill wondering what forces were at work moving it across the hands of people and continents. The market economy exists at such a remote scale to any particular unit of currency that the dollar bill would think some spirit of economics were at play, ordering its existence.

"This then, explains the origin of what we call 'spirits.' They are simply the epiphenomena of our world."

Jared stared at K'uhul intently. He had followed his argument carefully and was stupefied by its implications. Suddenly, he realized that all those silly scenes within ancient Greek plays of the Gods of Olympus meddling within the world of men were actually brilliant metaphors; they were analogous to K'uhul's example of warring humans affecting a remote world of atoms. There were other flashes of insight. K'uhul's theory could explain the underlying mechanism for all sorts of supposedly supernatural phenomenon. "So," Jared said, "if the heavens are just different but connected levels of organization that can feedback with this level, then that might explain the mechanism of astrology."

"Yes."

"More generally, it could explain many supposedly supernatural events as feedback from other levels of connectedness?"

"Yes."

Jared sat back in his chair and peered into the horizon. He had never given even the remotest credence to anything vaguely paranormal or occult, but realized now that his doubt had been so strong only because he had lacked a frame of reference to understand such things without having to resort to blatant superstition or magic. K'uhul had just given him that frame of reference. Suddenly Jared viewed the world with an even greater sense of wonder.

Jared and K'uhul headed back once the glory of the sunset had faded. At that point Jared hazarded another question. "Do you think I might be able to meet with my friends for a few minutes tonight?"

K'uhul hesitated for a moment, then smiled and patted Jared on the back. "Of course, why not?" He ordered his guards to escort Jared and said his goodbyes.

The response was instant. As soon as the guards opened the door to the prisoner's chamber, Chris and Katy leapt to their feet and nearly knocked Jared over with a hug assault. Alan smiled, obviously pleased that Jared seemed well. The guards closed the door and left the friends to catch up. For a brief moment, the group's bubble of joy floated above the room's sea of gloom, but as Jared scanned his surroundings, his cheer dissipated amidst worried eyes. He noted a new set of captives, already sporting forlorn expressions of doom. "Any sign of Sybil Lee?" he asked the others with concern.

"We haven't seen her since last night," Chris replied. "What happened to you?"

Jared explained what had transpired since they had last seen each other. He told his friends about his private room and his unusual sessions with K'uhul. He explained the madman's theories of balance and spirits, and noted that K'uhul was indeed both a doctor and former surfing champion. He also mentioned K'uhul's curious comment about cheating in order to win.

"You can't cheat surfing!" Alan exclaimed incredulously. "It's just you against the waves!"

Chris nodded in agreement. Jared shrugged – he

wasn't the one who had made the claim. He asked if the group had made any progress accessing the wireless network.

"No," Katy replied, "we tried a few more guesses but the batteries are running low. Maybe you should take the OnePod since you're getting so close to K'uhul. Maybe he's already given you a clue."

"Good idea," Jared concurred as he hid the unit in his special pocket. With some hesitation at causing unnecessary concern, he then told the others what K'uhul had said about healing the Earth of its human disease. Chris made a cuckoo bird noise. "I know," Jared said with exasperation, "the guy is certifiable, but he's also very intelligent and I'd be lying if I said I wasn't worried. He keeps making vague references to a larger plan."

The friends continued their discussion until late into the night. There wasn't much news to report from the prisoner's chamber beyond the usual insect rituals and VIP tortures. Chris, Katy, Alan and several other captives had, however, developed unseemly bruises where they had been bitten. They tried to play down their concern, but they were clearly nervous about their wounds.

"Maybe it's just an allergic reaction," Jared offered hopefully.

"Yeah, probably," Chris agreed half-heartedly as he scratched the crimson stain developing on his arm.

Jared did his best to calm his friends. He determined to scour every clue at his disposal to figure out what K'uhul was up to and what he could do about it. Too soon, the door swung open and the guards motioned for Jared to go back to his room. For a moment, his face melted like a pound dog realizing it wasn't going to be adopted. He gathered himself, smiled reassuringly, and promised to return to visit his friends again soon.

Chapter 16
Surfing

The next morning, Jared was summoned to the laboratory to meet with K'uhul over breakfast. As they chatted, a group of workers labored to move a pallet of small wooden boxes from what Jared had assumed was the ancillary laboratory to a workbench nearby. All of the containers were labeled with the same curious glyph. K'uhul noticed Jared's interest in the procedure and smiled wryly. "I am sure you are wondering what is in the boxes. You will know in due time. Come, today we will visit our serpentine friends."

A short while later they were trudging through the mist and trees. They zigzagged along various trails, stopping frequently to allow K'uhul to listen to his surroundings. Jared wondered what K'uhul was listening for.

"Bird calls," the giant said, as if he'd heard Jared's thoughts.

Jared stumbled over himself. Maybe K'uhul had seen his confused expression. Dear god, the man was frightening. "I thought we were trying to find snakes."

"The birds will tell us where the snakes are, first with their warning calls, then with the silence of the areas that they have abandoned in fear."

They continued their march, periodically listening for clues. Jared struggled to control his growing apprehension. The thought of an encounter with snakes only fueled his concern. Eventually, his anxiety boiled over and a steam of concern whistled from his mouth. "But what is it," he started, regretting his outburst immediately. He clamped his anxious steam back inside and cast his gaze to the ground.

K'uhul turned to face him. "What is what?"

Jared met K'uhul's eyes nervously. "What is it that you plan to do with us?"

"With you and your friends?"

"Yes." Jared wasn't even sure he wanted to know. He winced, as though preparing for a blow.

"You, my brother, will live in harmony with the new world and will be free in a matter of days. I am not sure what to do with your friends. I would like to let them go but they know the location of the lab. I cannot use them to spread the news."

"What news?"

"Patience, Jared."

"What about Sybil Lee?" Jared tried to act calm, but his eyes twitched with the intensity of his emotions. "What are you doing with Sybil Lee?"

K'uhul turned and continued walking. "Sybil Lee," he said wistfully, savoring a huge inhalation, "she is *special*."

I know that, dammit!

Soon enough, they heard a frantic squawk and flurry of movement. They walked in the direction of the ruckus to reach a clearing, now silent save for the babbling of a brook by its edge. K'uhul pointed to a branch swaying in the distance. Squinting, Jared realized the projection was, in fact, a cylindrical slab of writhing muscle, an enormous snake. K'uhul sat calmly on the ground and invited Jared to do likewise. The giant then wrapped his legs together and took a deep breath. His eyes narrowed to slits and his face softened as he slowly eased into a trance. Jared sat quietly next to him and fidgeted. In another place and time he might have been able to find peace in a setting like this, but not today.

Jared watched the snake ripple in the distance and listened to the flowing water of the nearby stream. He was suddenly reminded of waves, and their conversation of the previous day. His curiosity wrestled with his reluctance to disturb K'uhul. He cleared his throat conspicuously. K'uhul maintained his repose. Emboldened, Jared spoke. "I was wondering," he said, "about a comment you made yesterday. You said you cheated when you won those surfing championships. What did you mean? How can you cheat against the ocean?"

K'uhul's eyes crept across the leaf litter to meet Jared's body, then shifted their gaze to an indistinct area ahead. Something was moving toward them. Jared blinked. It was the snake. Its tongue flickered ominously from powerful jaws as it approached. Suddenly, Jared recognized the species and tripped over himself in retreat. The snake was a fer-de-lance, one of the most venomous creatures in the Americas. The guards, who had been hitherto held back unobtrusively, raced forward with machine guns extended. K'uhul motioned for them to put down their weapons. The fer-de-lance drew within striking distance. Jared watched with mouth agape as the giant extended an arm to the ground. The snake reared alarmingly, then slackened like a wilting leaf. Slowly, it weaved itself up K'uhul lowered limb. It spiraled deliberately, almost affectionately, around his torso, past his shoulder and neck, to the end of his other arm.

"I spoke yesterday," K'uhul said, his eyes half closed and voice a million miles away, "about the true nature of the spirits. I did not mention that to know them is to gain influence with them." The snake weaved gently from his outstretched arm, its eyes locked on his. "If you can succeed in becoming highly in tune with your environment, you can increase the breadth of your perception. Just as an array of dish receivers can pick up more complex signals from outer space than a single antenna, you can increase your awareness of the intricate layers of reality by utilizing a larger base of inputs. Feel pain when the animals about you feel pain and feel pleasure at the exuberant sun and you move that much closer to understanding. Realize that you do not need to see the moon to know that it exists or to predict its movements. Simply look at the tides."

K'uhul eased his hand to the ground and the fer-de-lance melted into the brush. The sputtering eddies of the stream nearby created a gentle sonic nest for his words. "When you expand your perception this way," K'uhul continued. "you may begin to glimpse how the spirits in the dimensions of connectedness above and below you interact, and you may begin to understand how to influence their feedback. The fact is that nothing in the universe is truly random. All energy and matter interact in predictable ways with patterns invariably emerging, standing waves of connectedness tying together vastly different scales and phenomena. It is a matter of finding the right wave, and surfing it to the next wave, all the way through the layers of emergence and back until you achieve your desired feedback in this reality."

Jared looked into the forest and tried squinting like K'uhul, wondering if that were part of the trick. "But how?" he asked. "I mean how exactly can you influence the levels of connectedness above and below you?"

"I am not going to say it is easy, but it is simple. It is the Butterfly Effect writ large."

"The Butterfly Effect? You mean like when a small change in the atmosphere caused by a butterfly flapping its wings in Rio ripples out to cause a storm a week later in New York?"

"Yes, precisely, but in your example there would be a severe time restriction. It would take days, weeks, or years for the disturbance to ripple through the system to create the eventual storm. What I am referring to can be instant. It's like taking a shortcut through the dimensions of emergence and back.

"You must understand that the actions we perform in this world may manifest themselves as vastly different phenomena in other levels of existence. Think back to our example of the conscious uranium atom. If we can believe that a man existing in some remote 'Otherworld' can simply press a button and cause you and your friends to explode, then how hard is it to believe that doing something equally trivial on this plane of existence can have a vastly different effect on other levels? The trick is to understand how our actions affect other scales and how the events at other scales relate back to us."

Jared could not decide whether he was hearing the pathetic dribblings of a lunatic or an insight of profound import. Everything the giant said made perfect sense and yet he was obviously batshit crazy...wasn't he? And what was this strange relationship developing between the two men? K'uhul was acting like a mentor, but he was a mortal enemy. Was it possible that he was a misunderstood genius with a singular vision? Perhaps he had really tapped into some fundamental unseen tides of reality. Jared was in murky territory with no clear answers. "I don't know," he said, "I suppose that could be true but I'd have to see some experimental support."

K'uhul turned to Jared with a sympathetic smile. "It is your choice to believe me or not, but I do recommend you beware of the blinding power of doubt. It never ceases to amaze me how little we see with our open eyes for lack of opening our minds. But come, that is enough for this morning. Let us return to the temple and continue our good works."

Chapter 17

Signs

Jared vacillated between hope and despair on their return walk to the temple. One moment he felt certain of K'uhul's insanity and hence believed the man's evil plans to be nothing more than fantasy. Then he recalled his captor's interactions with the viper. That was certainly quite a display. Still, the animal could have once been a pet and, in any case, snake charming was nothing revolutionary. Reflecting on the cold efficiency of K'uhul's laboratory, Jared's pessimism finally muscled aside his cheer. Perhaps the man had outlandish beliefs, but he was one hell of an impressive individual and he was up to something sinister.

"You know, I have been thinking," K'uhul said, jolting Jared out of his reverie.

"Yes?"

"You are one of the most talented filmmakers in the world, and I am about to unleash one of the most important transformations that the world has ever seen."

"Go on."

"I was going to make an announcement explaining my actions through a simple post on the Internet, but now I am thinking I could use your skills to come up with something a little more...sophisticated."

"I suppose if I had access to a computer I could put something together. I would need editing software, and we would need to determine what images to include, but I guess the real question is what I would be announcing in the video."

K'uhul dodged the query artfully. "How long would it take you to construct a three minute clip with narration?"

"That would depend on how much footage I'd

204

need to wade through to get to the final takes. Maybe a day."

"Good, because we have only two days until our current world dies."

    Back in his room, Jared put aside his torture box of thoughts to pick at his lunch. He browsed absently through a battered text as he did so. Its pages were surprisingly dog-eared and marked. *Someone must have thought this was important,* Jared thought. The book was called the "Encyclopedia of Predatory Fungi." Jared had never heard of fungi described as predators, but apparently many species within that kingdom made their living actively - they hunted. For instance, one species of yeast, typically unicellular, burst into multi-cellular growth mode once ingested, thus rupturing the body of its predator and feeding on its remains. Another species captured tiny nematode worms with lassos as they passed. His curiosity piqued, Jared read on to find one particularly blemished passage. Barely any text remained untouched and scribbles spilled over one another along the margins. The passage discussed a fungus that was a hyperparasatoid of an unusual parasite that had a life cycle alternating between insect and mammalian hosts. A line extended from the species name to the page margin where someone had drawn a curious symbol, a stylized skeleton in the embrace of a smiling corpulent creature.

    Jared studied the drawing, admiring its graceful lines. It was rendered in the same style as the glyphs he had seen carved into the ruins around the twin temple complex. The contrast between this little work of art and the hard science written in the pages of the text was extreme. Something about the symbol looked familiar…

    Jared's concentration was broken by the sound of a woman giggling flirtatiously. His ears leapt to attention.

It was Sybil Lee again, and K'uhul. Their laughs burbled with joy. Jared jumped to the door, his thoughts frothing in confusion. He heard the two chortling as they walked down the hallway toward the lab.

He stood there, choking in angst and betrayal while juggling flaming blades of paranoia. What the hell was K'uhul doing with Sybil Lee? What was she doing with him? What were they doing, *together*? Couldn't she see that the man was a monster? Had she not witnessed the same hideous murders Jared had? He wanted to tear the door from its hinges and beat K'uhul to the ground. But what was the use? K'uhul was charming in his own way, wasn't he? Maybe he was even good looking, if someone were into grotesquely muscular mad geniuses. He did seem to be passionate about protecting the natural world. These were all things Sybil Lee could be attracted to, and despite her many good aspects, loyalty was not her forte. But she couldn't be under his spell, could she? Maybe she was just playing K'uhul, like she always did, casting her spell on him? Jared wanted to believe that so badly, but his body and spirit seemed to know better as he crumpled to a heap on the floor.

Later that afternoon the guards came to retrieve Jared. When the group reached the lab, K'uhul was nowhere to be found. The guards led Jared inside the door with the window at the end other of the room, where they all changed into hazmat suits hanging from the wall. They proceeded to a small chamber where a flip of a switch turned on a blinding light, another activated fine mist sprayers, and a third brought an enormous fan roaring to life. Thus cleansed, the group continued past a door marked with a large red symbol. It took a moment for Jared to realize the sign was similar to the glyph he had just seen in the fungus text. In this case, however, the corpulent figure was missing from its design.

They found themselves in another laboratory filled floor to ceiling with terrariums and incubators. Rodents scurried about some enclosures, while insects swarmed within others. Jared tried to determine their various species but did not have time to do so before being led quickly through the room to another hallway. He was once again bathed in light and mist and hurried past another door with a large red sign. This time, Jared recognized the mark instantly. It was identical to the one in the fungus text.

The group entered a darkened cavern. K'uhul stood there in his own extra large contamination suit, along with several lab workers. Terrariums lay spread about, their contents obscured in the dim light.

"Hello, Jared," K'uhul said, his voice tinny through the vents of his helmet.

"Hi."

"I have to apologize, I thought we would have time to talk but we have had an unexpected technical problem and I will likely be predisposed for remainder of the afternoon."

"No problem." Jared saw movement in one of the terrariums.

"In the meantime, you could start on the video. Did you have a chance to capture much footage of the surrounding environment?"

"A fair bit, yes, maybe six or seven hours. I got some really nice shots."

"Good. If you could put together a three-minute montage of that footage, we would have a good start for our announcement."

"I'll need my equipment."

"It's waiting for you in the lab."

"And a computer with editing software."

"There is a Mac workstation ready for you. I believe Macs come preloaded with video editing applications?"

"Yes. I should be able to get started immediately. Otherwise," Jared ventured, "I can always download something from the Internet."

"Heh heh, I am afraid that will not be possible."

"Alright, I'll see what I can do with what I've got."

One of K'uhul's lab assistants walked with a flashlight past a terrarium, giving Jared a quick glimpse of the enclosure's contents. Petri dishes lay covered with tiny fruiting bodies, like miniature mushrooms.

"Very good," K'uhul said, "I'll check on you after I'm done here."

Jared sat at the computer terminal and fiddled with its settings. He was disappointed to find that K'uhul's men had not only disabled the machine's network hardware, they had removed it entirely. He went to work downloading footage from his camera. As he began to assemble the montage, he brainstormed desperately. Whatever K'uhul was up to involved the use of some mysterious insect. And that glyph on the door …the fungus that Jared had read about probably also played a role. Seeing the extent of this bizarre operation was unsettling. It didn't matter if K'uhul was insane, he was dangerous. This was dangerous. And whatever plan the man had, he intended to hatch in just two days.

Hours had passed when K'uhul emerged from the back chamber of the lab. "How is it going?" he asked.

"Good, good, check it out." Jared played a clip of the video he had crafted and watched K'uhul's eyes brighten.

"Exactly what I had in mind," the giant said. "When will you be done with the montage?"

"I should be able to finish in the morning."

"Good, then we can add the narration tomorrow afternoon and I will have my men upload it in the evening. Unfortunately, I will have no more time to spend with you today. I must handle some last minute contingencies. You may retire to your room whenever you please. I will have my men bring you your supper."

"If it's all the same to you, I'd like to visit with my friends again."

"Yes," K'uhul said, turning away to continue with his chores, "that would be fine."

"I was wondering if I might see Sybil Lee too."

K'uhul stopped. He did not turn back around to face Jared. "I will let her know you would like to see her."

Jared cocked his head. Did that mean he would get to see her or not? "Thanks," he said, half heartedly.

Back in the prisoners' chamber, Chris's once cheerful face had completed its metamorphosis to become a hauntingly gaunt mask. His fingers were caked in crimson. "But what do you think he's planning to do with the bugs?" he asked, scratching the wound from his insect bite.

"I don't know," Jared replied, horrified at the worsening condition of his friends. "I really don't."

Katy shuffled nervously. "And you say whatever he is planning is supposed to happen in the next couple of days?"

"Yes."

Alan was silent. He was playing with a tiny creature, letting it crawl from one hand to the other.

"What is that?" Jared asked.

"An ant. It's been here for days."

"Lost, probably," Chris added.

Jared stepped closer. Alan's little companion was another leaf cutter. Suddenly, Jared turned back to face the others. "Hey," he said to Chris, using a finger to draw on the filthy ground, "I saw this symbol earlier today and thought it might mean something to you." Jared carefully drew the stylized skeleton he had seen in the fungus book and on the entrance to the laboratory's back chamber. He had just begun to draw the corpulent figure embracing it when Chris spoke excitedly. "Oh yeah!" he said. "That's a famous glyph. It translates to something like 'Holy War' or 'Divine Wrath.'"

Jared was taken aback. He was happy that Chris had known what the glyph meant but hadn't even finished his drawing, and certainly didn't like the implications of the translation. He continued moving his finger through the floor until the symbol was complete. "What about his, then?" he asked.

"Well, the fat god you drew around the Wrath symbol generally represents forgiveness. I'd say both glyphs together translate into something like 'Mercy.'"

"Where did you see those symbols?" Katy asked.

"On a couple doors in the lab. And in a textbook about fungi."

"Really?" Chris asked. "A Mayan glyph in a science book?"

"No, I mean, it wasn't printed there - someone had drawn it in the margins, next to the name of a species of fungus." Jared squeezed his temples. "I'm trying to connect the dots, but all I'm seeing is scribbles."

The sound of heavy footsteps approaching interrupted their conversation. Jared's heart revved. Chris noticed the look of concern on his face. "I think they're just bringing dinner," he said reassuringly.

Jared looked back and forth between the door and Alan. He had an idea. He asked Alan to borrow his little pet, then raced to throw it past the crack under the door into the hallway. He had just enough time to stand up and look composed before the guards entered. They distributed supper to the prisoners.

"What did you do that for?" Alan asked glumly as Jared sat next to him. Entertainment, even in unexciting ant form, was hard to come by in the chamber.

Jared squinted and nodded his head to signal that he wanted the group to keep quiet about the topic. "Sorry, I just want to check something," he whispered. "Chris could you tell me when five minutes are up?"

"Sure."

Jared ate his food purposely, breaking his silence only to ask about Sybil Lee. Nobody had seen or heard from her. He wasn't surprised. "I asked K'uhul to bring her here," he said despondently.

"I'm sure she would have come if he had let her," Katy offered.

"Yeah..." Jared remembered Sybil Lee's flirtatious giggles outside his door. "Maybe."

Chris said time was up. Jared apologized and quickly took his leave. He asked a guard to escort him to his room. As they walked down the hallway, he scanned the ground intently. They passed the door to his cell and Jared continued to walk, feigning confusion and saying something about going back to the lab to do more work. Ignoring the guard's increasingly agitated demands, Jared continued to search the floor. Finally, when they reached the open door to the generator room, Jared turned and walked inside. The guard jabbed Jared with his bayonet. He'd had enough. Jared's eyes scoured the room frantically as he was dragged out by his shirt collar. Finally, they locked on to their target. He'd found what he was looking for. Alan's leaf cutter ant was scurrying across the room toward where the generator vent met the wall.

"That leads home doesn't it, buddy?" Jared asked under his breath.

The next morning, the laboratory teemed with its usual activity. Jared entered to find K'uhul leading a lecture on the opposite end of the room. The giant's face softened at the sight of him. Jared nodded and sat nonchalantly at a desk next to the one that he had been using the day before, hoping for an Internet connection. He was quickly asked to move to the proper space. *Couldn't be that easy.* He worked diligently for several hours, taking short breaks to pace about the lab and jog his brain. He thought only tangentially about the video and spent most of his mental energy trying to understand what was happening and what he could do about it.

Nearby lay the stack of wooden boxes he had noticed workers moving from the ancillary lab the previous morning. Jared now recognized the symbol imprinted on their sides. It was the fat god and skeleton glyph representing Mercy. What did that mean? What was in the boxes? A worker stood sorting through their contents. Strolling by casually, Jared stole a look at what the man was handling. He held a glass vial filled with a rust colored powder. Jared was more mystified than ever.

By lunchtime, he had completed his assignment. K'uhul smiled broadly as he watched the video. "Good work, my brother," he said, "even better than I had hoped, especially on such short notice. Shall we begin with the narration?"

Chapter 18
Revelations

Jared tapped the end of the microphone. "You're on," he said.

K'uhul cleared his throat with a rumble. "This is K'uhul Ajaw Kab," he started, his voice an oozing molasses of power, "Divine God King of the Maya and Spirit Incarnate of the Wild Earth. I am here to explain to you the dramatic loss of human life that you must now, assuredly, be witnessing around you.

"You see, on this most auspicious of days, everything will change. The fourth manifestation of our creation will end and we will be reborn into a fifth world of infinite beauty, harmony, and light.

"Unfortunately, not all will live through this cleansing. Only the righteous shall survive.

"The fact is that throughout human history, wherever Man has trod he has crushed something precious under the soles of his feet. Whatever he has touched has withered to dust. He has taken the generous gifts of our Earth Mother and desecrated them with his greed.

"I have heard the screams of our beleaguered forests and have heeded their desperate calls. It is on this auspicious day that they will have their revenge. It is on this day that I will release their Wrath.

"Those of you living out of step with the natural world in your god forsaken city hellholes of filth will all die miserable deaths, fittingly enough, by lethal parasitic infection. But those of you living balanced lives in harmony with pristine environments shall be spared. The parasitic virulence is activated only by an excess of industrial chemicals. Flee from your belching smokestacks and embrace your loving Earth Mother on her own terms and you will live.

"This parasite will be a permanent fixture of humanity going forward. The righteous shall thus awake to a new world in eternal balance. May we dance forever to its blessed rhythms and harmonies."

K'uhul turned to Jared. "How was that?" he asked sheepishly, as though he were a song writer who had just shared his first masterpiece in public.

Jared stared at him, stupefied. He felt as though the entire universe had slammed on the brakes. His every heart beat lasted a million years and every breath an eternity. He struggled in the frozen moment to think of an appropriate response.

"Well?"

"Wow," Jared said flatly.

K'uhul inhaled deeply, thrusting his massive chest forward and sitting up straight and proud. "Yes, isn't it incredible? Think of it - never again will anyone have to worry about environmental degradation. The governor for balance will now be a permanent part of our biology. The Earth will celebrate with a flowering of life the likes of which we have never seen. The entire world will be as pristine and fecund as this magical spot of rainforest."

"Yes... fecund."

"And it is only the transgressors who will suffer. Those who have lived in harmony with their environments will be spared. It is a just solution."

"Just."

"Well then, why don't you finish this up and we'll talk later? Tomorrow the metamorphosis begins!"

Jared snapped out of his funk.

"But how?" he asked. "How will you spread the parasite?"

"The parasite is already out there. That is the 'news' we have been spreading. We infected our prisoners before we released them. That was the purpose of the insect rituals. The carriers will have all reached their homes by now across the globe. Their parasites must have already sensed the intolerable pollutants in their environments and must as we speak be reproducing within their hosts in astronomical numbers. If our calculations are correct, their progeny will become infective at the most auspicious hour of the most auspicious day in history."

"Tomorrow?"

"Yes, late tomorrow evening our blessed Maize God will be born again high above our new creation. In time, the parasitic cleansing will spread and the spirits will rejoice. We will have saved the world."

"Wow. I mean, Wow! Glorious news, K'uhul!" Jared said, struggling for conviction in his voice. "Could I share it with my friends? I'm sure they would be so pleased to hear about your plan!"

"Let us wait to inform them, Jared. We may need more messengers to spread the news and they will be more effective if they do not know their purpose. You can rest assured that I will not sacrifice them unnecessarily."

Jared had to think, and he couldn't keep up his charade of complicity for long. "Of course, yes, that makes sense, and I'd certainly appreciate if you would hold off as long as possible on using them for that purpose. Maybe I could just retire to my room for a bit, I'm not feeling too great and could use a break."

"Of course, get some rest. We still have the remainder of the day and all day tomorrow before we really need to post the video."

Jared drowned in a torrent of conflicting thoughts and emotions as he was escorted back to his room. It all made sense now, everything - the pristine nature of the area, the disappearances, the insect rituals, the texts, K'uhul's scientific background, his vague references to a master plan. For better or worse, the madman really had figured out a way to save the environment, permanently. But the cost! The hideous cost!

"Jared!" Sybil Lee rushed toward him from the hallway ahead.

"Sybil Lee!" he cried. He ran to meet her and they embraced.

"Oh Jared, isn't it wonderful?" she exhaled wistfully. Her eyes were wild, her hair braided in an unusual style.

"Isn't what wonderful?" Jared asked, taken aback.

Sybil Lee stepped away. Her face registered confusion. "Didn't K'uhul tell you about his plan? He said he was going to tell you today..."

"Yes, yes, he just did."

Sybil Lee's smile spread like an opium rush across her face. "Isn't it fantastic?" she gushed. "He's our savior!' She twirled in circles as she spoke. "He's going to accomplish everything that we've ever worked for in one fell swoop, just like that, and it will be a permanent fix." She continued to float in circles as she repeated the words, "...forever and ever and ever..."

Jared grabbed Sybil Lee's shoulders and shook her.

"Sybil Lee! Billions of people are going to die! You can't tell me you really think that's a good thing."

Sybil Lee ripped herself free. Her expression changed in an instant. Suddenly her face was a dark storm and her words crackling lightning bolts. "What are you saying, Jared?" she demanded.

"We can't let this happen! It's too much! It's not right!"

Sybil Lee's face contorted in rage. "Oh Jared, you weak fuck. Ever since you sat in that damned tree you haven't had the guts to do what needs to be done. K'uhul has the guts. He knows that we need to sacrifice to achieve anything worthwhile. He knows he needs to do this dark thing to keep the world in eternal light. He's our savior, Jared, he's our God, and you're too damn stupid to see it!"

More gently now, Jared stepped toward Sybil Lee and extended his hands. "Please, we've got to do something. It's not right, it's just not..."

"Fuck off, Jared!" she said as she pushed aside his arms and blew past him like an angry wind.

Jared punched the wall of his room, hard. He hunched over cradling his hand and fell into his bed moaning in agony. What the fuck was happening? Sybil Lee had just taken the entire essence of his being and shoved it into a blender. A gigantic fraction of the human race was about to die a grizzly death and Jared couldn't do a damned thing about it. How could she be so blind? How could she be so heartless? Or was it Jared who was playing the fool? Maybe Sybil Lee was right, maybe the world did deserve to die. Maybe this thing was a necessary evil to ensure a brighter future.

Like K'uhul, Jared had heard the desperate cries of the forests and had devoted himself to answering their calls. He had done what he could, first by living as simply as possible, then with his ecowarrior pursuits, and now through his films. He thought he was having an effect on people. It seemed that his documentaries were getting more and more popular and he often felt as though the entire world were on the cusp of a new environmental consciousness. If just a few more people could be convinced of the sacredness of things and that we humans needed to change our ways only minimally in order to have enormous effects on the health of ourselves and our planet, then Jared's lifelong dreams would be achieved.

But K'uhul had found a violent shortcut to the crux of these dreams, and a permanent one at that. The protection of the environment would never again need to rely on easily overturned and neglected laws. Nature itself would do the regulating and the fines would be stiff. The juggernaut of industry would grind to a virtual halt. Only the bare minimum of manufacturing would be allowed to continue before the parasitic plagues would flare up again. Naturally, agricultural output would fall, leading to an even further decline of population, until humanity reached a truly sustainable equilibrium with the planet.

K'uhul was right. Nothing good came for free. His actions were unspeakably dark, but the outcome would be unimaginably bright. Jared pictured the disjointed habitats of the world, cleaved by human hands, slowly fusing back together, their populations of animals growing in a rapture of healing. He pictured the alligator that he had seen in Florida grow fat in a swimming pool now devoid of toxic chemicals. He saw legions of rhinos and pandas and tigers and all of the other endangered species of the Earth multiplying and carrying on with their grand pageant of life right where they had left off before their rude human interruption.

And then he thought of the people that would remain. They would live lives of plenty amid environments overflowing with fertility. Game would be prolific and exhausted fields reinvigorated after long fallow periods. The sadness and neuroticism so prevalent in modern society would disappear as people lived closer to their evolutionary design. They would feel more connected. They would once again become a part of the flow of the entire cosmos. They would once again sing in tune with the harmony of the universe.

Jared eased back into his bed. Maybe he should just relax and go with the flow. The fact was that K'uhul really did appear to be attuned to the spirit world. Maybe he really did communicate with otherworldly entities. Maybe he really was channeling the Earth Mother, and maybe this really was her plan, a natural result of the devastation that we humans had wreaked upon the balance of the world.

Yeah, that was it. Let it go. Let it flow. Wake up to The Rapture.

Jared closed his eyes and rode a dream into his subconscious. There, he found himself in the shade of skyscrapers and surrounded by throngs of phantoms. He knew the phantoms weren't real because they kept walking right through him, releasing frigid blasts each time as though icicles were exploding under his skin. Their words were cold too, all yammering and blabbering about stocks and fancy cars and jumping around like monkeys telling each other who was boss. Jared tried to scream but found his mouth was frozen shut.

He saw a small park at the end of the block, an oasis of greenery amidst the concrete and steel, and raced toward it. Once inside the comfort of the trees, he sat on a vine-covered stump to catch his breath. The sounds of the city's traffic and crowds diminished in the forest's embrace and were replaced by the singing of birds and the gentle rustling of the wind. Jared felt warmer now, connected, calm. He smiled as his legs grew roots, his arms sprouted leaves, and his skin roughened into bark.

As a plant, Jared perceived the world in an entirely new way. His leaves were his eyes, still sensitive to the light, he could taste the earth with his roots, and his entire body moved as one with the breeze. In this state, he interpreted the universe as gentle swirl of diffuse sensory waves.

He could tell there were small creatures scurrying around him but could not determine for certain what they were. With his roots he felt their vibrations as they moved along the ground and with his leaves he noted the way their minute bodies interrupted the flow of air. These little beings seemed to be moving with purpose, connected with each other toward some end. As Jared felt the six legs of one crawl up his side he realized what they were. Ants. He was perceiving ants, and by noting what each one was doing in relation to the others he was able visualize their colony as a whole.

Other sensory waves indicated an enormous creature was moving through the sky. No, Jared was confused. It wasn't a single organism; it was a number of smaller animals. Birds. He was sensing a flock of birds as though they were one entity.

His confusion continued as he found himself repeatedly thinking parts of things were wholes and wholes were parts. He perceived a cloud as made of individual drops of mist and the soil as individual particles of dirt and nutrients. He thought a drop of water was a whole, but then tasted its individual water molecules. Everywhere parts combined into wholes and wholes fell apart.

Emergence, thought Jared. What were parts on one level became wholes on another, what was mundane from one perspective became "spirits" from the next. He sensed endless waves of these interactions across scales all the way up, all the way down and felt connected, just another wave in the maelstrom of energy. He was One with...

One with what?

Suddenly Jared saw the entire universe before

him, the one true whole, like a giant Mandelbrot set, infinite swirls of complexity across infinite scales, and then all at once it hit him. Much like the majesty of the Mandelbrot set stemmed from a simple mathematical rule, the undulating branches of form and energy that comprise physical existence were just an unfolding of something much deeper. Then his roots shot back into his legs, his leaves retracted into his hands, and the bark sloughed from his skin. Tears of sadness welled in his eyes for at that moment he understood that the forest was not God. It was just one aspect, one reflection of something even more profound. All this time, he'd been worshipping a swirl of the Mandelbrot set and confusing it for The Truth.

Suddenly the woods around Jared seemed sinister and he felt bitterly cold. He watched in horror as his body shrank and he was once again just a small boy who had lost the warmth of his mother. Huge menacing eyes peered at him through the darkness and little Jared ran, terrified, with nowhere left to turn for comfort. Bawling and shivering he almost allowed the menace to overtake him, for he was lost and without hope. Then he heard the wind softly call his name. It was a woman's voice. Jared bolted through the trees toward it.

He reached a clearing filled with neat rows of crying babies. Sybil Lee sat there on her knees, hacking into the infants, planting seedlings in their wounds. She smiled at Jared with dark nubs for teeth. "They'll make good fertilizer," she croaked.

Jared ran for his life toward the soft voice calling his name.

"Come back here, you little shit!" Sybil Lee screamed. "Come back here and help me kill these vermin!"

Soon, Jared reached the edge of the forest and ran straight into a phantom. Only this must not have been a phantom, because it didn't pass through him like the others. This was a solid person, a woman.

"Jared!" she said.

"Katy?" he cried, his words muffled in her embrace.

"Oh, poor little Jared!" Katy hugged him hard and kissed the top of his head.

Jared was a small boy cradled in her arms. He looked up with huge eyes full of tears. "The forest isn't God," he said solemnly.

"It's okay, Jared. You haven't lost anything. You've just gotten a glimpse into the bigger picture. You've gotten closer to The Source. The forest is still beautiful, still worth cherishing and protecting. Maybe it's even more awe-inspiring now that you know it can provide a path to understanding something even more profound."

Jared began to grow.

"But you were silly," Katy continued. "As wonderful as nature is, as comforting as it may be, it isn't God, and it makes a poor substitute for the love of others. Home is in people, Jared. Home has always been in people."

With that she gave Jared a sweet kiss on the lips. He returned her affection, reluctantly at first, and then with passion as he wrapped his arms around her and grew back into the body of a man.

Jared woke with a start, drenched with sweat. A flash of images roared across the movie screen of his mind. He saw the poor man who had been killed on the highway trying save the family of ducks. He saw the sad faced man outside Abundancia charged with raising crocodiles. He saw Chris near death and Katy's big, sympathetic eyes, and then he saw his dog, ragged and hungry. Its caretaker, Jared's good friend, had died. Then suddenly Jared saw a million sad dogs staring at their fallen masters, a million children weeping at their mothers' graves. He saw all of these images at once, an explosive chorus of suffering and grief, a last desperate advertisement for the dregs of good left in people, a final plea from within Jared's own mind for mercy for the flawed world of humanity.

Tears of conflict welled in his eyes. How had it come to this? He'd come to save the rainforest! He'd always considered people a distraction at best, a stain on the beauty of the earth, and now here he was, the only one in the world of men with the knowledge that might be able to save it. He wallowed in confusion and, suddenly, heard a voice echo in his memory - something about a boy and a flood. And then it came to him - the two young brothers trapped in their car that he'd heard about on the radio back in Colorado. When faced with the wrath of nature in aquatic form, each had put their love of one other above all else. In that moment, that's all they had. At any moment, that's all we have. Nature is beautiful, alluring and beguiling, but ultimately, she is not God. Furthermore, beyond that beauty lays an unpredictability and heartlessness with no bound. Sweet Mother Earth is a tempestuous bitch. Home is in people because, in the end, that's all we can count on. Jared choked back his tears and stood tall. He knew at that moment there was no way he could let K'uhul succeed with his plan. The fact that he had even considered the option indicated that he had become as unbalanced himself as humanity was with nature. He could almost feel a blade render his heart in two as he mentally sacrificed what had been his greatest love for the sake of hope in humanity.

But what to do, what to do, what to do? Jared

was just one man surrounded by an army. He had a very limited time to affect any plan and he didn't even know where to begin.

He again reviewed everything that he had learned. K'uhul had genetically modified a parasite with which he had infected a number of prisoners. These parasites would reproduce and spread, probably by some insect vector, to infect other people when their hosts reached their polluted homelands. K'uhul called his creation the "Wrath" of nature. The "Wrath" was the parasite. The "Wrath."

So what was the "Mercy"?

Jared rushed back to the Encyclopedia of Predatory Fungi. He flipped to the passage with the symbol of Mercy scribbled at its side.

That was it.

The back room of the back chamber of the lab was the fungal growth area. There, they fed the fungi the parasites from within the animals that they were growing in the first room of the back chamber. The fungi were the Mercy. They were parasites of the parasites. They were the antidote and the cure.

Jared had to get his hands on some.

But how? And what would he do once he got it? What if he was wrong?

He had to communicate with the outside world. If he could do so in time he might be able to get the infected prisoners quarantined and avoid the parasitic plagues to begin with. If he failed in that, at least he would have the Mercy fungus as a backup. He could take it to a lab where they could analyze it. Maybe it was a naturally occurring organism. Even if wasn't, even if K'uhul had genetically engineered it, its gene sequences could be determined and it could be reproduced in massive quantities as a global cure.

Above all, Jared had to make sure that K'uhul

was put out of commission. If the man escaped he could simply modify another parasite for immunity against the Mercy fungus and go forward with his plan at a later date.

Jared couldn't use the lab computers to send a message. The only computer to which he was allowed access had no network connectivity. He couldn't use his OnePod to connect to the wireless network because he didn't have the password. Even if he escaped from the complex it would take him a week to get to get back to civilization...although... if he could get back to Sherpa he could reach town faster.

Actually, if he could get back to Sherpa he could use her onboard computer to send a distress message! If he left soon enough he could be at the truck by early the next day, possibly in time to put an end to all of this, and for better or worse, to save the damned.

To find his truck, he would need to use the GPS features of his OnePod. Jared reached into the waist pocket of his pants and pulled out the device. Only twenty percent charge remained. Not much juice, but maybe enough for a night of navigation.

What would he do for light, and for food and water? It would be a grueling march back to the truck in the pitch black at night. But he had to escape. He had to reach Sherpa as soon as possible and send a distress message. And he had to get his hands on the Mercy fungus. Now.

Chapter 19

Commitment

Jared pounded on his door until he attracted the attention of a guard. As they walked down the hall, he took care to note that the generator room was open. Once they arrived at the laboratory, he surveyed the scene closely. K'uhul and Sybil Lee talked intimately in a corner while workers moved about. Most importantly, the little wooden boxes of Mercy still lay stacked on a bench just a few meters from Jared's workstation. A man tended them whose purpose was unclear. Jared adopted an expression of stupid bliss and walked briskly over to K'uhul and Sybil Lee.

"Well then." K'uhul said, standing up. "It seems you have had a salubrious rest!"

"Oh, man," Jared replied, "I woke up with a sense of peace I've never felt before, and I have only you to thank." Awkwardly, he made a motion, half incipient hand shake, half hug. They smiled warmly to each other and embraced.

Sybil Lee bounced from her chair and squeezed Jared harder than she ever had, sending him spinning. "I'm so happy you've seen the light!" she said.

"Seen it?" Jared replied, "It's standing right before me!"

Sybil Lee and K'uhul demurred, embarrassed by the praise.

So far so good, thought Jared, he could see no obvious signs of skepticism in their faces. "Listen, I've been thinking," he said. "I should be done with the montage in no time. Why don't we play it for the lab workers as a sneak preview of all the wonderful events to come?"

"Sure," K'uhul agreed, "excellent idea. None of

this would have been possible without their diligent labors and they should share in the excitement."

"I wonder," Jared added, "if we could hook up some real speakers to my workstation. It just wouldn't sound right hearing your magnificent voice through that computer's little mosquito box."

"No problem, I'll have my men retrieve the loudspeakers from my own stereo."

"Great, then I'll get back to work."

And so he did. It was easy incorporating K'uhul's speech into the video. Jared then downloaded a particularly vigorous recording of natural sounds from his camera to add as background for the project. Next, he adjusted audio levels until he achieved a perfect balance. Then, exactly forty-five seconds into the video, he inserted a virtual trigger to raise the soundtrack volume to its maximum level. He made one last addition, pressed 'save,' and called K'uhul over excitedly to say that he was done.

Minutes later the loudspeakers were installed and the entire laboratory staff gathered around the computer's video monitor.

"Go ahead," K'uhul said proudly from the front row.

"No, please, you should have the honor," Jared replied. "Just press this button." With that, he stepped into the crowd.

K'uhul hit the "play" button and the spectators muttered in approval as a glorious sun rose from the bottom of the screen. Jared counted to himself - *one, two, three, four...,* and eased his way as unobtrusively as possible further into the crowd. He smiled and patted his neighbors on their backs as he pointed to the screen.

K'uhul's narration began, his powerful voice projecting the essence of apocalyptic gravitas. The sound fidelity was excellent. Jared had used a high quality microphone.

Thirty, thirty-one, thirty-two…just a little further.
Forty-one, forty-two…so close.

And then, right on cue, the speakers blared at deafening volume. Chaos ensued as workers tumbled over one another in a panic to turn down the sound and avoid angering their leader. The diversion would last only a precious few seconds. Within that time, Jared would need to open a box, pull out a vial, and shove it in his pants before anyone turned to look for him to fix the problem. With tremulous nerves quivering like jelly, he quickly retrieved a tube, stashed it, and rushed through the crowd.

"Sorry," he said, feigning confusion. "I'm not sure what that was about. I'll fix it."

By the time Jared got to his workstation he was so consumed with fear he had to muster the entirety of his will to overcome his instinct to freeze. The slightest loss of focus and he would give himself away. He forced himself to take a calm breath and hit the appropriate keys on the keyboard. There were no screaming accusations, no pointing fingers. No one had seen him taking the vial. The crowd continued to watch his video in wonder with its sound now adjusted to a reasonable level.

The die had been cast. Jared could not turn back. He did not know how long it would take for the missing tube to be noticed but, given how much attention the lab technicians had been lavishing on the boxes of Mercy, he knew he had limited time to enact his plan.

"Beautiful," K'uhul said, "a production worthy of the message." Sybil Lee gave Jared a warm look of approval. The audience clapped and cheered.

Jared smiled and bowed and sat back down at his workstation. He peered nervously at the bench full of Mercy as he added finishing touches to the video. A technician hovered over the area. Jared watched as the man reached for a different box than the one he had opened. *Good.* The man went through a series of mysterious checks and preparations. For a moment, Jared's heart sank when he considered the possibility that the vial he had grabbed might not have gone through some last minute activation process. It didn't matter, there was nothing more he could do about it.

K'uhul and Sybil Lee strolled about the lab and chatted with workers. Jared checked the time on the computer - it would be dark outside by now. He approached the two casually. "The video is done," he announced. "The file name is 'Channels of Light.' It's saved on the desktop."

"Interesting title," K'uhul replied. "Very good, thank you, Jared. I will have my men upload it this evening and we will bring it live tomorrow."

Sybil Lee caressed K'uhul's tree trunk of an arm as he spoke. Jared had to fight not to make a face when he saw the boundless admiration with which she drenched the giant, and then lost it and started grimacing when he noticed K'uhul's even more worshipful gaze toward Sybil Lee. He caught himself and waged a quick and mighty battle with his emotions to wrestle his snarl back into a smile. He didn't think anybody had noticed.

"I think I'll head back to my room," Jared said, "unless, of course, there's something else you'd like me to work on?"

"You have already done an excellent service," K'uhul replied, "Feel free to use your time as you wish."

"Very well, see you in a bit."

Just one guard, thought Jared, *good.* He chatted animatedly with his escort as they walked through the gleaming hallway of the laboratory wing and down the stairs to the lower level. He tried to get on the man's good side, but it was useless. They walked around a bend in the tunnel and Jared stopped in front of the generator room. He asked the guard if he wanted to hear a joke. The man grumbled and tried to nudge Jared forward. Jared insisted.

"You see," he said forcefully, "this guy walks into a bar holding a bowl of laughs." Jared's mimed his description. "He takes his bowl and makes like he's going to throw it." Jared moved his imaginary container in a rhythmic arc. "You wonder what's inside, what the man's going to do." The guard couldn't understand a word Jared was saying. Jared timed his next words just right. "And as he throws it," he said, again swinging his imaginary bowl toward the guard, "you realize the joke's on you."

Jared's swing transformed into a vicious punch to the guard's throat. The man tumbled to the ground. He tried to scream for help but succeeded only in releasing a pathetic series of gurgles. Jared had to act fast. If he went for the guard's rifle he would most likely get shot. At best, the weapon would go off in the ensuing struggle and the others would be alerted. He opted for a sweeping kick to the man's jaw.

Teeth cracked and bones shattered but the guard continued to flail. It was a lot harder to knock someone out in real life than in the movies. Jared leapt atop his adversary and pummeled him furiously. He didn't even bother with the gun; he knew no one could do anything when all they saw was stars. The guard sputtered and then lay still.

Jared scanned the hallway breathlessly, terrified that the commotion might have been overheard. He saw no one. As he dragged the guard into the generator room, he heard a clinking of keys coming from the man's pockets. He waffled. Perhaps one of those keys opened the prisoner's chamber. Jared might have been able to free the others, but there was no time, no time at all. If he was caught in the process everything would be lost. In any event, the uncertainties that he was about to face would be more dangerous for his friends than just staying put. K'uhul would be too busy chasing him to bother with them anyway. If Jared were successful he would send help. If he weren't... well, that wasn't an option.

He took one last peek into the hallway and closed the door behind him. "That'll do," he said, prying the assault rifle away from the guard's motionless hands. He crammed the weapon's muzzle into the crevice between the vent and the wall into which he had seen Alan's ant crawl earlier that day. "I hope you didn't steer me wrong, little buddy," he whispered.

With a groan the steel panels gave way and Jared was able to wrench the entire vent from the wall. In its place now stood an ominous dark hole. Jared glanced at the rifle in his hands. With its barrel bent it was useless. He dropped it. Taking a deep breath, he wriggled into the narrow passageway. He didn't know where the shaft would lead. He didn't even know whether it would be wide enough for him to crawl all the way through. He only knew that air must have found its way in from the outside, and with luck, he would reach its source.

Jared was a snake, a legless lizard, as he made his way through the pitch black chute. Within a short time, the passage narrowed such that he couldn't even move his arms. He had to ripple his body, like an inchworm, to proceed. He battled intense claustrophobia and nearly came to tears when he thought he had gotten stuck and could carry on no further. But he twisted and bent and contorted his body and somehow managed to squeeze through the tight spaces as though he were made of liquid.

Then, in the darkness, he felt a searing prick on his neck. He struggled to control his surging terror as he thought of tarantulas and scorpions, and then plummeted into a full-scale panic when he realized he might have crawled into an even worse fate. If he had reached the heart of the leaf cutter nest, he would soon be shredded by a ravenous swarm, one painful bite at a time.

Although he was bitten several more times, the feared horde never materialized. Calmer now, he wormed his way forward until his muscles ached in confusion at their unusual usage and his throat cracked in the acrid air. Onward he went, shuffling, squeezing, and struggling through the channel into the dark unknown.

He wriggled faster when he heard the sound of rushing water ahead. Tiny droplets of mist tickled his face and knew he was getting close. Suddenly, the smell and tone of his surroundings changed. The space had opened. He rose to stand in an expansive darkness filled with the echoing roar of a fast-moving stream. He could see nothing. That was about to change. He pulled out his OnePod and clicked open its protective case. Smiling, he pressed the device's power button. The glow of its screen might not have been impressive in broad daylight, but there, in the blackness of a cave untouched by a single photon its entire existence, it was like a miniature sun. Jared squinted as his eyes once again became useful organs of perception.

The OnePod provided only enough illumination to reveal an arm's length ahead. He moved the device in all directions, examining his environment. He could see now that he was in a large tunnel, wide enough to allow passage of a school bus. Directly ahead tumbled a powerful stream. Darkness obscured either end of the passageway.

Which way? he wondered. Following the river's flow might lead further into the cave, or it might lead outside. How could he know? Reasoning that he could move faster if he jumped into the water and swam with its current he decided to explore the area downstream first. He walked carefully along the water's edge until he was dismayed to find the ceiling of the tunnel descend to the top of the stream. To go further he would have to swim into the submerged channel. He had no way of knowing what would happen once he did. Would there be any open spaces for him to come up for air on the other side or was the passageway filled with water? Would he be able to fight the swift current if he changed his mind, or would it hurl him to a terrifying death by drowning in the dark?

He cursed himself and the world around him for this turn of events. He would do it, but only as a last resort. First, he would explore the area upstream for an alternative. He scrambled back to the passageway from which he had emerged and then continued ahead. After walking for several minutes, he stopped, discouraged. He didn't know what to do. There was just no way of telling which way he should go. He looked upstream and down, again and again. At either end he saw nothing but darkness and indecision.

Then something bit his ankle.

He yelped and jumped back. Something bit again, and then once more.

"Shit!"

Lowering his OnePod, he realized he was standing directly on a trail of ants. He leaned closer and was bitten yet again, but this time he didn't mind. He'd seen something heartening. A parade of leafcutter ants headed in opposite directions. They were foraging. The ants scurrying upstream held nothing in their mouths, but the ones moving downstream carried chunks of green plant matter. Plants didn't grow in caves. There was only one place the ants could have retrieved their precious cargos and that was on the surface. Jared raced along the edge of the stream toward its source, which he now knew must have been the rainforest outside.

Sybil Lee and K'uhul spoke softly, their faces only inches apart. They spoke of love and moved closer. They spoke of trees and beauty and justice and moved closer still. Now they were silent, just two sets of adoring eyes hovering over eager, parted lips. K'uhul leaned in for the sweet consummation of bliss.

"K'uhul Ajaw Kab!" squeaked a frantic little man. K'uhul looked up, the moment shattered. The man blurted something in Mayan. K'uhul shot to his feet. He looked confused, angry. He asked the man to repeat himself.

"What is it?" Sybil Lee asked, concerned.

"There was a message embedded in the video file."

"What message, how?"

"A hidden channel in the audio. Anyone downloading the video could have easily heard it using multi-channel audio software."

"What did it say?" Sybil Lee asked, though in her heart she already knew that Jared must have reverted to his spineless ways.

"It is a warning. It gives the location of the temple and talks of the parasite's cure."

"There's a cure? Did the message get posted?"

K'uhul seemed distracted. "No, it did not." He grumbled at his minion as he shot a look at the benches by the computer workstations.

Jared heard the sounds of the rainforest and knew he was getting close. The cave narrowed to barely the width of a man and Jared burrowed his way up anxiously. Once he felt the warm forest air on his face he turned off the backlight of his OnePod and sat silently, listening for danger. When he finally emerged, he found himself in a forest as dark as the cave he had just traversed. He waved his hands in front of his face, marveling at the complete opacity of the night. He listened intently for a few more moments before he felt comfortable enough to turn his OnePod back on.

Quickly, he navigated to the device's GPS screen and waited as it locked on to satellites. The unit beeped. Now Jared could see where he was in relation to the last waypoints he had entered. He stood just north of the twin temples, over twelve miles from Sherpa. He took a deep breath and crept into the darkness in the opposite direction as his truck.

The little lab worker ran back to K'uhul with a look of abject horror. At the same time a guard ran into the lab from the corridor outside. The worker spoke rapidly as he gestured to an area near the computer workstations where a group of men feverishly searched through a stack of wooden boxes. K'uhul's lips twitched into a snarl and the veins in his forehead engorged. He heaved the worker up by his neck and demanded that he repeat himself. The man stuttered and gasped as K'uhul closed his grip tighter with each word.

"What is it?" Sybil Lee pleaded desperately.

Meanwhile, the guard was frantically gesticulating to get K'uhul's attention. The giant turned to face him, listened for a moment, and then grabbed him with his other hand. The men trembled as K'uhul lifted them high into the air. His words were fireballs roaring out of clenched teeth. "There is an unaccounted for vial of the antidote," he bellowed, "and someone seems to have escaped through the generator vent." With that, K'uhul clenched his fists and collapsed the necks of both men with a sickening crunch. He growled as he hurled their violently spasming bodies across the room. Sybil Lee ran after him as he dashed toward the laboratory exit.

Chapter 20
Trial

The jungle wailed and buzzed and chirped and howled as Jared stumbled through the undergrowth. This wasn't a relaxing chorus, he thought, this was a horror movie soundtrack. He did not know if K'uhul was aware of Sherpa. He had not mentioned anything about driving and did not think that his friends had either. Nevertheless, he could not risk heading straight for his truck for fear of tipping off his pursuers as to his ultimate destination. Rather, he intended to hike for a time in the opposite direction until he reached the swamps and could turn back without leaving tracks. He knew the runny mud and standing pools of the lowlands would camouflage his path well. He just needed to get there.

He carried on in the pitch black using the light from his OnePod sparingly in order to conserve battery charge. It was absolutely essential that the device did not give out before Jared reached Sherpa. If it did, he would be completely lost. All would be completely lost. He checked its battery meter. It held at eighteen percent charge.

The going was hard through the dense ground cover in the dark. There wasn't even enough light to search for a line through the brush. Jared had to feel his way forward and wriggle his way around obstacles. He was ecstatic when he noticed peccary tracks below him, knowing they would likely lead him to a more established game trail. Sure enough, a short time later he was running through the forest along a well worn animal path.

K'uhul's dark silhouette glided through mist-shrouded trees. The men flanking him struggled mightily to keep up. Those that were able to match his speed did so at the cost of deep scratches and torn skin. The swarm of soldiers stopped as one when they heard their radios burst into chatter. Stragglers poured from the jungle to hear the news. "Did they find him?" Sybil Lee asked, leaning on her knees to catch her breath.

"They found fresh tracks," K'uhul replied, "headed in the opposite direction."

"He must be lost. I thought for sure he would head for his truck."

"Perhaps."

K'uhul barked an order and a group of men immediately took off along their initial route to Sherpa. K'uhul and the others turned and raced back toward the twin temples.

The animal tracks Jared followed grew increasingly obscure as the ground before his feet softened to mush. He was almost happy when he found himself getting mired in mud. Almost. The sucking muck might as well have been molasses for the effort required with each step. For a moment, he thought he had made a bad strategic error. He now had that much more exhausting swampland to traverse. Wallowing in doubt and self denigration, he turned his OnePod on and saw something reassuring in its dim light. Within seconds of pulling out his legs, the craters he was leaving behind filled with muck. His steps were producing no noticeable trail at all. Pleased, he marched on.

He walked until his thighs begged for mercy and calves promised never to complain again. Eventually, he thought he'd gone far enough, checked his OnePod for directions, and began his arc back to his trusty vehicle. The first two hours were difficult but manageable. Jared's adrenaline and conditioning served him well. By the third hour he was parched and exhausted. He stopped to lap water from the filthy puddles around him, knowing they would likely make him sick but desperate for the hydration. By the fourth hour he was stumbling though a haze of delirium, and by the fifth he simply could not go on. He had nothing left. He had used every last ounce of his energy and reserves.

Then he walked on for five more hours.

The jungle fell silent in the netherworld between night and day. Jared heard only the soft slurps of mud beneath his feet and his own labored breaths. In the darkness, he saw faint outlines of things, nothing more. His eyes, exhausted by their constant efforts, made up stories to fill in the blanks. They told him huge fangs and claws surrounded him. Periodically, Jared froze, certain that a monstrous predator stalked him in the darkness. Still, he battled past his foes of fear, fatigue, and forest growth and carried on.

He checked his OnePod for directions. The unit's low battery indicator flashed ominously. His guts twisted themselves in knots as he considered the possibility of all hope vanishing in a lifeless screen. Then he heard a noise in the distance, a person calling. The slurping of his steps ended abruptly as he stopped in his tracks and held his breath. He heard the call again, closer this time. Focusing the entirety of his remaining mental acuity on interpreting what his ears were telling him, he heard the voice once more and realized it sounded a lot like Sybil Lee.

Had she regained her senses and come to join him in thwarting K'uhul? If so, she would be lost and scared in the woods. Or was she trying to bait him to a ghastly death?

Now he heard the voice distinctly. It was definitely Sybil Lee. "Please help me!" she cried, "Where are you?" Almost despite himself, Jared sloshed through the mire toward her pleas. He heaved himself mightily, trying to home in on her, but no matter how far he walked, he could not get closer. Every time he thought he was making progress, her voice moved. One minute her calls seemed to come from a hundred yards ahead, the next two hundred yards behind. At one point, it even seemed her voice was coming from two directions at once. Just when he thought he was imaging the whole thing, her heard Sybil Lee's calls yet again, beckoning him further. "Please help me! Hurry!" The ominous shapes around Jared continued to lunge at him, and still he hurried after the calls. The mud deepened dangerously below feet, but still he struggled on.

Then, finally, she was close, very close, just up ahead. A few more exhausting steps, a few more shadowy monsters to pass, and he would be there to comfort her. Jared stopped and listened intently for the rustling of leaves that he hoped would tell him if Sybil Lee was alone or if he were blundering into a trap. Once convinced that she was by herself, he ventured a whisper.

"Sybil Lee?"

"Where are you? Help me!" she replied as loudly as ever.

Her voice sounded odd, tinny. Briefly, Jared wondered if he were hearing another woman, or perhaps a recording.

"Sybil Lee?" he said, more forcefully. She couldn't have been more than a body length away. She must have heard him, and yet again she repeated her call at full volume as though he had said nothing. Jared pointed his OnePod toward her voice. In its faint glow, he could make out nothing but branches and trees.

"Sybil Lee!" he called loudly.

Nothing. Then, a moment later, as his eyes adjusted, he realized something was moving ahead. He could just make out the outline of a large bird, perhaps a parrot or a macaw, perched on a branch. He noticed another bird off to its side. Both animals stared at him vacantly. He couldn't believe his ears when one of them opened its beak.

"Please help me!" it yelled. "Where are you?"

Then the other bird spoke. "Oh please!" it said, "Hurry!"

Panic surged from Jared's core. He tried to back up but could not move his legs. Shining his OnePod down he was horrified to find that he had already sunk to his thighs in the mud. With each desperate attempt at flight he succeeded only in further entrapping himself. The muck crawled to his waist. He had stumbled into deadly quicksand.

Another woman must have met the same fate in this spot, he thought, and the parrots had been simply mimicking her death cries. What an idiot he had been for confusing their squawks for Sybil Lee and blundering into this mess!

He racked his mind for a strategy but found none. What was one supposed to do in quicksand? Remaining motionless slowed his descent but accomplished nothing. Flailing around would provide a sure path to a quick death and would be the inevitable result of panic. Jared struggled to control himself. Calmly, he scanned his surroundings with his OnePod for a handhold he could use to pull himself out. Nothing lay within reach. The mud seeped to his belly. He tried to leap to his side and twist around, but just sank further in the process. Still calm, he had the presence of mind to snap his OnePod shut in its waterproof case and tuck it away. He then tried a sort of a swimming motion, but again, found it counterproductive.

The muck reached his chest and Jared began to lose his cool. He could just make out the silhouette of a huge tree nearby. It was his last shot. With all of his might he flailed and kicked and writhed toward it. With each motion he made miniscule progress, but sank that much further. *He could not fail!!* he thought as the mud reached up his neck, *he must not fail!* The mud oozed past his chin, past his mouth. *Oh Lord, what had he done?* The mud rose above his nose. *He had let his obsessive love destroy him. He had let the entire world down.* Bitter tears of despair mixed with the wetness of the earth that rose inexorably above his eyes.

Jared stood in inky blackness. He was expecting more of a white light, but there he was. As he heard the explosive crackling of large branches and crinkle of shuffling leaves, he thought for a moment that he must still be in the rainforest above where something gigantic was lurching through the trees. A trick of his dying mind, he realized. An awfully convincing trick.

He felt a rhythmic breeze and heard what sounded like the bellows of a steel mill furnace. The creature in front of him was breathing. Suddenly, two enormous eyes opened, crimson red and big as grapefruits. They glowered menacingly at Jared.

Apparently the forest, or Jared's projection of the forest, wasn't keen on his plan.

"I need to get past!" he said firmly.

The eyes squinted. A swarm of twisting shapes emerged from the blackness.

"I am not forsaking you," Jared continued.

The eyes narrowed further. The shapes wrapped around Jared like a boa, squeezing the air from his lungs.

He coughed as he choked on air too thick to breathe.

"We're on the right track. We do need to re-embrace the sacred, but by increasing our appreciation, not by leaping into zealotry."

The eyes opened almost imperceptibly.

"I heard your calls begging for mercy and did everything I could to help you. Now I'm the one that's begging. We just need a little more time. I promise you. Just give us one more chance…please…"

The eyes blinked. They blinked again, and then, with their third blink, they vanished. The shadows released their grip and suddenly Jared realized he was grasping something roughly textured and firm. He heaved himself up and emerged from the muck, gasping for air, clutching at the base of a giant tree.

Jared was an empty shell, depleted beyond what his body and mind should have been able to endure. He was encrusted in a shell of filth, and now, in the emerging light of dawn, he saw three of everything. Pulling out his three OnePods, he checked his position. He lay within a hundred meters of Sherpa. He trudged pathetically, stumbling to his knees every few steps. Then, he heard the crackle of radio static and fell to his belly. *Oh no, no, no! They're here! They knew I was coming the whole time!*

Something moved to his side. Jared scrambled into the brush. He lay trembling as men spoke Mayan nearby. With his pulse throbbing in his ears, he pealed down the leaves in front of him and peered out. A large group of soldiers stood stuffing their faces with glossy red fruits, viscous liquid dribbling down their necks. Another half dozen men scrambled around the grove gathering its juicy harvest. Jared looked back and forth between the trees, the fruits, and the men. "Thank you," he said quietly to the forest as he slipped toward his truck

Sherpa was in shambles, her tires punctured, her windows smashed, and her hood bent at an odd angle. Most likely, someone had tried to pry her hood open to damage her engine. The lock had held. Two men stood close by, monstrous assault rifles in hand. One looked over. Jared froze. He was well hidden behind the foliage, and from his adventures in the sunken earth he had gained the best camouflage possible - mud. The soldier turned away.

Jared had to do something quickly. The large group of soldiers would return once they had sated themselves with fruit. Sherpa was disabled, but Jared could still send a distress message. He needed to create a distraction of least a few minutes. He looked around desperately for a diversion. He could throw a rock, but that might give away his position and would buy him all of ten seconds. He was well camouflaged – he could sneak up on the soldiers and then…and then what? In his sorry state, he doubted his ability to handle one man in hand-to-hand combat, let alone two. In any event, they'd make swiss cheese out of him with their bullets before he ever even threw a punch. *Ah! Time was running out!*

An enormous and agitated wasp landed on Jared's arm. At the same time, he noticed a soldier looking in his direction. He chaffed under his reflex not to swat the insect away lest he alert the soldier to his presence. He was forced to watch in silent horror as the wasp stung him repeatedly, as did a second insect that landed on his nose. And yet he felt no pain. The wasp on his face appeared gigantic in close up. It thrust its abdomen again and again in a fury of aggression, crawling terrifyingly close to Jared's eyeballs. And yet still Jared felt nothing. And then he realized he'd received another gift from his fall into the mud, an armor of thick, caked earth. The soldier averted his gaze and Jared swatted away the insects, only to have a number of others replace them. He must be close to their nest, he realized. And then he had an idea.

He pulled his socks over his pants and tucked in his shirt, slathered any exposed parts of his body with mud, and then followed the line of wasps harassing him back to their waxy home. The nest was engorged with seething defenders. *Perfect.* Jared caked extra thick earth on his hands and knocked the nest free with a stick. It fell, heavy as a baby, into his arms and he was immediately consumed in a hail of frenzied attackers. His shield wasn't perfect - every once in a while he felt the searing pain of a sting - but it provided enough of a defense for Jared to control his panic as he raced through the undergrowth back to Sherpa.

He made an arc to approach the soldiers from behind. Carefully, he crept closer, worried that the buzzing surrounding him might give him away. His breathing grew labored and he suddenly realized he might be reaching the limit of his tolerance to the insect venom. His entire body roasted with pain. Finally, he stepped close enough. He shook the nest violently to infuriate any hesitant stragglers and hurled his sting bomb behind the soldiers' backs. One man turned to look at the nest briefly, apparently not registering what it was, and then looked up to see from where it had fallen. The second recognized the danger right away and pulled his partner's shirt in alarm. Within seconds a cloud of insect wrath flooded the area. The soldiers fled in panic, swinging their arms desperately. One man glanced wild-eyed in Jared's direction as he ran. Jared wondered if he'd been seen through the trees. What would the man have thought? At that moment, Jared would have appeared as an amorphous jumble of sticks, mud, and writhing wasps.

Jared race-limped to his truck. He estimated he had less than three minutes before the soldiers returned. He climbed under Sherpa to retrieve a hidden key. *Twenty seconds gone.* Now he could unlock the hood and reattach the truck's battery. *Forty seconds.* Hopping to the rear cargo area, he was glad to see that, despite its broken windows, nobody had been able to pull the boxes full of gear past the steel bars. He shoveled snack bars and water bottles into a sack as he connected his Onepod to Sherpa's onboard computer system. *One minute thirty seconds.* He only had time to provide a sketch of the situation.

"bioterror plot imminent," he typed," *leader dr rojo reino, aka k'uhul ajaw kab, recent. visitors to guatemala must be quarantined worldwide, headquarters in temple/cave complex."*

Jared typed in the GPS waypoint he had taken just outside the first temple.

"innocent prisoners inside, expect heavy resistance, antidote in lab labeled with skeleton/embrace glyph, have small amount."

Jared reached into the cargo area and pulled out the two-way radio he had found days before.

"have walkie-talkie, model prime b32-0226, will use frequency 25 for contact."

He typed his current coordinates and finished with, *"REAL threat, please, send help asap!"*

His three minutes were up. Still, he heard nothing but the angry buzz of wasps. He briefly reviewed his email. Who could he send it to that would believe him and be able to convince the proper authorities that the threat was legitimate? No time for perfection. He entered several addresses – family, friends, colleagues. Some, at least, would recognize the email account as belonging to Sherpa's distress system. He pressed "send," and took a moment to remove evidence that he had been there while he waited for confirmation that the email had been received by satellite. Suddenly, he heard a radio transmission. One of the soldiers must have dropped his two-way radio in panic. Jared shoved it into his sack, and raced into the jungle.

Chapter 21
Joint Task Force Bravo

Jared didn't know how long he had been sleeping, though judging by the forest's gloom it was late afternoon at minimum. His joints pined for lubrication, his muscles rioted, and his mind wallowed in haze. A blank screen greeted him when he pulled out his OnePod to check the time. The device had finally run out of charge. He checked his two walkie-talkies. One was set to K'uhul's channel and the other to the frequency Jared had specified in his email. Both devices lay silent.

Jared wolfed down snack bars and considered what would happen if nobody took his note seriously. Though he was a well known filmmaker, he worried that the authorities might think the old Jared Foster had returned and that this was just a prank. At least his close friends would believe him, he reassured himself. It seemed as though his entire life were spent just trying to get people to believe.

One radio growled. Jared's eyes rocketed to his pack. Which had sounded? He heard another transmission, distorted, but clearly coming from the walkie-talkie set to K'uhul's channel. As he pulled it to his ear, its sea of distortion parted to reveal a conversation in Mayan. The voices grew clearer. K'uhul's men were getting closer. Jared breaths grew irregular as his legs started to twitch. He had taken great care to cover his tracks and didn't think the soldiers even knew that he was in the area, but when he thought of K'uhul's preternatural tracking ability he realized that his efforts had probably been in vain. The giant must right now be noticing the lack of bird calls in the area. He would be upon him at any moment and when he found him....

Jared entered a running crouch, ready to bolt out

of his thicket at the first sign of trouble. He heard another burst of static, this time from the radio set to the rescue channel. With one radio pressed against each side of his head, he heard men speaking Mayan in one ear and amorphous static in the other. Nothing but static, static, static and then, suddenly, a muffled voice!

"....force....copy?"

Tornados of joy and terror swirled within Jared's pounding heartbeats. He turned up the volume and tried to swallow. Finally, he heard a clear transmission.

"This is Joint Task Force Bravo. Jared Foster, do you copy?"

Jared fumbled with the radio's controls until he found the transmit button. "This is Jared Foster! I'm here! I'm right here!"

"Roger, Mr. Foster. Where exactly is 'here'?"

Shit! Jared didn't know and his OnePod was out of commission. "Approximately three miles southeast of the second GPS coordinates that I included in my distress message."

"Roger, wait one."

Drops of sweat marked the seconds.

"Mr. Foster, do you mean the coordinates to the temple complex?"

"No, no, the others!"

"Roger, wait one."

Jared thought he heard sticks snapping. He definitely heard a rumble of heavy wind in the distance.

"Roger, Mr. Foster, we are approximately six klicks away from your location. E.T.A. less than two minutes. Out."

"Rog...er," Jared exhaled. Less than two minutes! Excellent! Jared was elated but now he was sure he heard the sounds of crackling twigs and shuffling leaves getting closer. His entire being dedicated itself to interpreting the signals falling on his ears. Was that his rescuers approaching, or his hunters? The roar of wind differentiated itself with a familiar thumping rhythm as the shuffling transformed into distinct footsteps. Suddenly the footsteps were a thunder hurtling toward Jared.

"This is Joint Task For…"

Jared didn't wait for the transmission to finish. "Is that you coming on foot?"

"Roger, that's a negative, we are airborne."

Airborne. The thumping wind was the sound of helicopter rotors. That meant the footsteps rushing toward him were…

Jared sprung like a rabbit from its burrow, leaving everything but his rescue radio. Bullets screamed passed as he desperately leapt over stumps and vines. "Help! Help!" he yelled into his radio. "They're on me! They're right on me!"

"Roger, we are scanning for your position right now."

"Hurry! Please hurry!"

The roar of the helicopters grew louder as bullets punished the undergrowth.

"Mr. Foster, we believe we see you. I take it your pursuers mean to do you harm?"

"Yes!"

"……..hundreds of them……."

"What? Fuck!"

A voice boomed from the tree tops. "This is the U.S. Army Joint Task Bravo, 228th Aviation Regiment. You must cease your pursuit immediately or we will be forced to open fire."

"Just do it!" Jared screamed to the canopy above.

The voice repeated the message, this time in Spanish.

"Ahhh! Fuck! Do it!" Jared tripped over a sapling and tumbled to the ground. The moment he hit he heard such an immense crash that he expected to see his brains splattered around him. In fact, he had just heard the first salvo of a tremendous onslaught of destruction. Sunlight poked its way through the dense foliage as helicopter chain guns and rockets tore through the canopy. Trees groaned as they split in two and crashed to the ground. Fiery explosions sent ear-splitting shock waves in every direction. From the midst of this smoldering confusion, a man emerged from the undergrowth running toward Jared with the muzzle of his rifle extended. Jared leapt as bullets boiled the ground before him. He heard a loud explosion and turned to search for his attacker. Nothing but wisps of smoke marked the spot where the man had been just moments before.

The sounds of warfare crept into the distance as all of the helicopters but one moved to pursue their fleeing targets. Jared could hear the lone straggler hovering close by but could not see it through the treetops. He clutched his radio and listened. The helicopter swept closer until it was directly overhead. Jared's radio crackled to life.

"This is Orange Two, Jared Foster, do you copy?

"This is Jared."

"Hold tight, Mr. Foster, we are coming to get you. Please do not move from your current position"

Jared scanned the canopy above. How would they know where he was? A fireball ignited atop the canopy a short distance from where he stood. He watched as the ball burrowed its way to the ground, burning a path through the foliage as it fell.

"Mr. Foster, please make your way to the extraction point, do you copy?"

"You mean the hole you just burned?"

Something dropped through the new clearing - a rope, quickly followed by a man.

"Roger, affirmative."

Jared rushed to meet the soldier as he descended to the bottom of the rope. The man wore a helmet and goggles and had a flag of the United States sewn in the arm of his army fatigues. "Let's get you the hell out of here!" he grunted.

The harness squeezed Jared's waist and groin as he was heaved up. He cleared the forest canopy to meet a surreal blend of poetry and horror. The setting sun hurled sweeping rivers of vermillion across the top half of the universe while a sea of emerald green filled the lower half. Swift military attack helicopters and slower, double-rotored transports buzzed like dragonflies through the air. Expansive swaths of land lay scorched and burning. Explosions grumbled in the distance.

Jared looked up. He was being hoisted to one of the large transports. The air from its twin rotors pummeled him like a hurricane as he rose. Finally, he cleared the side of the airship and was helped into its cargo area. A soldier smiled in greeting and said something unintelligible. Hearing only rotor blast, Jared pointed to his ears and made a cutting motion. The soldier handed Jared a helmet. The next time the man spoke, Jared heard him clearly through his helmet's headset.

"Afternoon, Mr. Foster! I'm Chief Warrant Officer Niles. Quite a hornet's nest you've kicked up here!"

"Thank you for coming," Jared replied, shaking the man's hand. "Thank you for doing this!"

"It's our job, Mr. Foster. Come on, let's strap in. Follow me."

Niles led Jared further into the hold, where a crew of soldiers sat wearing full battle regalia. Glancing at their bristling bandoliers of ammunition, Jared felt strangely reassured. They seemed calm. One man read a newspaper, as though this were just another day at the office.

Niles motioned to two empty seats. "You OK?" he asked as they sat. Jared's motley collection of wounds would have made a soldier proud.

"I'll live, thanks."

"We'll get you home soon enough. Just got a little clean-up to take care of..."

Jared nodded.

"That message you sent sure got a bunch of Bigwigs in a tizzy. Looks like they'd been after that Reino character for a long time. We scrambled just about our whole regiment up here outta Soto Cano."

Jared's eyes registered confusion.

"Soto Cano, Honduras, home of Joint Task Force Bravo."

Jared nodded understanding.

Niles pointed to the control box dangling from Jared's helmet. "You can tuck that into your belt. We're on channel six-three right now. That's for internal communication within this bird. Turn the dial to one twelve and you can hear all the action."

Jared gave the OK sign and flipped his headset to the combat channel. It was instant information overload.

"...Tango, Oscar, Papa, One, Six, Four, Four..."

"Roger! Hellfires off!"

A number of powerful explosions echoed in the distance.

"Red Four, this is Red One, status please."

"Roger, Red One, got 'em."

"This is Orange Three, we're taking hits!"

"Roger Orange Three, this is Orange One. I see 'em. You got ten at 11:00."

"Roger."

A chain gun shredded the air.

"Got 'em."

Jared turned to Niles to ask him a question, forgetting that there was no way to hear without the headsets. Niles indicated two numbers with his fingers, six and three. Jared flipped to the correct channel. "How can they see through the foliage?" he asked.

"Night vision. Shows up green but works like a charm."

Jared flipped back to the combat channel.

"Orange One, this is Red One. What is your status?"

"Roger, Red One. We have one hundred sixteen enemy dead or wounded with approximately forty left on the ground."

"Roger Orange One. Think Orange Flight can handle the rest?"

"That's affirmative."

"Roger, out."

"Red Flight, Yellow Flight, this is Red One. Maintain your attack formations. You will follow me to target Hotel Quebec on my signal."

Jared's head spun from the jargon. Hotel Quebec? He peered through the port window behind him and saw a group of helicopters assembling in the air. He flipped channels. "What's Hotel Quebec?" he asked.

"Hotel Quebec," Niles replied, "H Q - stands for headquarters. They're breaking to take the temple."

Oh man. Jared thought of his friends and hoped the assault would not involve as many high explosives. "Are we going there too?" he asked.

"Negative."

"I could help, I know the layout of the complex. There are innocent prisoners there."

"Don't worry, we got your message about the prisoners. We'll be joining them soon enough. Just a little more clean-up here..."

"What about the quarantine? Did you get my message about the quarantine?"

"Yes, Mr. Foster. We're doing all we can on that front."

Jared nodded and flipped back to the combat channel.

"Roger, I *am* trying to hit 'em!"

"Orange Three, Orange One. What is the problem?"

"Roger Orange One. I don't know! He's a big son of a bitch but I have *never* seen a man move that fast in my life!"

"Roger, want some help?"

"No, I got it. I'll sting 'em in just a second."

Jared heard repeated chain gun fire. He had a good idea who they were after.

"Orange Three, Orange One. Status please."

"Dammit!"

"What *is* the problem Orange Three?"

"It's the night vision, sir, there's clearly a malfunction!"

"Roger. What is the specific malfunction of your night vision unit Orange Three?"

"The screen's not working right. My target is now displaying as an animal, a big...dammit!...a big fucking cat that I cannot seem to hit."

"Orange Three this is Orange Two. Is that a joke?"

"No, I'm telling you, my imaging system is hosed. My God that thing is quick!"

"Orange Three, this is Orange One. You are cleared to use Hellfire against your kitty cat target if you feel it is necessary."

The voice was clearly condescending. Apparently the army did not like to waste missiles.

"Orange One, Roger Wilco."

Jared heard a powerful blast close by, followed by silence.

"Orange Three, Orange One. Status please."

The channel was silent.

"Orange Three, Orange One, repeat, status please. Did you grease 'em?"

"Uh, Roger, this is Orange Three. I have a malfunctioning imaging system."

"Orange Three, what is the specific malfunction of your imaging system?"

"Well it showed that I, uh, I greased him all right, but he sort of...he sort of vaporized before the missile even hit."

"Could you repeat that please, Orange Three?"

"Nothing. I greased 'em. That's all. Orange Three out."

Jared's body slumped with relief. It must have been him. Who else could have been that big and agile? They had blown up K'uhul into a vaporous cloud. He would never again be able to threaten the world of men. Nor would he ever again risk everything in order to protect the world of the wild.

With that last thought, Jared's emotions leapt into somersaulting freefall. He felt intense joy and stabbing guilt, overwhelming dread and small pangs of hope. K'uhul was dead as a direct result of Jared's actions. Did that make him a hero or a villain, a savior or a murderer? Was it a good thing that K'uhul was gone? Of course it was! But now humanity could go on raping and pillaging the Earth as it always had. *Argh!* Jared put his face in his hands and moaned.

"Orange Flight, this is Orange One. Let's finish this up."

"Roger."

"Roger."

The three helicopters swept over the area. Eventually, Jared heard another transmission. Though it contained no identifying call line, its accent sounded like Orange Three's southern drawl. "Man oh man, weren't there just about thirty o' those little buggers running around here?"

'Yeah. Oh, hey....will you take a look at that? Looks like they're assembling around the edge of that giant hole over there."

"Roger, now which hole--y shit! Look at the size of that thing!"

"Let's check it out Orange Flight."

"Roger."

"Roger."

Jared felt his stomach drop as his transport moved to follow the attack helicopters. After a short flight, the helicopters began circling.

"This is Orange Three. What *is* that thing?"

"Orange One here. I don't know, maybe a giant sinkhole? Jesus, I can't even see the bottom of it. Orange Three, what is the status of your imaging system? Can you visualize the enemy?"

"Roger, imaging appears to be working again, however, the enemy has taken refuge inside natural formations around the hole. I am not able to visualize their exact whereabouts."

"Roger, I'm having the same problem. Orange Two this is Orange One. Do you copy?"

Niles looked at Jared and pointed his finger at the floor. They were riding on Orange Two.

"Roger."

"Orange Two, I think we're gonna need to put some boots on the ground to flush the enemy out. We will clear you a wide landing zone at the southern perimeter of the hole. You are to drop off troopers at that position on my order."

"Roger Orange One."

Jared winced at a sustained series of explosions close by. His headset crackled back to life.

"That should do it. Nobody could have lived through that."

"Roger, alright Orange Two, this is Orange One. We have cleared the LZ for you. You may proceed to land your troops."

"Roger."

Jared's helicopter moved into position. Two troopers raced from their seats to open the sliding door on the side of the cargo hold. A blast of warm air laced with the sickly sweet smell of turbine exhaust shot inside. Jared's eyes widened at the dramatic view now exposed. The sun lay in its grey death throes and dark clouds raced so quickly from the horizon that Jared thought he must have been watching time-lapse photography of a weather shift. Below this ominous sky, where the ground should have been, sprawled a gaping hole in the earth. It was as wide as ten stadiums and descended indefinitely. Ragged formations of limestone extended from its edges to meet a solid wall of jungle at its perimeter. Two dark grey attack helicopters circled like sharks above the black ocean. On one end of the hole lay a wide patch of scorched earth, the landing zone the other helicopters had just moments earlier stripped of life.

"Orange One, this is Orange Two. I have examined the LZ and determined that it is too uneven to set this bird down. Request permission for a rappel dismount."

"Roger, Orange Two, you may proceed. We will provide cover."

A group of soldiers heaved an enormous coil of rope out the cargo doorway. After assembling his battle gear, Niles motioned to Jared's channel switcher. Jared flipped frequencies.

"Wish us luck," Niles said, handing Jared a pair of binoculars. "You can watch the action with these."

Jared switched back to the combat frequency, put the binoculars to his eyes, and watched the final battle ensue.

Chapter 22

Nature's Last Stand

The sky darkened ominously as the soldiers rappelled to the ground. Rolling clouds smothered the setting sun and lightning jabbed at the horizon. Powerful blasts of air rocked the helicopter. *Strange*, thought Jared, in all the time he had been in the Petén he had rarely felt the even faintest breeze.

"Orange Three, do you see someone on the ground at 12:00?"

"Roger, at the other edge of the hole?"

"Affirmative."

"I believe so but he's just kinda standing there isn't he?"

Jared focused his binoculars. Atop a limestone formation at the opposite end of the chasm, an unusually large and well-built man stood with arms extended.

The lightning moved closer.

It couldn't be him. Could it?

"Affirmative Orange Three, he certainly does not appear to be doing much. Why don't you go ahead and...whoa!...what the hell was that?"

Several black objects whizzed across Jared's field of vision. He put his binoculars down to look outside directly. Hundreds of small animals flapped through the air. Of course, Jared realized, huge numbers of bats must live in the crater below. They would be emerging now for their evening forage.

He lifted his binoculars back to his eyes. The man in the distance weaved his arms in front of him. Violent lightning and thunder alternated with hurricane gusts of wind. The helicopters battled to maintain their positions in the air.

"It's just a few bats, Orange One."

"Just a few? What the?"

The gunships scurried from the center of the hole. Looking down, Jared understood. The depth of the chasm's blackness rippled and seethed. He glanced directly below his helicopter. The rappelling soldiers floundered against the wind. Peering back at the hole, Jared saw the writhing mass of darkness slowly circling as it extruded itself into the air.

Thunder crashed all around and lightning pummeled the ground. Jared focused through his binoculars again. The man in the distance was moving his arms theatrically now, like a conductor. Jared watched him, transfixed, until the whizzing objects obscuring his view coalesced into a solid black mass. He pulled the lenses away and stepped back in awe.

Before him, sprawled an enormous colossus, as wide as the chasm and tall as the clouds. Around and around it swirled, like some monstrous elemental summoned from the depths of the Earth to wreak havoc upon the universe.

Bats, thought Jared, it was composed of millions upon millions of bats.

The tumult of thunder now dwarfed the roar of the helicopters' rotors. A barrage of lightning beat back the darkness of the falling night.

Still the cloud of bats grew larger and more ominous.

The helicopters wavered against the angry winds.

And still the cloud grew.

And then, unexpectedly, a torrent of bats burst from the cloud toward Jared's transport. The ship groaned from the impact. Another river of animals exploded forth in the direction of a gunship. The helicopter attempted to dive but was hit head on. It lurched dramatically as its rotors found themselves spinning in a virtually liquid medium. The helicopter's engine stuttered and coughed from the strain.

"Jesus Christ! Let's get the hell out of here!" someone yelled on the radio. The colossus swung an arm at the second gunship, knocking it back as far as it lifted it. Blood rained from its rotors. Still it did not stall. The helicopter turned to flee but just then a second wave struck. Now its blades turned lazily. And then a third wave hit.

"Oh shit, they're clogging the air intakes! They're clogging the air intakes! Mayday! Mayday!"

A giant fist of black rocketed from the cloud to Jared's ship, launching his helicopter into a violent spin. For a moment Jared saw nothing but swirls of bats and trees outside the cargo doors. He heard a catastrophic explosion, followed by booms receding into the distance.

One of the helicopters had crashed into the chasm.

"Son of a bitch!" shouted an aviator. Jared's view swung back to face the colossus and he caught a glimpse of the second helicopter unleashing a rain of bullets into the swarm. The view swung away and Jared's stomach dropped in terror as he realized his ship was falling too.

'Mayday! Mayday! Orange Two going down!" he heard just before impact.

Jared wasn't sure how long he had been unconscious but there was no mystery about his pain or the sickening smell of his own burning flesh. He rolled to escape the heat and opened his eyes. He lay in the wreckage of the transport helicopter, darkened but for spasms of electrical shorts along the fuselage. Machine gun fire and thunder attacked the air outside as a strobe light of pyrotechnics illuminated the night. Blood poured from Jared's forehead. Reaching up, he realized he had lost his helmet. Suddenly, he heard an ominous whoosh as the rear of the helicopter burst into flames. He scrambled to a rocky crevice outside just in time to avoid getting torn to pieces by the ship's violent last gasp.

The explosion cast the scene into sharp focus. He was at the edge of the crater. Lifeless bodies lay atop a ground knee deep in bat carcasses and blood. The smoldering remains of the second gunship lay crumpled in a heap on the other side of chasm. Men shouted and screamed in all directions. Jared felt hideously exposed. He had to get his hands on a weapon, or at least a headset. Would the communication system even work now that the helicopters were damaged? Maybe he needed a walkie-talkie, in any event, he needed something!

He crawled to a fallen soldier, then grimaced. It was Niles. A twig snapped alarmingly nearby. Jared whipped his head around to see one of K'uhul's men stalking in his direction. The man hadn't noticed him yet. Jared rooted through the bats next to Niles for a weapon. He would be discovered any second. K'uhul's man turned away briefly. Jared gave up his search and sprinted to the edge of the perimeter. Bullets soon took chase. One hit his shoulder hard, punching him into the jagged rocks. Turning, he saw his attacker in pursuit. Jared shuffled on hands and feet, like an airplane gaining flight velocity, until he finally reached enough momentum to burst full speed into a run. And then he was at the rainforest's edge. He ran inside, turned, and stopped. Pressed against a tree, he listened as his pursuer ran straight into the jungle. Jared's evasive maneuver had worked, for the time being.

He analyzed his wound. It didn't hurt much, but his body was pumping out such copious quantities of adrenaline that he would have scarcely noticed losing an arm. His blood seeped rather than spurted which meant that the bullet had most likely missed any major arteries. He stood, panting and listening. The sounds of machine gun fire grew sparser. Either somebody was winning, or both sides were losing. He wondered about the helicopters that had gone to assault the temple complex. Hadn't they heard the mayday calls? Shouldn't they now be on their way back to assist? Maybe they were running into their own problems. He had to assume the worst. Nobody was going to come to the rescue and the American soldiers were all dead or dying. He patted his pants pocket. The vial was still there, unbroken. It was the only good news for the moment.

Unexpectedly, he heard the shrill scream of a woman.

Sybil Lee?

He scurried to the edge of the jungle and peered into the battle zone. Sybil Lee stood, a twenty second dash away, facing an American soldier. Behind her loomed one of K'uhul's men. Jared held his breath and hoped against hope that the American would save her. In the distance he saw K'uhul, gesticulating for some unclear purpose. A large blue butterfly seemed to appear from nowhere just off to the side of the American. As the man aimed his rifle, the butterfly fluttered about his face. In the moment he took to swat it away, he was riddled with bullets.

K'uhul's man approached Sybil Lee. She turned and embraced the soldier. She was thanking him for saving her.

Jared winced and turned away. A flash in the distance caught his eye. K'uhul was running at a sprint. Wearing his ceremonial loincloth and a stone pendant on his chest, he glided like a jungle creature across the ground in the direction of a group of soldiers engaged in hand-to-hand combat. One of the Americans at the edge of the fray tried desperately to reload his rifle. Jared watched in fascination as K'uhul slowed to a stalk. What did he intend to do? He appeared unarmed. Jared wanted to scream a warning to the soldiers, but just then he heard a rustle of leaves behind him. The next instant K'uhul emerged to stand behind the American at the edge of the fray. He punched straight through the man's back, then sprang into the battle. Jared had to avert his gaze as the giant savagely tore into the American soldiers.

The battlefield grew silent, dominated by K'uhul's triumphant silhouette over a sea of lifeless bodies. Jared knew what he had to do. As the crunching behind him drew closer, he recognized his opportunity. The man who had shot him had not given up his search. Jared moved like a shadow past his side. He made a sound so the man would turn around. When he did so, Jared channeled ten years of rock climbing brawn, five years of jujitsu training, and the angst of a very, very bad week into the power of his fist. The soldier snorted as he tried to breathe. Jared kindly relieved him of his weapon as he fell.

How did one stalk a predator? Was it even possible? Jared focused on his prey at the edge of the abyss and imagined himself just a casual breeze blowing in that direction. When he reached a patch of shrubs he became just a plant himself, visiting old friends, and when he passed the smoldering wreckage of the attack helicopter he was just another column of smoke. K'uhul lay just ahead now, searching the pockets of an American soldier. Jared had a good idea what he was looking for.

One last, beautiful obstacle stood between them, Sybil Lee flanked by one of K'uhul's men. Jared crawled closer and closer until he could see the fingernails of the soldier's fingers wrapped around his rifle. He took a deep breath. He had to do it. He had no choice. He aimed his rifle at the man's head.

His finger stalled on the trigger.

He'd never actually killed anyone. This wasn't a damn video game. Funny, he thought, for a brief moment he'd entertained the idea of letting K'uhul murder countless people. And yet Jared couldn't even stand the sight of a wilting plant.

Readjusting his aim, he first shot the man in one arm, then the other, and then both legs. The soldier fell like a puppet released one string at a time. Sybil Lee shrieked in anger and grabbed the man's firearm. Its bayonet dug deep into Jared's gut as he jumped to wrestle the weapon away and throw it into the chasm.

"No you stupid son of a bitch!" Sybil Lee screeched. "You don't know what you're doing! He's our last chance! He's our only chance!"

Jared felt a chill on the back of his neck and whipped his head around to see K'uhul towering before him. "You have something of mine," the giant seethed.

Jared aimed his rifle "I'm sorry, K'uhul, you're sick. I know you meant well, but you went too far. I'm so sorry." With that, he pulled the trigger.

Click.

Nothing. Jared had checked his ammunition. There was no way he had just used a full magazine. He pulled the trigger again.

Click.

Click-Click-Click

K'uhul grabbed the barrel of the rifle and ripped it free. "Give me the vial, Jared."

Jared stumbled back. "I don't have it."

"Give it to him you sack of shit!" Sybil Lee hissed.

Jared sneered. "I don't have it!" he repeated.

K'uhul swung the rifle like a man trying to fell a giant sequoia with a single blow. Jared's ribs shattered as he was launched back, sending sharp slivers of bone into his gut. K'uhul grabbed him by his collar and hurled him into the rocks. Jared rolled on the ground, pathetic, helpless.

"Check him," K'uhul said.

Sybil Lee rooted through Jared's clothing, growing increasingly frantic when she could not locate the vial full of Mercy. "He doesn't have it!"

"What?" K'uhul growled. His eyes were demonic as he pounced on Jared. "Where is it?" he bellowed, though Jared could hardly respond with the weight of K'uhul's hand crushing his neck.

"I...don't...have it," he gasped.

The earth shook as K'uhul raised his fist in the air and roared. In Jared's peripheral vision he saw something slither toward him. It was an enormous viper, as long as a man and thick as a fist. It climbed K'uhul's body to the end of his outstretched arm and coiled around his wrist. Its fanged head weaved menacingly in front of Jared's face.

"The little dipshit, he probably lost it," Sybil Lee sniped. "He's weak."

Jared struggled to speak. "They'll find it...anyway...in the lab."

"No," K'uhul said. "They will not. The lab will be dismantled by the time the Americans get there. Now, I will ask you one more time, Jared, you traitorous little worm. Where...is...the vial?"

Jared fell silent. He looked at the snake undulating above him and closed his eyes until it became a blur. Amidst the frenzy of his situation, he slowed his mind to a gentle swirl. He saw images of Greek gods juggling uranium atoms and waves of wrathful forest spirits. Then he saw the one true whole, the universe itself, radiant, endless, an infinity of color and form extending in all directions forever. K'uhul's gods were but tiny infants throwing tantrums in the midst of an endless pageant. He opened his eyes again, calm, sure.

The giant screamed as he whipped the snake down. He looked quite surprised when Jared moved ever so slightly and the viper swung its head back around to sink its venom deep within K'uhul's own jugular. "Yarrrrgh!!!" he yelled as he rose and stumbled back. He blinked in confusion at the snake and Jared. The animal struck again and then slithered to the ground and away.

Sybil Lee wailed hysterically. "What have you done? What have you done?!"

Jared shuffled to his feet and suddenly Sybil Lee was upon him, clawing at his eyes and hurling high pitched vitriol at his ears. He glimpsed the furor in her face and at that moment understood that his obsession with her was as obscene as her obsession with nature. Beautiful and alluring as she was, beguiling and fascinating as she could be, ultimately, at her core, Sybil Lee was just a tempestuous bitch. Finally, he threw her off his back, flinging her toward the fallen king. K'uhul's legs buckled as she bowled him over. His eyes rolled back in his head and he stumbled, off balance, into the abyss.

Chapter 23

Rebirths

Sybil Lee lay unconscious. She'd hit her head on a rock as she fell. Jared checked her wounds. Her lip had a nasty gash and her head a swollen lump, but she would eventually heal. Even with her injuries, she was stunning in the moonlight. Jared's heart felt sick. He knew he could never trust her again. Despite her treachery, he wondered if he still loved her.

He limped to the wreckage of the attack helicopter and fished out the vial of Mercy from a crevice in the cockpit, right where he had left it to be discovered in case he had died. Gazing at the sky, he noticed the clouds had dissipated. The full moon was trying to prove itself that night, treating the world to an especially bright rendition of its glow. Hearing no more explosions, Jared assumed the battle for the temple complex had ended. He returned to Sybil Lee to tend to her injuries and waited hopefully for the other helicopter team to arrive.

A short time later, a formation of airships circled overhead with powerful search lights. He patted the precious tube of Mercy as he watched the first helicopter land. A group of soldiers ran out cautiously and scanned the environment. It was only when they saw firsthand that there were no threats that other airships landed. When the soldiers reached Jared, they barraged him with questions. Jared looked at them and then back at the helicopters. Civilians were stepping out of one. The soldiers repeated their questions. Jared squinted. *Was that? Could that be?* It was! Chris, Katy and Alan hurried across rocks in his direction.

Jared glanced at the soldiers and nodded toward Sybil Lee, who was just regaining consciousness. "Ask her," he said. With that he hobbled as fast as he could to joyfully embrace his friends.

"Jared," Katy said with concern, registering that the blood soaking his clothes had seeped from his own body. "Are you okay?"

"I'll be fine," he replied. He searched through his pocket for the vial of Mercy. "Hey, this is important. This is the cure for the parasite. I wanted to make sure you all got it before I handed it over."

"What are we supposed to do with it?" Chris asked.

Jared lifted the vial to his eyes. "I'm not sure. It's a powder of fungal spores. I don't think they'll work if you eat it."

"Maybe we should snort it?" Alan suggested.

Jared chuckled. Leave it to the rich guy to think of snorting a drug. Then he realized it was actually a good idea – pathogenic fungi often infected animals through inhalation. He reached in his pocket for something to spread the powder on and found a used energy bar wrapper. Once they had finished, Jared absentmindedly threw the wrapper to the ground. Alan picked it up. "I don't think you need to take anymore," Jared said.

"I know," Alan replied, "I just don't want to leave any trash."

Jared gave him a quizzical look. He turned to the others. Calmer now, he smiled broadly as waves of relief spread over his beaten body.

"We were so worried about you!" Katy gushed. "We didn't know what had happened. You're a hero, Jared!"

"More like a superhero!" Chris said.

"Well done!" Alan added.

Two older military men joined the group. The helicopters would be leaving in just a few minutes, they said, as soon as all the casualties were collected. Jared handed the vial of mercy to the most senior of them and explained what it was. He was told that the quarantines he had suggested had been enacted and had proved effective, thus far, but the officer thanked Jared profusely for securing the antidote as a backup. A medic came over as the other military men went back to work. He examined Jared's wounds. "Oh Boy," he kept repeating as he attended to one festering gash after another.

"So you know, I don't live far from Boulder," Katy said to Jared suggestively, her smile a warm sun rising amidst the stars of her eyes. Even after all that time in captivity together, Jared had never noticed just how pretty she was. "You could come visit me sometime," she added, her eyes locked on his.

"That would be nice," Jared replied, holding her gaze, basking in it, "that would be really nice."

A gust of wind blew a piece of paper against Jared's leg. Reaching down, he discovered it was the charred remains of the sports section of a newspaper. *Must be from that poor soldier in the transport,* he realized. He looked at the date. It was only a couple of days old. "Hey Chris," he said, "check it out, special delivery of the sports page for you."

To his surprise, Chris waved him off. He was busy talking with Alan. Jared overheard their conversation and noticed Chris pointing animatedly at the sky. When he looked up, he saw the silhouette of a soaring bird framed by the constellation of the Maize God's rebirth.

"That's the same kind of eagle I was telling you about," Chris exclaimed, "the one that got the sloth!"

Alan watched it intently.

"Coooool," he oozed.

Jared looked back and forth between Alan and the smoldering remains of the rainforest around him. He smiled. "You'll be OK," he whispered to the trees.

The End

About the Author

Mark D. Longo recently spent several months exploring the wilds of Central America. It was during this trip, while trapped knee-deep in the mud in a Guatemalan jungle and being assailed by screeching monkeys, that he realized Nature might just have a temper. Mark holds a degree in foreign affairs from Georgetown University and is currently pursuing a doctorate in evolutionary biology at Stanford. This is his first novel.